What readers are saying about After Eden

Please return / renew by date shown.
You can renew it at:
norlink.norfolk.gov.uk
or by telephone: 0344 800 8006
Please have your library card & PIN ready

NORFOLK LIBRARY
AND INFORMATION SERVICE

"Once I started reading I couldn't put it down. I love it everywhere." Chioma

"This book is a masterpiece ... It takes you on a rollercoaster ride of love, secrets, deadly discovery and time travel." Grace

"After Eden is absolutely amazing ... and has everything which you could want: romance, action and so much more!!" Aadya

"'Light-hearted', 'fun' and 'pure brilliant' are the words I would use to describe After Eden. It leaves you starry-eyed and with questions that keep you up at night. This is definitely on my favourite books of the year list." Niamh

"Adventurous, exhilarating, plot-twisting, heart-warming book. You love each and every character. A Must-Read!" Ella

"This book is about planets and literally took me out to space because I forgot what was around me as I was so interested in the book." Beth

"A very thrilling story with twists you never expect and an element of romance. This all comes together to make a perfect book you can't put down until you've turned the last page. I read it all in one night." Regan

AFTER EDEN

HELEN DOUGLAS

BLOOMSBURY

LONDON   NEW DELHI   NEW YORK   SYDNEY

Bloomsbury Publishing, London, New Delhi, New York and Sydney

First published in Great Britain in November 2013 by Bloomsbury Publishing Plc
50 Bedford Square, London WC1B 3DP

A CIP catalogue record for this book is available from the British Library

ISBN 978 1 4088 2869 4

Typeset by Hewer Text UK Ltd, Edinburgh
Printed in Great Britain by CPI Group (UK) Ltd, Croydon CR0 4YY

1 3 5 7 9 10 8 6 4 2

www.bloomsbury.com

For Jack and Eden

PROLOGUE

Perran – June 2012

She was dancing with somebody else.

She looked different. Her auburn hair had been pinned up so that the waves that usually fell below her shoulders fell just below her chin. The beads on her green dress swayed as she moved across the floor. She caught his eye and smiled.

Flicking his hair out of his eyes, he pushed through the crowd towards her without thinking, without allowing the fear to stop him.

'Will you dance with me?' he asked.

She grinned. 'Thought you'd never ask.'

She placed one of her hands loosely around his waist, the other one lightly on his shoulder. She was close, but their bodies didn't touch, not the way Amy and Matt were pulled together so that every inch of them joined. Connor pulled her gently towards him, encouraged her head towards his shoulder. He breathed in the green-apple scent of her hair. The warmth of her skin. The faintest smell of soap or perhaps perfume. All around him was the music, the swirling lights, the mass of people dancing and laughing and shouting over the music. But all he knew was the feel of her warm breath on his neck, the thumping of his own heart, his hand as it moved around her waist and settled on her rear.

'Connor?' she said quietly.

He looked down, found her neck with his lips and began kissing her; small light kisses.

'What are you doing?' she asked.

'Something I should have done long ago.'

He kissed his way up her neck towards her lips. This was it. The moment he had dreamed of for the last two years. The moment when he would finally have the courage to kiss the girl he'd loved for ever and tell her how much he loved her.

'Stop!' she shouted above the music.

He froze. This was not the way things played out in his daydreams. Out of the corner of his eye he could see some of the couples near him staring, waiting to see what would happen next.

'What's wrong?' he asked.

'Connor, you're my best friend. I don't feel that way about you.'

'But you're my date,' he began.

'I thought you understood.'

She had raised her voice loud enough for him to hear it over the music, but it felt like she was broadcasting it to the whole world. Tears tickled the back of his eyes. There was no way he was going to stand there and cry in front of just about everyone he knew.

He pushed past her and headed out of the room. He would have gone outside, but Mr Chinn, the science teacher, was between him and the door and the last thing Connor needed was some teacher asking him if he was OK.

Instead, he took the other direction.

CHAPTER 1

Perran — March 2012

Megan was late. The five-minute bell had rung and everyone else had made their way to assembly. I was standing at the front gate waiting for her.

It was a frosty March morning with a clear blue sky. High above the school campus, two buzzards were circling anticlockwise, like the hands of a backwards turning clock. As I squinted into the distance, searching for a glimpse of Megan's purple coat, I saw him for the first time. He emerged from the dazzling whiteness, a tall boy with light brown hair that glinted silver in the pale winter sun. Striding towards the school gate, he unzipped his leather jacket to reveal his school jumper and white shirt, then draped a school tie around his neck and loosely knotted it, as though avoiding the discomfort for as long as possible.

He glanced in my direction before heading into the main building. It took about thirty seconds for him to pass through the school gate and into the main entrance. It took

4

considerably less time for me to figure him out: gorgeous, confident, unattainable.

By the lunch break, it seemed that the entire female population of Year Eleven was talking about the new boy. I heard snippets of conversation all the way from my appointment with the careers adviser to the canteen.

'He's Canadian.'

'He's South African.'

'Apparently he's so good at football that Mr Tucker wants him on the team.'

'He has a tattoo.'

'He has a really hot blonde girlfriend who lives with him.'

'He drives a silver sports car.'

'Chloe Mason is going to ask him out.'

My careers session had run over and the canteen was nearly empty by the time I arrived, but there was still a small queue at the till. I waited impatiently, running back over the meeting in my head.

Mrs Mingle's office was hidden away upstairs in the admin block, away from the rest of the rooms. She was a middle-aged woman with flamboyant glasses and a frizzy head of red Afro curls. 'So, Eden,' she had said enthusiastically, once we were both settled in our armchairs with a plate of chocolate biscuits and two mugs of tea balanced on a footstool between us. 'Tell me where you see yourself in the future.'

I hadn't given much thought to the future. Not the long-term future anyway. I'd thought as far as taking my exams in the summer and then going to the local college in the autumn. I would study hard during the week and on Saturday nights I'd go to parties. Not the sort of parties that Amy liked – the sort where everyone drank cider out of cheap plastic cups and fumbled in dark corners with boys from school – but the sort where people drank wine from real glasses and talked about books and politics and tried to change the world.

'Imagine yourself as a ninety-year-old woman,' said Mrs Mingle, dunking her chocolate biscuit into her mug of tea; she held it there so long I expected to see the biscuit break away, 'and you're looking back over your life. What sort of story will you have to tell?'

I tried to imagine myself as an old lady, grey and wrinkled, with my life behind me. And suddenly I knew what I wanted. Not in the details, but the broad sweep of things. I wanted my life to be like one of my favourite books: a big, fat novel, each page filled with small typewritten words as though the only way to cram so much life in was to make the writing really small. I wanted to be brave, take risks, make a difference, fall in love. The characters would be colourful, the landscapes exotic. I wanted my life to be a page-turner.

The problem was, I knew no colourful characters, had never been anywhere exotic and courage was something I lacked. As I sat there in the armchair in Mrs Mingle's office, I had a dawning realisation that if I didn't start to think about my future, my life story would end up like a half-empty notebook, blank page after blank page, interrupted only by an occasional shopping list or note for the window cleaner.

'What's that?' said a low, male voice beside me.

I looked up, startled from my daydream. It was the new boy. He was frowning at the special of the day.

I shrugged. 'Your guess is as good as mine. I'm guessing it's supposed to be curry.'

'What about that?' he asked, pointing to the pizza. 'The round thing with the red stuff.' His accent was difficult to place. Something between American and Australian.

'Do you mean the pizza?'

He nodded. 'What's on top?'

The canteen food was often a terrifying mixture of un-identifiable ingredients, but pizza was a recognisable and generally safe option. I turned to him, looking for a sign that this was a joke of some sort – perhaps a wink or a smile – but he was staring at the pizza slices, a crease between his eyebrows.

'It's just normal pizza. Tomato sauce and cheese.' Did he really not know what pizza was?

'Yeah,' he said, grinning suddenly. 'I knew that.'

I took a jacket potato and some sweetcorn and an apple. He took exactly the same.

'That looks nicer,' he said, shrugging one shoulder.

I paid for my food and strode across to the table where Megan and Connor were sitting. We were an odd bunch. We weren't part of any of the main tribes at Perran, like

7

the surfer and skater crowd, or the pony-club girls, or the musicians, although we hung around on the periphery of the main groups from time to time. Megan had a beautiful singing voice and mixed well with the other musicians. Connor was learning to surf – although he wasn't part of the surfing crowd – and he went to astronomy club on Fridays after school without being a fully paid-up member of the science geeks. As for me, I was part of the cross-country team but avoided all other sports and everything to do with them. Connor and Megan were sitting with Connor's neighbour, Matt, and Matt's girlfriend, Amy.

Matt was OK. He played guitar and was pretty laid back. Amy was a drama queen, always performing, always rein-venting herself, always the centre of attention. Her latest look was, in her words, vampire chic. She had dyed her naturally fair hair jet black, which made her pale skin look almost green. It was an improvement on her last persona, when she had bleached her blonde hair platinum, and affected a southern Californian vocabulary.

'I'm thinking, like, a beach party would be totally awe-some?' Amy was saying, as I pulled out a chair.

Megan looked at me and surreptitiously rolled her eyes. Amy had been planning her sixteenth birthday party for weeks. Megan didn't really like beach parties, but I could already picture the fire burning bright in the inky night, a skyful of stars and, with a little luck, the moon.

'Amy, it's the beginning of March. How can you have a beach party in March?' Connor asked. 'It's practically the middle of winter.'

'Actually, it's spring,' she said. 'Anyway, it's not going to be bikinis and trunks. Have you never partied on the beach outside of summer?'

'No,' said Connor, shrugging. 'Why would anyone do that?'

'Because there are no parents on the beach. I could have my party at home with Mum and Dad in the next room – I'm sure they'd just love to serve pizza and lemonade – or we can party at the beach with no parents and drink whatever we like.'

'I get your point,' Connor said. 'But it'll be freezing.'

'We'll build a bonfire,' said Amy. 'It's going to be so great.'

I tuned out and sliced into my potato. Out of the corner of my eye I watched the new boy sit alone at a table in the corner. Three Year Ten girls at the table next to him giggled, flicked their hair and upped the volume of their conversation. Something told me he wasn't going to have any trouble fitting in, even at this late stage in the school year.

'What do you think, Eden?' Amy was asking.

'Huh?' I hadn't been listening. 'Sounds great.'

Amy turned to where I'd been looking. She winked at me. 'Checking out the new guy?'

Connor groaned. 'Not you as well.' He nudged me. 'Is he dreamy? Does he make your heart flutter?'

'Get lost, Connor,' I said, nudging him back. 'You're just jealous.' I bit into my apple, embarrassed to have been caught.

'He's clever,' said Amy. 'He was in my science class this morning.'

'He's not that smart,' said Matt. 'I had history with him

and he'd never heard of Hitler. For God's sake, who hasn't heard of Hitler?'

'Or pizza?' I muttered under my breath, but nobody heard me.

'It's not his mind I'm interested in anyway,' said Megan with a giggle.

'I don't get it,' Connor said, shaking his head. 'What does he have that I don't?'

'Muscles,' Megan began. 'And great cheekbones. And . . .' Connor groaned again.

Megan ignored him. 'And gorgeous hair.'

'You have to be kidding,' said Connor. 'It sticks up in every direction. Doesn't he know how to use a comb?'

'Says the boy who doesn't even own a comb,' I said, tousling Connor's shaggy blond mop.

'Maybe that's how they wear their hair in America or wherever it is he's from,' said Megan.

Amy frowned. 'I don't think he's American. I think he sounds Australian.'

'Definitely not Australian,' Megan argued back. 'There's a hint of a twang there. Maybe he's Canadian. Or Hawaiian.'

'Or South African,' said Amy. 'Their accents sound similar to Australian.'

'Why don't you just ask him?' said Connor, a hint of irritation in his voice. 'He's coming this way. I'm sure he'll put you out of your misery.'

Sure enough, he had finished his meal and had to walk past our table. I studied my apple, hoping Connor wouldn't do or say something embarrassing.

Connor stood up, just as the boy approached, blocking his exit. 'Excuse me. I wonder if you would mind settling a discussion.'

The boy smiled warily. 'If I can.'

'The girls here were just trying to place your accent. We've got Australia, Canada, Hawaii and South Africa.'

The boy smiled a little more. 'Close,' he said. 'America.'

'America. Now that's settled. Thank you so much for your assistance.'

The boy raised an eyebrow. 'You're welcome.'

The bell went for fifth period and I sighed. Double art with Mrs Link.

'What class do you have next?' Connor asked the boy. 'I'll point you in the right direction.'

In his hand the new boy was holding a map of the school, which he had clearly folded and refolded several times already that morning. 'Art. Mrs Link.'

'Eden has art with Mrs Link,' Megan said, winking at me.

I cringed. Why did Megan have to be so blunt? I swallowed the piece of apple I was chewing and picked up my tray. 'You can walk with me.'

'Eden. That's a beautiful name,' he said as we walked towards the Godrevy Building. 'Is it popular in England?'

'No. I don't know anyone else with my name.'

'Is that so?'

I didn't reply. I couldn't think of a thing to say. I glanced at him from the corner of my eye. He was looking at me with an amused smile. The warmth on my face told me that I was blushing. I have reddish-brown hair and the palest skin that blushes fiercely, all the way from my chest to my forehead.

'What brings you to Cornwall?' I asked eventually, as I held open the door.

He hesitated. 'Work. My dad's work.'

'It must be tough arriving halfway through the school year. With exams and stuff.'

'It's not so bad. Everyone is so friendly.'

Mrs Link was in the classroom, meeting and greeting and watching us swipe in. As usual she was wearing a kaftan that accentuated her enormous hips. And she reeked of the hazelnut coffee that she always drank.

'You must be Ryan Westland,' she said, shaking his hand vigorously and beaming. 'Now, where are we going to put you? Eden here doesn't have a partner. You can sit with her.'

I sat down in my usual seat and looked away while Ryan sat next to me. I heard the scrape of stools and whispers as several of the girls angled themselves for a better look.

'So you're from America?' I said after a while.

'Yeah.'

'My aunt's boyfriend is from America. His accent is way different to yours.'

'It's a big country.'

'Which part are you from?'

'You ask a lot of questions, don't you?'

I got the hint so I took out my sketch pad and flicked through the last few pieces we had worked on. Hands, feet, eyes. All embarrassingly badly drawn. I closed the pad with a snap, afraid that Ryan would see.

'I'm from New Hampshire,' Ryan said softly. He was smiling. 'A small town in the countryside.'

'Take out your sketch pads,' Mrs Link interrupted, handing a blank one to Ryan. 'Today we will be sketching portraits. Face and upper torso.'

I felt my stomach clench. This was awful. I was going to have to sketch Ryan's face. I was terrible at art in general, but I was particularly bad at drawing people. Mrs Link chose a boy from the front of the room as her partner and then modelled how to approach the task.

'Thirty minutes each,' she told us.

'Do you want to model first or draw first?' Ryan asked.

Both options sounded bad. I figured that if I sketched last, I might not have to show him my effort. 'I'll model.'

I didn't know where to look. I looked out of the window. I looked at the art on the wall and then at the door.

'Do you think you could keep still?' Ryan asked.

'I'm sorry. I find it hard not to fidget.'

'Maybe you could find something to look at.'

I shrugged and looked around the room, trying to find something interesting. 'What would you like me to look at?'

'You could just look at me.' He must have spotted the look of horror on my face. It would be impossible for me to maintain eye contact with him without blushing brightly. 'Or you could look out of that window.'

I chose the window. There wasn't a lot to focus on: just a palm tree swaying slightly and a breeze-block wall. Mrs Link put on some slow jazz that was clearly designed to be relaxing. Piano and trumpet. I tried to think myself somewhere else. I thought about the beach party that Amy was planning. I thought about my Aunt Miranda and her boyfriend, Travis, who she was crazy about. And then I thought about the good-looking boy opposite me who was intently sketching my image. I could feel the colour burning my cheeks still.

'Why don't you take off your sweater?' Ryan said after a few minutes.

'Excuse me?'

'You look like you're burning up. Are you feeling OK?'

'I'm fine,' I said. 'Just a little hot.'

His attention was making it so much worse.

'Then take off your sweater.'

'Won't that mess up your sketch?'

He shook his head. 'I'm still working on your face.'

Slowly, I pulled my sweater over my head, ensuring my school shirt didn't rise up with it. I unbuttoned the top of my shirt and loosened my tie, knowing full well that it wouldn't make the slightest difference to the colour of my face.

'I have high colouring,' I said.

Ryan skimmed his eyes from my chest to my face, finally resting on my eyes. He smiled and continued drawing. I tried to focus on the music, but it was slow and achingly romantic and, ridiculously, I found myself imagining what it would be like to dance with Ryan, the two of us barefoot, the sun setting over the sea, while this piece of music played in the background. I picked up my sketch pad and waved it in front of my face, trying to cool myself down.

'Does the school have a science club?' Ryan asked.

'There's a revision club after school. It's for people who need to improve their grades.'

Ryan frowned. 'Isn't there anything else? A club for people who love the subject?'

'Not really. Unless you count astronomy. I guess that's science. My friend Connor goes.'

Ryan put down his pencil and looked at me. 'Connor?'

'You met him at lunch. He's the blond boy who stopped you and asked about your accent.'

Ryan nodded. 'That sounds perfect. When does it meet?'

'Fridays. Mr Chinn runs it. Connor will be able to tell you more.'

Ryan was looking at me intently. 'That's just what I'm looking for. What's Connor's surname? I need to catch up with him.'

'Penrose. He's one of my best friends. I'll introduce you.'

'Thanks.' He picked up his sketchbook and began to scratch his pencil across the paper. I looked at the palm tree again.

A waft of hazelnut coffee alerted me to Mrs Link's approach.

'Very good, Ryan,' she said. 'You've captured her expression beautifully.'

After thirty minutes of unbearable self-consciousness, Mrs Link told us to switch roles. I wasn't sure whether to be relieved or mortified.

'How do you want me?' Ryan asked, his eyes twinkling playfully.

'I don't mind.'

I didn't know where to begin. I looked at his eyes: brown. Not muddy brown or coffee brown or dirty brown. His eyes were all the colours of autumn leaves brown. Closest to the pupil they were a rich chestnut, further out a deep copper. Near the whites of his eyes they were almost gold. They were the most beautiful eyes I'd ever looked at, and they were looking at me with amusement.

'Actually, maybe it would be better if you looked out of the window,' I said.

'At that tree?'

'That would be fine.'

'What sort of tree is that?'

'Just a palm tree,' I said with a shrug.

I tried to capture the shape of Ryan's eyes. But I couldn't. They were just eye-shaped. I could explain in words that they were open, warm, smiling, but I couldn't transcribe those thoughts on to paper.

I tried to sketch his hair. It was light brown, with a rich warmth. If I was talented, I would have chosen twelve different shades of brown and blended them together. It was pushed back from his forehead so that it fell in all directions. I used my pencil to try and show the various

16

directions that his hair fell, but the result on my pad just looked chaotic.

I went for a generic oval face shape, confident that I wouldn't be able to capture anything resembling his cheekbones and square jaw. The face on the page looked like the efforts of an eight-year-old child and I toyed with the idea of ripping my pad into shreds. Sighing inwardly, I moved on to his body. He was angled slightly away from me, gazing at the lone palm tree outside the art room window. He had taken off his jumper and rolled up his sleeves and I noticed the golden hair on his forearms. His arms were slightly clenched and his hands in fists. The muscles stood out, like taut rope. I followed his body upwards. The shape of his chest was clearly defined through his shirt. It looked hard and muscular.

'Do you work out?' I asked.

'No,' he said, sounding a little confused. I saw him notice me looking at his chest.

'You seem pretty muscular.' The words slipped out before my internal censor had a chance to stop them.

He raised an eyebrow. 'Is that good?'

I blushed. 'It doesn't make a difference. I won't be able to draw it. Art is my weakest subject.'

'Can I see what you've done?'

'Absolutely not.'

All too quickly the minutes passed and it was time for us to peer-assess our portraits. Mrs Link wanted us to identify what had gone well, and a target for development.

'Here you go,' Ryan said, pushing his sketch towards me.

It was good. The girl in the picture was biting her lower

lip while gazing into the middle distance. Her long wavy hair was unruly and her eyes were intense. The shading on her cheeks suggested a slight blush of embarrassment. It was me all right. A much more attractive version of me.

'So what went well?' Ryan asked, smiling crookedly.

'I like the movement in her hair,' I said. 'You've captured that really well.'

He smiled and thanked me. 'So what's my target?'

'I don't know. She looks too perfect. She doesn't look real.'

'I draw what I see.'

I bit my lip, unsure how to respond. 'I wish I looked that good,' I said eventually, shrugging my shoulders and smiling in what I hoped was a self-deprecating way.

'Let's see your sketch then.'

I pushed my sketch pad in front of him. 'I'll be happy with two targets for improvement. I'm well aware that nothing went well.'

Ryan smiled and met my eye. 'Evidently human. But I must do something with my hair.'

'Next week,' Mrs Link told us at the end of class, 'we'll be taking a field trip to the Eden Project to sketch plant life. You will be excused from your morning classes and we'll be back in time for the buses at three thirty.'

'What's the Eden Project?' Ryan asked.

'These large domes, like greenhouses, built in abandoned clay pits in St Austell. Each of them houses plants from a different biome. It's cool.'

'And it's called Eden?'

I nodded. 'As in the garden of Eden.'

'I got the reference.'

The bell went and I put my sketch pad in my bag. Ryan slid off his stool quickly and began to walk out. He hesitated at the door and turned to look at me.

'Thanks, partner,' he said with a smile.

CHAPTER 2

Megan walked me to the bus stop at the edge of town. After school we'd been to see a film and then grabbed some chips. Now it was horribly dark and cold. 'I'll wait with you.'

'I'm fine. Go home. I'll see you at the beach tomorrow.'

'Text me when you're home safely,' she called when she was halfway down the street. I waved back, suddenly feeling very alone.

In summer Perran was always busy with tourists but in winter it was desolate. A ghost town. You could walk in the middle of the seafront road because the shops were closed and cars had no reason to drive along there.

I didn't usually hang around after school in the winter, because of the cold and the dark and the fact that there weren't many buses, but this Friday I didn't feel like going home to watch Miranda and Travis canoodling in the kitchen while he prepared some gourmet meal for two.

The seafront was empty. There was no sign of life except for the lights shining through the window of the Fisherman's Arms. I stamped my feet and clapped my hands to get my circulation moving. The next bus wasn't due for another twenty-five minutes.

For a second I thought about calling Miranda and asking her to drive into town to get me, but I knew she wouldn't be happy if I disturbed her Friday night date. I thought about a taxi, but I didn't have enough money for the fare. In the end I decided to walk a couple of miles and pick the bus up further along the route. It would be a lot less cold than standing around in the draughty bus shelter.

I was only five minutes out of town when a car slowed alongside me. I put my head down and increased my pace. This had been a mistake. I should have stayed at the bus stop. Out here on the coast road, no one would hear me scream. The car pulled up against the kerb, then a door opened and slammed behind me. I reached inside my school bag for my mobile phone.

'Eden!'

I turned. It was Ryan.

'You want a ride home?' he said with a smile.

'You don't know where I live.'

'You go to Perran School. How far can it be?'

'About five miles. I live in Penpol Cove.'

'I live there myself.'

Something occurred to me. 'You have to be seventeen to drive in this country.'

'I know.'

'And you're sixteen.'

He grinned. 'I know that too.'

I hesitated. But the night was cold and the next bus a twenty-minute wait.

Ryan opened the passenger-side door. 'Jump in.'

Wondering if I would live to regret this, I climbed inside.

He turned the ignition and pulled on to the road. The car lurched and jerked until it gained speed. He turned the heater up high and warm air blew over me. What a sudden change in circumstance I thought. One moment I was cold, on my own, and a little anxious, and now I was warm, with Ryan, and very anxious.

'So the rumours are true,' I said.

'Which rumours would they be?'

'The ones about you driving around town.'

Ryan frowned. 'People have noticed? That's not good.'

Of course they'd noticed. Every girl in the school had him on their radar. Perran was a small town.

'Is that a problem?' I asked.

'Like you said, I'm not old enough for a licence. I don't really want to attract too much attention.'

'So how come you drive?'

He looked away from the road and met my eyes. 'I don't like walking in the dark on cold nights.' He turned back to the road. 'What are you doing walking in the dark on your own anyway?'

'I hung out with my friends in town after school,' I said. 'And there's no bus for ages, so I decided to walk.'

He smiled but, mercifully, kept his eyes on the road.

'Did you go to astronomy club?'

'Yeah. It was fun.'

'Was Connor there?'

Ryan nodded. 'I had no idea astronomy was so popular over here. The club was packed.'

'Really? Connor's always given me the impression that it's three nerds and Mr Chinn. No offence.'

He laughed. 'Do you think I'm a nerd?'

We had reached the turn-off from the main road that led down to Penpol Cove. Ryan shifted quickly down through the gears, making the engine roar.

'Sorry. I haven't got the hang of these gears yet,' he said as we passed the small shop at the edge of the village. 'Whereabouts exactly do you live?'

'The other side of the village,' I said, giving him directions.

'I'm just further down the lane. In the farmhouse by the cove.'

'That place has been for sale for ever,' I said.

Ryan shrugged one shoulder. 'My dad likes it. It's quiet.'

I knew the house in question. It was a large granite building right at the end of Trenoweth Lane with views over the cove. Once it had been part of a working farm, but now it was just a big house with a very large garden. No one had lived there for years.

Ryan pulled up in front of my house and switched off the engine. My heart began to thud. Why had he switched off the engine? I could feel the redness begin to blossom across my chest. It would only be a minute or so before it crept up my neck and on to my face, like a flower blooming in a time-lapse photo. I wondered if I could say goodbye and escape before that happened.

'Thank you for driving me home, Ryan,' I said. The words came out all wrong. I sounded like an old-fashioned girl who'd been for a drive with her beau. It must be obvious that I didn't usually do things like this.

He shrugged. 'You're welcome. I had to pass you anyway.'

I opened my door and then paused. 'Are you going to the party tomorrow?'

'I haven't been invited.' He looked at me. 'Unless you're inviting me now?'

I nodded. 'It's Amy's birthday. She's invited everyone.'

'What do I need to bring?'

'I'm taking a load of food. You don't need to bring anything. She's holding it on Perran Towans, the beach just outside town. At two o'clock.'

'Shall I pick you up at a quarter of two?'

He was offering to pick me up? My heart repeated the squeeze from earlier, and yet I knew I couldn't accept.

'You're too young to drive.'

'Apparently I'm not.'

'Miranda – she's my aunt, I live with her – there's no way she'll ever let me get into a car with a sixteen-year-old driver,' I said. 'We could take the bus?'

Ryan shook his head. 'You just said you're taking lots of food. My sister Cassie can drive us. She's seventeen.'

I shrugged. 'OK. See you tomorrow.'

I slammed the car door and walked up to the house, trying not to skip. Ryan Westland was going to the beach with me tomorrow. OK, it wasn't exactly a date, but still, we would be going together and I wouldn't have to wait until Monday to see him again.

Miranda was in the sitting room watching the television with Travis. Two large wine glasses were on the coffee table in front of them.

'Did you have a good evening?' she asked, pressing the mute button on the remote control.

She had dressed up. She worked as a legal secretary for a small firm of solicitors in Perran, and always wore a neat, black suit to work. Before Travis, she used to come home from work and change straight into sweatpants and slippers. Tonight, though, she was wearing a red dress I'd never seen before.

'Yes thanks. We went to the cinema.'

'How did you get home?'

This was a question I knew to expect. Miranda's approach to parenting consisted mainly of checking up on my transport arrangements and keeping me clear of wild parties.

'Megan's dad gave me a lift,' I said, the lie rolling easily off my tongue. If I'd mentioned that a sixteen-year-old boy had driven me home, I would probably have been grounded until Christmas.

'See if you can finish this,' she said, passing me the newspaper.

I knew without looking that it was the crossword.

'Have you eaten?' Travis asked. 'I cooked teriyaki duck with quinoa and rocket salad. The salad is all gone but there's a little duck left if you want some.'

I glared at Travis. He knew very well that I was vegetarian. 'I'm not hungry,' I said, 'but thanks for thinking of me.'

'It's tasty,' he said. 'And fatty. You look like you could use some more meat on your bones.'

'I'd prefer to be skinny than eat a decomposing corpse.'

He curled his lip in a half-smile. 'I wonder when you'll outgrow your vegetarian phase and start enjoying some good food.'

'I wonder when you'll stop patronising me,' I said, smiling back.

'Travis is an amazing cook,' said Miranda. 'You really are missing out.'

Travis was a chef. Originally from California, he had been living in Perran for a few months now, planning to open a fish restaurant on the seafront. He had met Miranda when her firm did the conveyancing on the building.

'I picked up some food for tomorrow,' said Miranda. 'Some courgettes, red peppers and button mushrooms in case you want to make some veggie kebabs.'

I smiled. 'Thanks, Miranda.'

'And I also picked up some soft drinks.'

She glanced at the empty wine glasses on the table. Before she started going out with Travis, she had never brought alcohol home. 'Eden,' she began, 'can you promise me that you'll be sensible at this beach party?'

I nodded. 'I won't be drinking, if that's what you mean.'

She nodded slowly. 'And how will you be getting there?'

'I'm getting a lift with a friend.'

She frowned, a severe crease appearing between her eyebrows. 'Which friend?'

'Ryan Westland. He's new at school. His sister's driving us.'

Travis sat forward. 'Westland? I've heard about them. Father's a writer.'

I shrugged. 'I don't know about that.'

'He lives around here somewhere, doesn't he?'

'Yeah,' I said. 'In the farmhouse down at the end of Trenoweth Lane.'

'How old is his sister?' asked Miranda.

'Eighteen,' I said, adding a year for insurance.

'I suppose that's OK.' Miranda smiled and turned up the volume on the television. 'See if you can finish the crossword,' she said, nuzzling up to Travis.

CHAPTER 3

I pounded down the empty lanes of Penpol Cove, the cold air ripping into my throat and lungs until my chest felt raw. The first mile was always the worst. My limbs felt weak and rubbery, my breathing was laboured. Experience told me that if I could survive the first mile, I would soon get into the zone, find my stride and lose myself in the rhythm of my run.

My usual route took me through the village and then down the lane to Penpol Cove, past the farmhouse where Ryan Westland now lived. The thought of him seeing me run past his house was just too embarrassing to imagine. I shuddered at the thought and took the other route.

Images of him kept appearing in my head. His leather jacket slung on top of his school uniform. His messy brown hair. The picture he drew of me in art class. And then I could hear the sound of his voice, his unusual accent. I began to run across the cliff top. I turned up the music on my iPod and picked up the pace. I needed to push myself so hard that all I would be able to think about was breathing. I would not be a lemming. I would not, like almost every other girl in Year Eleven, spend my time daydreaming about Ryan Westland. It was pointless. Ryan Westland was gorgeous. He had about a hundred girls throwing themselves at him. And there was nothing especially interesting about me.

I pushed all thoughts from my mind. Breathe in, two three. Breathe out, two three. Just breathe. My thighs ached. My stomach grumbled. As I approached my house, I could feel myself reaching for those hidden reserves of energy, the sudden burst you get when the end is in sight. Breakfast.

By half one, I had tried on hundreds of different outfits. Finally, frustrated and irritable, I decided to wear my favourite jeans with the thin green sweater that Miranda said matched my eyes. I straightened my hair, applied some mascara and lipgloss and went downstairs to wait for Ryan.

A red car pulled up outside at one forty-five exactly. I fetched the cool bag from the kitchen and opened the door. Ryan was standing on the doorstep about to knock. He was dressed in jeans, a white T-shirt with a red flannel shirt on top and his black jacket and boots. He looked older than he did in his school uniform.

'Hi,' he said, smiling.

I felt myself blush. Why the hell couldn't I be cool? 'Hi.'

Ryan took the bag from me and put it in the boot while I locked the door.

'Cassie, this is Eden,' he said as I climbed into the back.

Cassie turned to look at me. She had long blonde

ringlets that coiled over her shoulders and chest like a nest of albino snakes. 'So you're the girl from astronomy club?'

'No,' I said, shaking my head. She had me confused with someone else. Everything suddenly made sense. Ryan had told her that he was going to the beach to see a girl from astronomy club. That was why he had agreed to go with me. I wondered which of the girls he was interested in.

A slight frown formed between her eyebrows and she turned to Ryan. 'You said . . .'

'I know,' Ryan interrupted. 'Eden is a good friend of Connor.'

'I see,' she said. She turned the ignition, flipped on the radio and pulled on to the road to Perran. 'And how long have you known Connor?' The question sounded more like an interrogation than polite chit-chat.

'Since we were both four. He's one of my best friends.'

This seemed to satisfy her. I saw her check me out in the rear-view mirror and then she gave Ryan a look and turned the music up loud. I got the uncomfortable feeling that I was the object of a bet or a dare.

Cassie and Ryan didn't speak to each other or to me until the car stopped in the car park at Perran Towans.

'Behave yourself,' she said to Ryan, as she switched off the engine.

He laughed. 'Not a chance.'

She put a hand on his knee. 'Call me when you want me to pick you up, OK?'

He put his hand on top of hers and removed it firmly. 'Thanks, Cassie.'

Ryan opened the car door and climbed out. As I reached over to open my door, Cassie turned to look me up and down. I knew what she was thinking. *Why is he going to a party with this girl?* I was thinking, *What kind of girl puts her hand on her brother's knee?*

'Nice to meet you, Eden,' she said, without smiling.

I stared back at her. 'Thanks for the lift.'

Ryan had already got the cool bag out of the boot. We said nothing as Cassie turned the car around and pulled away.

'I'm really sorry about her,' Ryan said.

'She doesn't like me.'

'It's not that. She's just not good with people.'

I shrugged and reached for my bag. 'I'll carry it,' Ryan said, throwing it over his shoulder.

We looked down over the beach from the cliff-top car park. Although it was only two in the afternoon, the sun had begun its descent, casting a deep bronze glow over the sand. It was easy to spot Amy and her friends at one end of the beach. There were about thirty of them gathered around a huge pile of wood. The rest of the beach was deserted. The sea was flat, so even the hardcore surfers had stayed away today.

As we walked across the sand, I could see them one by one turn and stare.

Amy spoke first. 'Hi, Eden. You brought Ryan.'

'Happy birthday. I hope you don't mind me coming along,' Ryan said. 'Eden invited me.'

'Did she?' Amy said, the surprise clear in her voice. She glanced at me. 'The more the merrier.'

I looked around. Connor and Megan were stretched out on a big, red blanket. Matt was bending over a cool box filled with bottles. Amy's friends from drama were milling around the unlit bonfire, swigging from bottles and laughing. As though watching a slow-motion film sequence, I saw Amy's girlfriends checking out Ryan. They whispered to each other and I could tell they were trying to work out why Ryan and I had arrived at the same time. Finally, one of them, a girl called Scarlett, made her way over to us.

'Come and get a drink,' she said, linking arms with Ryan and steering him towards Matt and the cool box.

I walked over to Connor and Megan and plonked myself on their blanket.

'What's going on?' Megan whispered. 'How the hell did you end up coming to Amy's party with Ryan Westland?'

'I'm not sure myself,' I said. 'Ryan gave me a lift home last night and I mentioned Amy's party. He asked if he could come along.'

'He gave you a lift home?' Megan asked. 'Explain that?'

I shrugged. 'It would seem those rumours about him driving around town are true. He drove past me last night and he gave me a lift.'

'Why would you, of all people, get in a car with an under-age driver?' Connor asked, locking eyes with me.

I met his gaze. 'Because I was cold and alone and the road was dark.'

'Why didn't you get the bus?'

'Because I had to wait thirty minutes for the bus.'

He turned to Megan. 'You left her alone at the bus stop?'

Megan looked at me uncomfortably. 'Eden said she was OK.'

'I *was* OK,' I said. 'Stop acting like you're my dad, Connor.'

Connor shrugged. 'No worries. You want to get in a car with an under-age driver from another country, you go ahead. It's none of my business.'

I looked at Megan and she rolled her eyes. 'Connor was just telling me about astronomy club,' she said, clearly attempting to move the conversation on to safer ground.

'Was it a good night?' I asked.

Connor pushed his hair out of his eyes. 'Different. Usually it's just five of us and Mr Chinn. Yesterday, Westland showed up and eight Year Eleven girls also decided to join. Quite the coincidence.'

'So what did you do?' I asked.

'We looked at Venus and Jupiter.'

'That sounds good,' I said. 'I'd love to do that.'

Connor smirked. 'Yeah, right.'

'I would.'

'That's why you've always shown such an interest in the past.' Connor lay back on his elbows. 'To be fair, Westland was mostly interested in the telescope and talking to Mr Chinn. He more or less ignored his groupies. Chloe Mason was throwing herself at him all evening. He didn't seem to notice. I think he paid more attention to me than any of the girls.'

'Maybe he's gay,' said Megan.

Connor shook his head. 'I don't think he's interested in boys or girls. He's a science geek.'

Megan snorted. 'He doesn't *look* like a science geek.'

Connor pulled himself back up into a sitting position. 'And what exactly does a science geek look like?'

'It's just that he's pretty muscly,' she said. 'He looks as though he belongs on the rugby team, not in the astronomy club.'

'So you can't be muscular and into science? The two are mutually exclusive?'

'Of course not,' Megan sighed, rolling her eyes.

Ryan was making his way across the sand to us, swinging a full bottle of beer in one hand.

'Hey, Ryan,' said Connor. 'Did you enjoy astronomy club last night?'

Ryan sat on the blanket next to me. He pushed the bottle of beer into the sand so that it stood upright. 'Yeah. It was good.'

I nudged Ryan with my elbow. 'According to Connor, the membership tripled yesterday.'

Ryan grinned and nudged me back. '*You* haven't signed up.'

'I don't know anything about astronomy. The only object I can identify in the night sky is the moon.'

'Maybe you should join then. You might learn something.'

Connor scowled. 'Don't waste your breath. Eden will never join. She thinks science is for geeks.'

'I didn't say that!'

'It's true though, isn't it?' said Connor.

'Not at all,' I said, beginning to get annoyed.

Megan stood up. 'Come on, Connor. Let's go and get a drink.' She grabbed him by the arm and dragged him over to Matt and the cooler full of bottles. Ryan and I watched in silence.

'So you and Connor have been friends for a long time,' he said eventually.

I nodded. 'I sat next to him in reception class. I've actually known him longer than anyone. Even longer than I've known Megan.'

'He really likes you.'

It was a statement, not a question.

'We're close,' I said, sifting the cold sand through my fingers. 'We're like brother and sister.'

Ryan smiled. 'I'm not sure Connor thinks of you as a sister.'

'Oh, he does,' I said. 'We know each other much too well for anything else.'

Ryan raised an eyebrow. 'You're very unperceptive.'

'What's that supposed to mean?'

'He has a huge crush on you. It's so obvious. Just the way he looks at you.'

I shuddered involuntarily. 'Eugh! Don't say that. Connor is really great, but he's like a brother to me. Anything more would be . . .' I paused, trying to find a word that explained how I felt. 'It would feel disgusting.'

Ryan laughed a short, strange laugh. 'Poor guy. No wonder . . .'

'What?'

Ryan was gazing out to sea, his eyes glazed, as if he were

miles away. He spoke softly. 'You are going to break his heart.'

'Actually, I think Connor and Megan would be good together.'

He gave me the flicker of a smile. 'If you say so.'

Matt came running over, kicking up sand in his wake. 'Frisbee. Girls versus boys. No excuses, Eden.'

Ryan leapt to his feet and offered me a hand up.

'You go ahead. I'll just enjoy the view,' I said.

I lay back on the blanket and shut my eyes. Although it was only the beginning of March, there was enough strength in the sun to warm me through my jeans and sweater. After a few minutes a shadow fell across my face and I heard someone sit down next to me.

'Well, well,' said a voice. I didn't have to open my eyes to tell it was Connor. 'It's always the quiet ones.'

'Get lost,' I said, shoving him playfully.

He didn't move. 'Aren't you going to sit up and watch your boyfriend showing off?'

'I don't have a boyfriend.'

'You could have fooled me.' Connor and I teased each other all the time, but this seemed different. He seemed really annoyed by all the attention Ryan was getting.

I sat up. 'I hardly know him. We couldn't even be described as friends.'

'But you like him, don't you?'

I could feel myself blushing. Even if I hadn't, Connor knew me well enough that I wouldn't attempt a lie. I shrugged. 'Too much competition. I wouldn't want to have to try that hard to get a boy to notice me. I'll leave him to the sharks.'

'Oh, I think he's noticed you,' Connor said. 'He came to this party with you.'

'That doesn't mean anything. We live near each other. Anyway, he's way out of my league. I haven't even thought about him that way.'

Connor smiled and leant towards me. 'He's not out of your league. You're beautiful.'

I couldn't speak. I thought back to what Ryan had said just a few minutes earlier.

'Well, thanks, Connor,' I said, in the end.

I stood up to put some space between us and Connor stood up too.

'I'm going to go and start the barbeques,' he said. 'You want to help?'

When the frisbee game ended, Ryan walked up to the barbeques and stood next to me. 'Thanks for the invite,' he said. 'I'm having a good time.'

'I can see,' I said, pushing veggie burgers around the grill and deliberately not looking at him.

'What are you cooking?'

I was reminded of the first day I spoke to him, at lunchtime when he had seen the pizza. 'Veggie kebabs and veggie burgers.'

'What are veggie burgers?'

I smiled. 'You don't know what veggie burgers are? Are they all hunting, shooting, fishing types in New Hampshire then?'

Ryan looked at me as though he didn't know what to say.

'They're made from soya beans,' I said. 'You should try one.'

'OK. Is Connor cooking the same?'

I shook my head. 'No, he's grilling beefburgers.'

'As in cow?'

I laughed. 'What planet are you from?' And then I noticed his expression. He looked sickened. 'Are you a vegetarian?' I asked.

'Yes.'

I couldn't work him out. He seemed so normal and yet at times, so strange. How could he not know what burgers were? He was American. Burgers were like their national dish or something. And Matt had said something about Ryan not knowing who Hitler was. Maybe he was a member of a strict sect like the Amish who didn't allow any connection with the modern world. But that didn't make sense. He didn't look Amish and he drove a car. Or maybe he was part of a religious group that forbade the eating of all animals? Animal rights campaigner? Child of commune-living hippies? Member of a cult? I checked out his shoes, which were on the sand by his backpack. They looked like they were made of tough leather, like his jacket.

'How long have you been vegetarian?' I asked.

'Always.' He breathed in deeply and looked me straight in the eye. 'What will you be eating?'

'The veggie stuff like you – I'm a vegetarian too.'

He breathed out. 'Good.'

'Does it matter that much?' I asked.

He was still looking at me intensely. 'It matters to me.'

The afternoon passed quickly. We ate and then Matt and Amy lit the bonfire and everyone drank bottled beer or Juiska, little pink or blue bottles of vodka and juice.

As the sun slipped below the horizon and the temperature dropped, everyone gradually drew their blankets closer to the bonfire. Connor and I were alone on our blanket, sitting as close to the fire as we dared. I was ready to go home.

'There's Venus,' Connor said, staring up at an unblinking point of light in the sky.

'How do you know that?' I asked. 'It just looks like a normal star to me.'

'Do you see any other stars in the sky?'

I looked around. It wasn't yet dark enough for the usual spread of stars.

'Venus is the brightest object in the night sky after the moon,' said Connor. 'And she doesn't flicker like the stars do. Her light is steadier.'

'What does it look like through a telescope?'

'She, not it,' said Connor. 'Venus is named after the goddess of love and beauty. Through a telescope you can see her disc shape. Right now, she's a crescent shape.'

'Connor!' I heard Megan call.

I looked up and watched as Megan slurred her way over to us. She half stumbled on to the blanket and put her arm around Connor. 'You ready to walk me home?' Her words tumbled over themselves.

'Yeah. It looks like you've had enough.'

Megan leant against his shoulder.

'How are you getting home?' Connor asked me.

'I'm not sure,' I said, looking for Ryan.

'You're not going to let him drive you home, I hope,' said Connor. 'He was drinking beer earlier.'

He didn't need to say Ryan's name for me to know that was who he was talking about.

'He hasn't been drinking,' I said.

'I saw him with a bottle of beer.'

'He hasn't taken a single sip.' I pointed to the full bottle of beer, still standing in the sand.

Connor snorted. 'How do you know that's the same bottle?'

'I just do. Anyway, his sister's going to drive us home.'

Connor pulled Megan to her feet and put an arm around her. 'Are we still revising tomorrow or have you made plans with Westland?'

'Of course we're still revising tomorrow,' I said. 'I wish you'd stop making assumptions just because I happened to get a lift with Ryan. It's ridiculous. Anyone would think you were jealous!'

'I'm not jealous of him. I'm just bored with you and Megan – and every other girl within a ten mile radius of Perran – acting as though there's a total eclipse every time Ryan Westland sits down.'

I rolled my eyes. 'Next week he'll be old news. We'll all go back to worshipping you.'

'If only that was true. I'd better get Megan home. I'll see you tomorrow, OK?'

I nodded. 'Feel better, Megan,' I said.

'I feel fine,' she said, her words thick.

I watched as she stumbled along the sand, leaning hard against Connor. If I didn't know better, I might have thought they were together. Megan had left her red blanket behind. I shook out the sand and folded it up.

'You ready to leave?'

I turned. Ryan had crept up on me. I nodded.

'I'll call Cassie.'

'Why don't we walk home?' I said. 'It's a beautiful evening.'

As soon as the words left my mouth, I realised I'd made a huge assumption. There was no *we*.

'I'd really like that,' he said. 'Let's get your bag and say our goodbyes.'

We followed the coastal path above the beach until it was too dark and then headed inland to the road that wound its way along the cliff edge to the village.

'That's Venus,' I said after a while, to break the silence that had grown between us.

Ryan laughed. 'I know. I thought you said you couldn't identify anything in the sky except the moon.'

'I can't. But Connor pointed it out earlier at the beach.'

'Venus?' He laughed again. 'I wonder why he chose to identify Venus, named for the goddess of love and beauty.' He stopped and looked up. 'He could have identified Jupiter or Sirius or Polaris. But he chose Venus.'

'Oh, stop,' I said through chattering teeth.

'You're cold,' he said, slipping off his jacket.

'I'm fine when we're walking.'

He helped me into his jacket, which was much too big but warm and smelt like lemons and metal.

'So you don't mind wearing leather?' I said, zipping up his jacket.

'The jacket's not leather.'

I ran my palms down the front of it. It was supple like leather and felt super-strong. 'Is it plastic?'

'It's a synthetic material similar to Kevlar. It's strong, but also flexible.'

'So,' I said. 'Connor showed me Venus. What would you have shown me?'

I could see his smirk in the moonlight, but he didn't make any of the obvious innuendoes, the way the boys at school would have. He looked around. We were passing the golf course that lay halfway between Perran and Penpol Cove.

'Come here,' he said, taking my hand. He helped me climb over the low wooden fence and we walked to a sand bunker just a few metres from the road. 'Lie down.'

Something about the serious look on his face told me that he wasn't about to suggest we hook up out here in the cold winter night. He lay next to me, close, but far enough away that no part of our bodies touched. Above us, the sky was a hard black, thousands of pinpricks of light shimmering.

'You can't really blame Connor for starting with Venus,' Ryan said. 'It's the brightest object after the moon. You can also see Jupiter tonight.' He pointed to another bright light in the sky. Like Venus, it shone steadier and brighter than the surrounding stars. 'You need good binoculars or a telescope to see her moons. But I would start there with Orion.'

'Why Orion?'

'It's easy to identify. Give me your hand.'

I held out my hand. He covered it with his and extended my index finger.

'You're cold,' he said. He moved my hand across the sky, using my index finger as a pointer. 'These three stars in a row make up Orion's Belt. They're easy to find and you can use them to locate lots of others stars and constellations.' He moved my finger down slightly. 'That's Orion's Sword. The hazy star in the middle is the Orion Nebula.'

'The what?'

'Orion Nebula. Do you see how fuzzy the middle star is?'

'Yes.'

'It's because it's not a star, it's a nebula. Where stars are born.'

'Stars are born?'

'They're born, they shine for a few billion years and eventually they die.' He moved my hand again and made the shape of a rough square. 'These four stars also make up the constellation Orion.' He moved my hand slowly around the square. 'Betelgeuse, Bellatrix, Rigel and Saiph.'

Suddenly there was a pattern, a shape, among the nameless chaos of stars in the sky.

He took my hand back to Betelgeuse. 'Betelgeuse is a red supergiant, one of the largest, most luminous stars in the sky. It's about sixty times bigger than our sun. It's going to die soon. It will explode into a supernova and, when it does, we'll be able to see it on Earth. It will be like Earth has two suns.'

'When you say *soon*, how soon are we talking?'

'Soon in astronomical terms. Maybe tomorrow, maybe in a million years.'

'I won't hold my breath.'

'Don't,' he said with a laugh. 'But there's something else cool about Orion and you'll only have to wait a few months. If you look towards Orion in late October, you will see the Orionids, one of the most beautiful meteor showers of the year.'

'Shooting stars.'

'Yeah. Well, it's actually dust from Halley's Comet hitting the upper atmosphere. But it's spectacular.'

I'd never thought about the stars as being anything more than a bewildering disarray of beauty, like glitter scattered on to black sugar paper by a child. I'd never thought about the patterns they made or their size, or the fact that they were born and they died. 'Show me another constellation.'

Ryan moved my hand across the sky, stopping at a w-shaped formation. 'Cassiopeia.' He traced its shape with my hand. 'Another constellation that's easy to find.'

I found the pattern in the stars, drawing imaginary lines between the dots.

44

'And that cluster is the Pleiades.'

He pointed my finger to a small fuzzy area of the sky.

'Just keep looking,' he said.

I stared at the hazy shape and then it was as though the haziness disappeared and seven separate stars emerged.

'Also known as the Seven Sisters,' said Ryan. 'Through a telescope or binoculars you'll see loads more. There are more than five hundred stars in that cluster.'

I looked back and found the three stars of Orion's Belt easily. Out of the corner of my eye, I could see Ryan looking at me. I turned towards him. Our faces were so close, his hand still held mine. For a couple of seconds we stayed right there, looking at each other, the stars pulsing and flickering above us.

'Who needs astronomy club?' I said.

Ryan laughed softly and I could feel the warmth of his breath on my face. 'You know, when stars explode, they release their debris into the universe and this stardust forms new stars and planets and all the life forms on those planets. Everything on Earth, even you and me, is made from atoms that were once inside a star. We're made of stardust.' He held my gaze for another long second and then pulled me to my feet. 'That's enough stargazing for one night. Come on, we better get moving before you freeze to death.'

We clambered back over the fence on to the pavement and continued home. When we got to the bus stop near my house, I tried to say goodnight but Ryan would have none of it.

'It's very chivalrous of you to want to walk me home. But it's fine. I've walked home alone from here hundreds of times.'

'Are you embarrassed?' he asked. 'Don't you want your neighbours to see me?'

'I'm trying to save you the bother of walking out of your way.'

'In that case, please humour me. I'd feel much better if I saw you safely home.'

The theories began again. Non-meat-eating, Kevlar-wearing, out-of-date manners. A cult of some sort, probably.

We stopped at the front gate.

'Are you doing anything tomorrow?' he asked.

Despite every cell in my brain and body urging me to say no, I told him about my plans to spend Sunday with Connor. 'You could come too,' I said. 'I think he'd like you a lot if he got to know you.'

'I think he'd like it a lot if I stayed away from you.'

'You're wrong about Connor. I've known him most of my life. If there was anything like that going on, I'd know.'

'We'll have to agree to disagree,' he said with a laugh. 'I'll see you on Monday.'

He closed the gate behind me and waited until I was turning the key in the lock before disappearing into the star-studded night.

CHAPTER 4

Connor lived in an old fisherman's cottage with a view over the harbour beach, a tiny two-up two-down with the world's smallest bathroom. Despite the cramped conditions and the damp problem, Connor's mother had made the place into one of the cosiest homes I'd ever been in. The whole house smelt like fresh bread and biscuits when I arrived and Connor's mother was cutting up a tray of home-made shortbread.

'Here you go,' she said, carefully arranging the shortbread on a plate. 'Connor's upstairs. I'll bring you up some tea in a sec.'

'Thanks, Mrs Penrose,' I said, taking the plate and heading up the stairs.

The door was wide open and Connor was sitting on his bed reading a *Simpsons* comic.

'Working hard?' I said, clearing a space on his desk for the shortbread.

'My brain is aching.' He tossed the comic on the floor.

Connor's room was its usual mess. His desk was covered with textbooks, an ancient computer, a pile of overdue library books, and a collection of empty water glasses and coffee mugs. Discarded clothes were strewn across the floor and a poster of a rock band I'd never heard of hung from his bedroom wall by a single pin.

'It's sweet of you,' I said, kicking his clothes into a pile so that I could find somewhere to sit on the carpet, 'but you really shouldn't have gone to the trouble of tidying your room.'

'I didn't do it for you,' he said. 'I did it for Megan. But she's stood us up.'

'She's not coming?'

Connor chucked me one of the pillows from his bed. 'Sit on that. She's come down with a virus. Symptoms appear to be a raging headache, the shakes and vomiting. Not unlike a hangover from what I hear.'

I laughed. 'Poor Megan. She never knows when to stop.'

Connor shrugged and passed me the shortbread. 'Actually, I'm kind of glad that it's just you and me.'

I suddenly felt very aware of the fact that we were alone. 'You are?'

'We almost never get to spend time with just the two of us any more.' He smiled. 'You know what this means?'

I stopped breathing.

'It's my go,' Connor said, reaching for the Scrabble board.

The last time Megan couldn't make our revision session, Connor and I had started a game of Scrabble that we'd never had time to finish.

Connor gave me a look. 'Are you all right? What did you think I was going to say?'

When the door opened, and Mrs Penrose came in with a tray of tea, I realised I'd been holding my breath.

'I'm popping over to see Nan and Grandad,' she told Connor. 'I'll be back this afternoon.' She looked around the room with disgust. 'I suggest you clear your dirty clothes off the floor and put them in the washing machine if you want a clean school uniform tomorrow.'

Connor grunted. 'OK, Mum.'

Mrs Penrose left and we were alone again. I poured the tea.

'So how did you get home last night?' He was frowning at his row of tiles.

'Walked,' I said.

Connor looked up from the game. 'In the dark? It's five miles to Penpol Cove.'

'It wasn't that dark in the moonlight.'

He snorted. 'Not that dark! I bet that was Westland's genius idea. Walking you home in the moonlight.'

'Actually, it was my idea.'

'Your idea!'

'Connor, are you going to repeat everything I say?'

'I suppose walking home in the moonlight is very romantic.'

'In fact,' I said, 'Ryan thought you were the one with the romantic ideas. He said that showing me Venus was a classic move.'

Connor blushed. 'Venus was the only light in the sky at the time.'

'That's what I told Ryan. I had to explain that you were my oldest friend and that there was nothing remotely romantic going on between us.'

'That must have made him happy.' He glared at his tiles.

'He doesn't care one way or the other.' I sighed. 'Come on, Connor. Are you going to make your move or not?'

Connor looked up from his tiles and met my eyes. The blush was still on his face. For a split second, I tried to imagine how I would feel about him if I didn't know him so well. He was attractive in a beach bum kind of way – wavy blond hair, smattering of freckles on lightly tanned skin, clear blue eyes – and maybe if he wasn't so familiar I would have liked him that way. The problem was that I knew Connor. Not just as the good-looking boy in front of me. I knew him as the little boy who had once had an obsessive interest in *Star Wars*, who still left dirty underwear all over his bedroom floor and had enjoyed a lengthy childhood habit of digging for nose gold and tasting the nuggets.

'Eden,' he said. He opened his mouth to speak again, but I cut him off.

'I'm going to go and wash my hands before I eat any of that shortbread. If you haven't made your move on the board before I get back, you'll have to forfeit your turn.'

I dashed down the stairs and into the tiny bathroom at the back of the kitchen. After bolting the door shut, I filled the basin with cold water and splashed my face. Connor and I were friends. We played Scrabble together. We prepared for our exams together and sometimes went to the cinema. There had never been the hint of anything more from either of us and I probably wouldn't even be considering it if Ryan hadn't put the idea in my head.

Ryan hardly knew either of us. I had allowed my

imagination to run away with me. Connor wasn't going to say something embarrassing or try to kiss me. Smiling at my own paranoia, I unlocked the door and headed back up the stairs.

CHAPTER 5

The bus for the Eden Project was already waiting by the time I got to the school gate. A group of shivering students was milling around and Mrs Link was ticking names on a register. I couldn't help noticing Chloe Mason was, despite the rain and cold, dressed in very short shorts and a flesh-baring crop top. Her navel was pierced with a fake diamond on a long silver pin.

'Here he comes,' I heard Chloe say to her friend.

Ryan was strolling down through the yard towards us. He seemed utterly unselfconscious in a way that I knew I would never be.

'Wait up, Picasso!' Ryan called.

He walked straight past Chloe and her entourage and up to me, a huge smile spread across his face.

'Picasso?' I said. 'Didn't anyone ever tell you that it's unkind to poke fun at people's weaknesses?'

'Picasso drew strange-looking people,' he said, shrugging.

'Picasso meant them to look strange.'

He put his arm around my shoulder, sending tingles down my spine. 'I can't wait to see how you draw plants,' he whispered in my ear.

We took a seat towards the back of the bus. As the rest of the art students ambled on the bus and found their seats, several clocked Ryan and me sitting together and I picked up snippets of gossip about the two of us arriving and leaving Amy's party together.

'So what weaknesses do you have?' I asked. 'You know mine.'

'None,' he said, grinning.

'Everyone has weaknesses.'

He sighed dramatically. 'Beautiful girls. That's my weakness.'

'Well, you seem to be resisting, from what I've heard.'

'Have you been talking about me?' He smiled at me in a way that made my heart jump.

Predictably, Chloe Mason and her friend Melissa took the seat in front of us. As the bus pulled away, Chloe turned around and stuck her face between the two seat backs.

'Hey, Ryan,' she purred. 'How was your first week at Perran?'

'Educational,' he said with a smile.

Chloe frowned, clearly unsure whether he was being sarcastic. 'I know the Eden Project really well,' she said. 'Melissa and I go ice-skating there in the winter and there's live music in the summer. I could show you around.'

'That's nice of you, Chloe,' Ryan said, 'but I already have a tour guide.'

Chloe gave me a quick look. 'Eden won't mind if you come with us, will you, Eden?' She didn't wait for me to respond. 'You can spend the day with anyone you want; you don't have to stick to your art partner.'

53

'But I want to spend the day with Eden.'

Her smile dropped and she flicked her eyes from Ryan to me and back again. 'Are you two going out?'

'No,' I said quickly.

She pouted at Ryan. 'If you change your mind, come and find me.'

She turned back to Melissa, leaving Ryan and me alone again.

'She's scary,' Ryan whispered in my ear, close enough that I could smell his warm skin and the odd combination of lemons and metal. 'Why is her skin so orange? Does she have jaundice?'

'That's her make-up,' I whispered back. 'And fake tan.'

'She made it look like that deliberately?'

I nodded.

The bus reached the A30 and picked up speed. Through the windows, green fields and thick grey drizzle sped by in a blur.

'How was your study session with Connor?' Ryan asked.

'It would have been much better if you hadn't said all those things about Connor liking me. Every time he said something I kept wondering if there was some double meaning.'

Ryan laughed softly. 'I'm sorry. I shouldn't have said anything.'

'No, you shouldn't.'

'But he does like you and he will ask you out.'

I let it go.

*　　*　　*

We arrived at the Eden Project just after ten. Mrs Link gave us our pads and assignments for the day and told us to be back at the bus for two o'clock.

'Do you want to eat or drink or go straight to the biomes?' I asked.

'The biomes,' he replied immediately.

'Which one do you want to visit? We have a choice of the Mediterranean or the tropical. I like the tropical dome because it's exotic and warm.'

'Show me the way.'

We strolled through the café to the tropical biome. Immediately we were hit with the thick humidity and the rich smell of damp soil.

Ryan shut his eyes and breathed in deeply. 'Whoa! This place smells amazing!'

I laughed.

He walked ahead of me, up the path, through the lush green foliage and sultry air.

'Look at that.' He'd stopped in front of a large plant with thick shiny leaves. He rubbed one of the leaves between his fingers. 'It's so glossy.'

'You're really into plants, aren't you?'

He tilted his head towards the roof of the biome. 'Is that a waterfall up there?'

Without waiting, he strode ahead, along the path that twisted through the steamy jungle up to the canopy-level at the top. I caught up with him by the waterfall which crashed down from the summit of the biome.

'Let's start here.' He pointed to a large-leafed plant. 'We can sketch this and let the waterfall cool us off.'

Ryan sat cross-legged on the ground, flipped open his sketch pad and began to move his pencil across the paper.

'The green is so vibrant,' he said. 'This is such a healthy plant.'

I laughed at his enthusiasm. 'What is the vegetation like where you come from?'

Ryan paused, his hand hovering over the sketch pad. 'Where I'm from there's a lake,' he said, his eyes far away, as though searching through his memories for a picture. 'Once it was surrounded by trees. Maple and birch and pine. In the fall the maple trees would turn yellow and gold and red.'

'I've seen photos of New England in the autumn. It looks amazing.'

Ryan nodded. 'It was. People would come on vacation in the fall to see the colours. And in the winter they would come to ski. And in the summer they would come to fish and swim and boat in the lakes. And everywhere there were trees.'

'It sounds great,' I said. 'What's it called?'

'Wolfeboro,' he said. 'But it's not like that any more.'

'What happened?'

He shut his eyes. 'I don't know. Pollution. Some sort of industrial accident, I guess. The trees are all gone. Just the rotting remains of what was once a tremendous forest.'

'That's terrible,' I said. 'But one day they'll grow back.'

'I hope so.'

We continued sketching. From time to time, I glanced at Ryan's pad. He was outlining the shape of the plant, somehow capturing the glossiness of its leaves and the sun pouring down through the hexagonal panels on the roof of the dome. He flipped the pages of his pad and began another drawing. This time he drew the same plant, but closer. He described the shape of the leaves, the veins in each frond, little details I would never have noticed. I focused on my own sketch. I was attempting the same plant. I had an outline that was roughly the same shape as the plant itself. It was probably the best sketch I had ever produced. The next step involved filling in the details.

Ryan leant over and grinned. 'Do you want me to do your sketches for you?'

'It would be pointless. Mrs Link would know it wasn't my work. I am officially the least talented artist in the history of Perran School.'

'Did she say that?'

'Not in those words, but she's made it plain that she doesn't believe anyone can really be this talentless without trying hard.'

He looked back at my drawing. 'She does have a point.'

I smacked him across the head with my sketch pad and stood up. 'I'm hungry. Shall we go and get some food?'

He snapped his pad shut and we strolled back to the café.

'I have to warn you, Ryan,' I said. 'They will be serving meat here. Cornwall is not as evolved as Wolfeboro.'

'You must think I'm strange,' he said, smiling to himself.

'A little,' I said as I took a hummus sandwich for myself

and one for Ryan. I picked up two bottles of sparkling elderflower and pushed the tray to the checkout. Ryan insisted on paying. I made a mental note to pay next time we went out. Next time? Maybe I was imagining it, but it did feel as though there was something between us.

'Can I ask you something?' I asked, as we took a seat by the window. 'And do you promise not to be offended?'

Ryan smiled. 'You can ask me anything you like, but I can't promise not to be offended.'

I decided to take the risk.

'Are you and your family members of a cult or religious group or something?'

His face paled and he stared down at his sandwich. 'Sort of,' he said. 'My dad is part of an environmental group. It's committed to protecting indigenous species and vulnerable habitats. So we spend a lot of time campaigning and plant-ing trees, and very little time watching television or eating out at fast food restaurants. Which is why I'm not always *au fait* when it comes to popular culture.'

When he had finished speaking, he looked up and met my eye. The whole speech had sounded wooden and over-rehearsed, as though he knew I was going to ask him that question.

'I'm sorry if you think I'm rude,' I said. 'I've just never met anyone like you before.'

He shrugged. 'I don't suppose you have.'

After we had finished our lunch, I made a quick visit to the loo. I was locked in a cubicle, thankfully, when I heard Chloe Mason's voice.

'Undeniably gorgeous,' she was saying. 'And he looks even hotter in his own clothes.'

'That T-shirt he's wearing is really clingy,' said another voice I recognised as Melissa. 'You can see his muscles. I bet he has a six-pack.'

'He could have had any girl in the school,' said Chloe. 'Why is he wasting his time with Eden Anfield and her loser friends?'

I stopped breathing when I heard my name. I thought about opening the door and walking out, but quickly changed my mind. It was too late. To walk out now would be awkward for all of us.

'She's pretty,' said Melissa.

'If you like skinny, flat-chested and ginger!' said Chloe. 'I would have thought he would be into something sexier.'

'Like me,' said Melissa. She burst into giggles.

'I thought Eden was with Connor Penrose,' said Chloe. 'I guess she must have dumped him.'

'That would explain his miserable face lately,' said Melissa. 'Does my hair look OK from the back?'

'It looks great. Ready?'

I heard the door open and shut again. I waited another minute before I came out of the cubicle to wash my hands.

'Your friend Chloe was just admiring your physique,' I said, back in the café. 'She thinks you look hot today.'

Ryan raised an eyebrow. 'And what do you think?'

I felt myself blush. 'I think you should stop fishing for compliments.'

CHAPTER 6

'Double maths and then it's all over,' said Megan, dropping her lunch tray on the table.

It was the last day of school before study leave started and I wasn't sure whether to be sentimental or overjoyed. I was looking forward to the long summer holidays and then college after that, but there were things I would miss about this place.

I glanced at Ryan. Over the last few weeks, he had infiltrated our tight little group. At first he just sat with us on Monday lunchtimes before our art lesson, but recently he'd started sitting with us every day. He caught me looking at him and smiled.

'What's the probability of a fun last lesson with Stevens?' asked Matt.

'Absolute zero,' said Megan, sprinkling salt over her double helping of cheesy chips. 'He'll make us go over past papers. Guaranteed.'

I prodded at the vegetables sitting underneath a thick grey pool of congealing sauce, trying to find something I recognised. I should have known better than to risk a veggie curry.

'You want to share mine?' asked Ryan, wrinkling his nose at my food. He pushed his tray between us and moved closer to me.

'Thanks,' I said, stabbing a piece of his pasta with my fork. 'You can't go wrong with pasta. My curry looks like dog vomit. What was I thinking?'

Connor looked at me. 'Just get yourself something else to eat, Eden.'

'It's fine,' said Ryan. 'I don't mind sharing.'

Connor glared.

'What shall we do tomorrow to mark our first day of freedom?' asked Megan.

'The beach,' said Matt. 'The forecast is good.'

'What do you think?' Amy interrupted, waving a poster in her hand. 'Melissa Whitlock did the artwork, but I designed the layout.'

She thrust the poster on to the middle of the table, where it absorbed a grease spot and turned translucent.

Leavers' Ball
Saturday 23rd June
Tickets £15

There was a silhouette of a couple dancing and the entire poster was printed in silver and pink.

'That looks great, Amy,' I said.

She sat next to Megan and stole a chip from her tray.

Megan slapped her wrist playfully. 'Get your own lunch. I didn't get this gorgeous figure by sharing my food.'

'Help yourself to Ryan's lunch,' said Connor. 'He doesn't mind sharing.'

Ryan smiled to himself.

'What's so funny?' I asked him quietly.

He leant close to me. 'If I tell you why I think Connor is being an asshole, you'll just tell me that I'm wrong and imagining things. But I'm pretty sure this is all to do with who is going to pair up for the ball.'

'It's rude to whisper,' said Connor.

Ryan caught my eye. I tried not to smile.

'Tickets are on sale now,' said Amy, stealing another chip from Megan's plate. 'Obviously Matt and I will be going together. Although he hasn't asked me yet.'

'You could ask him, you know,' I said. 'This is the twenty-first century. Women don't have to wait to be asked.'

'I could ask him, but I shouldn't have to.'

Matt rolled his eyes. 'Amy, will you go to the ball with me?'

'I'd love to, Matthew,' she said, smiling smugly. 'What about you, Eden? Who are you going with?'

I shrugged. 'I haven't really thought about it.'

'Yeah, right,' she said, rolling her eyes. 'Everyone's been talking about it for weeks.' She took another chip from Megan. 'Who do you want to go with, Megs?'

Megan's cheeks dimpled as she smiled. 'I have someone in mind.'

'Megan?' I said.

She laughed. 'Tell you later.'

'What about you, Westland?' Amy said, turning to Ryan. 'Will you finally put Chloe Mason out of her misery?'

Ryan laughed. 'I'm not that brave.'

Amy nudged him. 'You have to go.' She glanced at me. 'Chloe won't be the only girl in Year Eleven who will be disappointed if you don't.'

'When is it?' he asked, dragging the grease-soaked poster across the table towards himself.

'The twenty-third of June,' said Amy.

Ryan's eyes lit up. 'Actually,' he said. 'I think I will go.'

'I saved a special place for you,' Connor said with a smirk as he passed me a black felt-tip pen and gestured at his chest.

'Your left nipple?' I asked, pulling a face.

'My heart,' he said, clutching his chest with both hands and sighing melodramatically. 'You are my oldest friend. I sat next to you on my first day in reception.'

'The happiest days of our lives,' I said. 'Why do people say that? Are we supposed to think that now our schooldays are over, it's all downhill?'

I removed the pen cap and wrote on his shirt *Connor and Eden 2000–2012.*

'I remember the first day of school so clearly,' said Connor. 'You arrived with your mum. You left her at the door and picked up a jigsaw puzzle and brought it to the table. You forgot about her right away but she stood there and watched you for ages.'

I wished I could remember that myself. I had no real memories of my mother, just things that Miranda told me when we looked at old photographs.

'I remember you too. You wet yourself.'

'Thanks, Eden. I can always rely on you to remember the good times.'

'That's what friends are for,' I said, handing him back the marker. 'Your turn.'

He looked at my shirt. Almost all the white space was filled with comments and signatures. 'There's no space left.'

'The inside of my arm,' I said, twisting my arm to expose the underside.

There wasn't much room. He wrote the same as I did: *Connor and Eden 2000–2012*.

'Not very original,' he said. 'But inspired by one of the best.'

'Let's capture the moment,' I said, pulling my phone out of my bag. 'Go and stand by the steps, under the sign.'

He walked over and turned towards me, a big happy grin on his face, his blond hair full of sunshine and light.

'Say, cheese,' I said, holding my phone up and snapping a few shots.

'My turn, I want one of us together.' He put his arm around my waist and held me close to him, the other arm stretched out, holding the phone.

'Promise you'll delete them if they're terrible.'

'No way. These photos will be online before dinner-time.'

The school bus sighed into the parking bay in a cloud of grey diesel fumes.

'This is it,' I said. Sentimentality was threatening to rear its sickening face.

'We've still got exams to look forward to,' said Connor.

I gave him a look.

'And the leavers' ball.'

'Now you're talking,' I said. 'That will be a fun night.'

Connor kicked at the ground. 'Have you thought about who you might want to go with?'

I shrugged. I suppose I'd assumed that Connor would ask me. Like he said, we'd been friends for ever and neither of us had a boyfriend or girlfriend. It would make a sweet ending to twelve years of schooling. Me and Connor: best friends for ever.

'Well,' I began.

And then I saw Ryan. He was striding straight towards us, his shirt covered in scrawled signatures, his tie knotted halfway down his chest.

'Eden!' he yelled. 'You haven't signed my shirt yet.'

I smiled. 'Doesn't look like there's any room.'

'There's always room for you.'

I could feel myself blushing.

'I guess I'll see you tomorrow,' Connor said.

'At the beach,' I said. 'Can't wait.'

'In a sick sort of way I'm going to miss this,' he said softly.

The tide was high, leaving only a narrow strip of warm, dry sand. Ryan and I had arranged to meet the others on the harbour beach, at our usual sheltered spot under the wall. They were already there, Amy hiding her milky skin in the shade of a beach umbrella, the others stripped down to shorts and T-shirts, basking in the unseasonably warm glow

65

of April sunshine. Connor saw us first. He stared as we walked across the beach towards him.

'Did you take the bus?' he asked, checking his watch.

'I drove us,' said Ryan.

'You're making quite a habit of driving around with under-age drivers,' Connor said, glaring at me.

Ryan looked from Connor to me and back again.

'Did you take the bypass or the coast road?' Connor asked Ryan.

'The coast road,' said Ryan. 'What difference does it make?'

Connor smiled thinly. 'She hasn't told you, has she?'

Ryan shrugged one shoulder. 'Told me what? How can I answer that question?'

'Shut up, Connor,' I said. 'The buses aren't convenient and Ryan's a good driver. Anyway, it's my decision.'

'Don't argue, children,' said Megan.

Matt stood up. 'We've been waiting for you two. The tide is high and you know what that means.'

I groaned.

'We're gonna jump off the harbour wall! First jump of the year. Coming?'

'You go ahead,' I said. 'We'll come down in a minute.'

Matt clucked like a chicken. 'The tide is high, Eden. It doesn't get any safer than this.'

'It's not just the water, it's the height,' I said. 'And the rocks.'

'The rocks aren't dangerous at high tide,' said Matt. 'You just have to know exactly where to jump. If you watch where I jump, you'll be OK.'

'And if I don't jump where you jump?'

Matt mimed his head exploding. 'It's game over!'

'Exactly. No thanks.'

He threw a shortie wetsuit towards Ryan. 'I brought my spare if you want to borrow it.'

Ryan pulled off his jacket and threw it on the sand. 'I'll keep Eden company.'

The four of them ran across the sand to the harbour wall. It towered above the water, even at high tide.

Ryan raised his left arm to push the hair out of his face, and the sleeve of his T-shirt rose up revealing a tattoo on his bicep. It was a large, blue sphere and a smaller white sphere cradled in the black branches of a tree.

'What's your tattoo?' I asked.

He glanced at it. 'It's a symbol. An environmental thing.'

'Did it hurt?'

'Not really.'

'Can I look at it?'

He held his arm out and I touched the tattoo with my fingers. I expected it to feel different to the rest of his skin, but it didn't.

'It's beautiful.'

Ryan covered it with his sleeve. 'Thanks.'

'You sure you don't want to go with them?' I said. 'I don't mind sitting on my own.'

He shook his head. 'I don't want to jump off the wall. I want to spend time with you.'

'You do?'

He looked at me with a bemused expression. 'Yes. I like you. You're interesting.'

I didn't feel remotely interesting, sitting on the beach, too scared to join in with the fun my friends were having.

'But you hardly know anything about me.'

Ryan laughed, just as Megan launched herself off the harbour wall with a scream. I watched as she swam towards the shore. From experience, I knew that they'd all repeat the jump four or five times before they tired of it and swam across the bay to Lucky Cove on the opposite headland.

'Are you going to educate me?' said Ryan.

I looked at him, lost. 'What do you want to know?'

'Everything.' He was still smiling at me with his big, warm smile, a smile that was amused and friendly and just on the cusp of being flirtatious without quite crossing into it.

'That could take a while,' I said, feeling myself blush.

'I don't mind.'

I lay back on the sand and closed my eyes, enjoying the gentle caress of the April sunshine on my skin.

'Everything is a big subject,' I said. 'How about you get to ask me three questions.'

'Like three wishes in a fairytale?'

'Mmm. Exactly. And then I get to ask you three.'

'OK,' he said. 'Only three questions. I'll have to make them count. So let's start with the perfect date.'

'That's a good question,' I said, stretching my arms above my head. I'd never considered it before. My perfect date. I'd never been on any kind of date, good or bad. 'I'd like to drink cold champagne and eat warm, sweet strawberries while the sun sets over the sea.' I'd never had champagne before, but I liked the way it sounded.

Ryan laughed. 'Very romantic.'

'I hope so. I mean, for it to be the perfect date, it would have to be with someone I love.'

'That leads on perfectly to my next question. Have you ever been in love, Eden?'

Both the question and the way he said my name made my heart stall. I was pretty sure my blush must be in full bloom by now, from chest to forehead. I put my hands over my eyes to shield them from the sun and my embarrassment, and then parted my fingers slightly so I could look up at him. He was looking down at me, the sun weaving through his hair and lighting up his face.

'No,' I said, although I was beginning to wonder if the acute mixture of nerves and embarrassment I felt whenever he was near might be one of the symptoms.

He held my gaze, a half-smile on his face. 'What are you afraid of?' he asked.

For a moment I thought he was still talking about love, but then I realised that this was question three.

'Heights,' I said. 'Deep water. And missed opportunities.'

'Missed opportunities,' he repeated. 'I agree. OK. Your turn.'

I thought for a moment, unsure what I most wanted to know about him.

'What's the worst thing you've ever done?' I asked in the end.

Ryan exhaled slowly. 'Whoa. Right in with the serious stuff. How about a gentle warm-up question first to help me relax.'

'I only have three questions.'

'You'll probably be disappointed by my answer. I haven't done anything really bad. I guess the worst thing I've ever done is pretend to be someone I'm not so I could fit in with a group of people.'

I couldn't imagine Ryan struggling to fit in. It made him sound vulnerable in a way that didn't add up.

'Second question?' he asked.

'What do you want to do when you grow up?'

'I don't know,' he said, shrugging one shoulder. 'Probably something with the environment. With animals or plants. Study ecosystems. Protect fragile habitats.'

'Like a job at the Eden Project?'

He smiled. 'Something to do with Eden. Yeah. That would be perfect.'

'Last question,' I said. 'Who is your hero?'

Ryan chuckled. 'Connor.'

I looked up at him through my fingers. He was laughing of course.

'Connor?' I asked.

'Why not? He's smart, he's independent, and he doesn't care what anyone thinks. And he has you for a best friend.'

'Be serious.'

'Fine. I don't have heroes. I don't believe in them.'

'Why not Gandhi or Nelson Mandela or Martin Luther King? Surely they've done more to earn your admiration than Connor?'

Ryan said nothing. Out of nowhere came the memory

of Matt telling me that Ryan had never heard of Hitler. I sat up. 'You *have* heard of Gandhi and Mandela?'

'Of course,' he said. He dug his heel into the sand and frowned.

'Who are they then?'

Ryan looked at me and exhaled deeply. 'I have heard of them. I recognise their names, but I can't remember why they're famous.'

'History lessons in New Hampshire must be so bad. What did they teach you?'

'You've had your three questions,' said Ryan.

'Answer it and you can ask me one more.'

'They taught us about the Greeks and Romans mainly and the history of discovery and exploration.'

'Like Columbus?'

He nodded. 'Can I ask my final question?'

'Fine,' I said, expecting another general question about my loves or hates.

'What did Connor mean earlier?'

'You mean when he began his Mr Health and Safety routine?'

Ryan nodded.

I hesitated. I hated talking about what happened. People never knew what to say. 'Ten years ago, I was in an accident. I was in a car with my parents and we were driving home from a wedding. My dad was driving. He'd had a lot to drink apparently. We were on the coast road, halfway between Penpol Cove and Perran. He lost control of the car. It skidded off the road and into the sea.' I pointed to the headland across the bay from the harbour. 'That's where it happened. It's known as Lucky Cove. Both my parents drowned.'

Ryan said nothing, but I noticed on the drive home later that afternoon that he stayed well below the speed limit for a change.

CHAPTER 7

Ryan knocked on the door at eleven o'clock on the dot, just as the beeps on the radio signalled the hour. I smiled to myself at the military precision of his timekeeping. How had he managed that? I'd been watching for him from my bedroom window, half expecting him to call and cancel. It was my turn to host the Sunday revision session and although I'd invited Ryan every week since we met, this was the first time he'd accepted.

I'd seen his silver car reach the top of Trenoweth Lane before heading around the corner, out of sight. A minute or two later, he'd strolled along the road, his backpack swinging from one shoulder, as though he didn't have a care in the world. Part of me hoped to catch him doing something self-conscious – like checking his reflection in the wing mirror of a car – but he had just ambled along the pavement, hands stuffed in the pockets of his jacket.

Miranda got to the door before me and I guessed she had been planning that all along.

'Hi,' I yelled, running down the stairs two steps at a time.

Ryan looked up at me and smiled. 'I wasn't sure what

we were studying, so I brought everything,' he said, holding up his backpack.

I was stunned for a moment by just how great he looked in his shirt and black jeans, and then I remembered my manners. I jumped to the bottom of the stairs.

'Ryan, this is Miranda, my aunt.'

'How do you do?' Miranda said, shaking his hand enthusiastically. 'Come inside and meet Travis, my partner.'

Partner. That was new. Travis had somehow skipped the boyfriend stage, jumping directly from friend to partner, passing Go and collecting two hundred pounds without me noticing. Not that I minded too much. Despite the vegetarian jibes, Travis was OK and he seemed to make Miranda happy.

Travis was sitting at the kitchen table drinking a coffee and reading the food section of the Sunday newspaper. He stood up and held out a hand. 'It's nice to meet you, Ryan.'

'Likewise,' said Ryan, shaking Travis's hand.

'Take a seat,' said Miranda.

Inwardly I cringed. Miranda had warned me that she wouldn't let Ryan and me go up to my room alone. What did she think we were going to get up to with her and Travis downstairs and Connor and Megan on their way over? And if she objected to me being alone in my room with a boy, why did she allow me to spend hours alone with Connor? It was typical of her random, half-thought-through rules that held no logic.

'What part of the US are you from, Ryan?' Travis asked, as he sat down again.

For a second Ryan looked alarmed, as if he'd been asked a trick question, but then he pulled out a chair and joined him. 'New Hampshire.'

'Live free or die,' said Travis with a smile. 'I'm from California myself.'

'Eureka,' said Ryan, smiling back.

'Would one of you like to explain what you're talking about?' I asked.

'No,' said Travis, winking at me. 'You like puzzles. You work it out.' He turned his attention back to Ryan. 'What part of New Hampshire?'

'Wolfeboro. Do you know the area?'

'Not at all,' Travis said. 'But my college room-mate came from that area, so I've heard a little about that part of the country. What's the hunting like out there? Mike used to shoot deer. He invited me but I never did make it out.'

'Ryan's vegetarian,' I said. 'He doesn't hunt.'

Travis smirked. 'Well then, this really is a match made in heaven. Shall we put an announcement in the paper?'

Ryan looked at me, one eyebrow raised in a question.

'Just ignore Travis,' I said. 'It's his aim in life to irritate and embarrass me as much as possible.'

'You have an unusual accent, Ryan,' said Travis. 'You're not originally from the east coast, are you?'

'We move around a lot. Dad's a writer and he likes quiet places. Every year or so we move. Wolfeboro is home, but I grew up all over the place.'

Miranda was pouring orange juice into a jug. 'That sounds exciting.'

75

Ryan shrugged. 'It's OK.'

'Has he written anything we might have read?' she asked.

'Not unless you enjoy books on palaeoclimatology and astrophysics.'

'What's that?' asked Miranda, reaching for a set of tall glasses.

'It's the study of long-term climate change.'

'He must be very clever.'

My phone vibrated with a text message. 'Connor and Megan have just got off the bus,' I said. 'They'll be here in a couple of minutes.'

'Well then, you'd better take this up to your room,' Miranda said, passing me a tray laden with biscuits and cakes and juices.

That morning I had tidied, dusted and vacuumed my room and even picked a bunch of daffodils from the garden to make the room smell nice. Miranda had noticed and she and Travis had teased me all through breakfast.

'*Voilà*,' I said, kicking the door open. '*Chez moi.*' I put the tray down on my desk. Ryan shrugged off his black jacket and hung it on the hook on the back of my door.

He turned a full circle, taking it all in with a smile. 'So this is where you dream,' he said, almost to himself.

He leant on the window sill and gazed down into the back garden. A cool wind was blowing in from the Atlantic. Miranda had pegged out the washing and the sheets billowed and snapped on the washing line like sails.

'Choose a seat,' I said.

As well as the single bed, there was a desk with a chair, an armchair with a reading light and a beanbag on the floor. Plenty of options.

Ryan chose the bed. He leant back against the head-board.

'Sorry about the interrogation,' I said, sitting next to him.

'They seem nice.' He picked up a small framed photo from my bedside table. 'Are these your parents?'

I nodded. It was my favourite photo of the three of us. We were standing in the back garden on a sunny day. My mother was wearing a pair of thin, rectangular sunglasses and her bright red hair, which fell almost to her waist, gleamed like copper. My dad, tall with wavy brown hair was grinning at the photographer. I was in between them, my darker auburn hair tied into two neat little plaits, squinting through the sun.

'Your mother is beautiful,' said Ryan. 'You look like her.'

It was a sweet thing to say. My mother was beautiful but we didn't look alike. Nor were we alike in personality. She was as vibrant and confident as the colour of her hair and, according to Miranda, was as reckless as I was cautious. My mother had jumped out of an airplane for charity when she was twelve and had once been rescued by the coastguard when her rubber dinghy floated more than a mile out to sea as she slept. Although Miranda had never said so, I was certain she would have been one of the kids jumping off the harbour wall as a teenager. The most reckless thing she'd done, however, was drop out of school aged sixteen when she'd discovered she was pregnant with me. Against everyone's advice she had married my dad, who was only seventeen himself.

Ryan put the photo back on the bedside table and turned his attention to the books piled up next to my bed. 'You've been working on Shakespeare.'

I nodded. 'English is one of my first exams. I have a list of revision topics for Shakespeare.'

'Let's hear them.'

I shuffled through a file of papers. 'Who is most responsible for the deaths of Romeo and Juliet?'

'The apothecary?' suggested Ryan. 'He sold Romeo the poison.'

'I think that Shakespeare is the most responsible.'

Ryan raised an eyebrow. 'Because he wrote the play?'

I shook my head. 'Shakespeare spells out what will happen in the play at the beginning, in the prologue. The chorus tells the audience that "a pair of star-crossed lovers take their life". I think that he means that their future was already written. It didn't matter what they did, or what anyone else did, they were destined to take their lives. I guess I'm talking about Fate.'

'You could be right. Romeo and Juliet frequently see omens that suggest their fate.'

'Evidence, please, Mr Westland,' I said, mocking Mr Kennedy, our English teacher.

Ryan lay back on the bed and stared at the ceiling. 'Just before going to Capulet's ball, Romeo has a premonition that things will end badly – "my mind misgives some consequence yet hanging in the stars,"' he said quietly, his eyes still gazing at the ceiling as though the words were written there. ' "Shall bitterly begin his fearful date with this night's revels, and expire the term of a despised life, closed in my breast, by some vile forfeit of untimely death." '

'I take it you studied this play back in New Hampshire?'

Ryan nodded.

'It seems they teach literature more thoroughly than they teach history.'

'That was a backhanded compliment,' he said, swatting my thigh with a copy of *Romeo and Juliet*. 'So, Miss Anfield, how does Shakespeare explore the theme of Fate in his plays?'

'That's a massive question,' I said, groaning. 'You'll have to narrow it down a bit.'

'In *Macbeth*, is Macbeth the victim of Fate or his own ambition?'

'Macbeth believed in Fate. But he also tried to prevent Fate from determining his destiny. Like when he tried to kill Banquo's sons. But the prophecies all came true.'

'Forget Shakespeare. Do you believe in Fate?'

'No. I believe we make our own destiny. I hate the idea of Fate. It's a cop-out. It stops people taking responsibility for their actions. I think that, until we make a choice, the possibilities are infinite.'

Like the choices I was faced with now. He was lying on my bed; I was sitting next to him, mere inches separating us. I could stay where I was, and ask him what he thought about Fate. Keep it friendly and platonic. Or lean over impulsively and kiss him.

'And once you've made a choice?'

'All the other possibilities disappear.'

Ryan sat up, leant towards me and gently placed one hand on my arm. 'So imagine this,' he said, a mischievous twinkle in his voice. 'Imagine you travel back to the Victorian period. And imagine you walk in on your great-grandfather meeting your great-grandmother. Would you look at them and think that their possibilities were infinite? Or would you think that Fate had already determined their future? That they were bound to make choices that would eventually lead to you being born?'

I hesitated, thinking through his question. Downstairs, I heard the ring of the doorbell, registered vaguely that Connor and Megan had arrived. 'I don't know about that,' I said eventually. 'That's different. And ridiculous.'

'Humour me. Imagine that you were able to prevent them from meeting at all?'

'I don't suppose I *could* do that,' I said. 'Because if I prevented them from meeting, then I would never be born, in which case I would be unable to travel back in time and prevent them meeting.'

Ryan grinned. 'And there's the paradox.'

I smiled back. 'Do *you* believe in Fate?'

'I don't think so,' he said. 'Ask me in a hundred years.'

A herd of elephants stampeded up the stairs and my door swung open. Connor came in first, with Megan right behind him. Ryan removed his hand from my arm. Connor was all smiles until he saw Ryan sitting on my bed.

'Great,' he said. 'You're here.'

Connor sat in the armchair and pulled a physics text-book out of his backpack. 'Let's warm up with some science, shall we?' he said.

'We've already warmed up,' I said.

Connor looked at Ryan and then at me. 'Bet you have.'

'What's that supposed to mean?' I asked.

Connor shook his head. 'It doesn't matter. I'll test you.'

Science – physics in particular – was his strongest subject and I suspected he chose this so that he could spar with Ryan in some silly intellectual showdown. Ryan answered every question Connor threw his way, in detail, a bored expression on his face.

'If you already know all the answers,' Connor said eventually, 'why don't you go home?'

'Connor!' I said.

'It's OK,' Ryan said, standing up. 'I'm quite good at science. Not so good at twentieth-century history. Let me know the next time you plan to study that and I'll come along.'

He picked up his backpack and I walked him to the front door.

'Wish you wouldn't go,' I said.

Ryan shrugged one shoulder. 'I don't want to, but Connor is going to be a jerk if I stay.'

'I'll tell him to leave.'

Ryan shook his head. 'Don't do that. Study with him. Maybe you and I could spend some time together tomor-row?'

My heart literally skipped a beat and I held on to the door frame to steady myself. 'Let me give you my number.'

I picked up a marker from the phone table in the hall.

'Do you have a scrap of paper in your backpack?' I asked.

Ryan held out his hand. 'Just write it on the back of my hand.'

His hand in my hand felt warm and almost too intimate. I dragged the pen across his skin, taking care to make the numbers clear.

Ryan read the numbers back to me. 'I'll see you tomorrow then,' he said with a smile.

Back upstairs, Connor and Megan were tucking into biscuits and juice. Megan smiled sympathetically as I walked in.

'What was that all about?' I asked Connor.

He shrugged. 'He's such an asshole. Why come to a study session if you don't need to study?'

'He didn't know we were going to be studying science,' I said. 'You chose the subject.'

'He just came to show off.'

'No. You tried to show off and it backfired.'

'Why did you invite him anyway? You know how I feel about him!'

'No, I don't know how you feel about him, although it's become quite clear this afternoon. What's your problem with Ryan?'

'He flirts with everyone. And it's just irritating to see you fawning over him like every other girl in our year.'

'I don't fawn over him,' I said.

'Yes you do. And then I come over today and he's lying on your bed.'

'He doesn't flirt with me,' said Megan.

'He flirts with most girls,' said Connor irritably.

'But not fat girls,' said Megan.

'You're not fat,' I said.

Megan laughed soundlessly and reached for another biscuit. 'I'm just big-boned.'

Connor ignored her and glowered at me. 'Are you going to the ball with him?'

'No.' I glared back at him.

'You said no?' His tone was disbelieving with the faintest flicker of a smile.

'I didn't have to. He hasn't asked me.'

Connor looked confused. 'But Friday, at the end of the day, I thought . . .'

'You thought wrong. Ryan hasn't asked me to the ball. Which is fine. Because I'm not going anyway.'

Both Connor and Megan looked at me.

'You have to go,' said Megan. 'Everyone goes to the leavers' ball.'

'It's a rite of passage,' said Connor.

'I'm not going,' I said. 'But since you two obviously feel so strongly about it, why don't you go together?'

CHAPTER 8

Connor and Megan had been gone for nearly an hour when I noticed Ryan's black jacket hanging on the back of my bedroom door. I ran my fingers down the material. Impulsively, I pulled the jacket down off the hook and buried my face in it, breathing in the scent of him through the fabric.

'Eden!'

I stuffed the jacket into my backpack and picked up the tray of glasses just as Miranda poked her head around my bedroom door.

'Ryan left early,' she said.

'Ryan and Connor don't get on very well. He thought it would be better if he left.'

Miranda raised her eyebrows in surprise. 'Travis and I are going to walk to the shop to pick up some milk. Won't be long.'

She took the tray from me.

'Actually, I'm going to go out too,' I said. 'Ryan left his jacket behind. I need to return it.'

'Fine. Wrap up warm. The wind is cold.'

*   *   *

My eyes stung as the wind blasted against my face. I blinked and marched on, keeping my head down. The wind's sharp teeth ripped through my thin clothing. Despite Miranda's warning, I hadn't dressed for the weather; I'd stayed in the tight blue top I'd worn earlier, the thin one that hugged my body and made me look like I had curves. I'd straightened my hair again, touched up my make-up and sprayed perfume behind my ears.

It was pointless. Standing in front of his door, I ran my fingers through my hair, trying to sort out the unruly tangle of curls. My heart thudded harder in my chest. Would Cassie be there? What was his dad like? Why had it never occurred to me to ask about his mother? Just as I was about to knock, Ryan opened the door, catching me with my fingers knotted in my hair.

'Eden! What are you doing here?'

I had the horrible feeling he wasn't pleased to see me.

I unzipped my backpack and pulled out his jacket. 'You left this,' I said. 'I thought you might need it.'

Ryan stood aside to let me in. 'Looks like you could use a jacket yourself. Come inside.'

'I should go.'

'No. Come in.'

He smiled and my nervousness evaporated.

I followed him through the hall and into a room on the right. Heat blazed out of a fireplace in the opposite wall.

'Warm yourself by the fire,' he said. 'I'll make us hot drinks. What would you like?'

'Whatever you're having.'

I crouched in front of the fireplace, rubbing my hands together. Once I could feel them again, I took a look around the room. The walls were covered in a pink florid wallpaper that had yellowed in places and was smoke-stained around the old fireplace. The carpet was bottle green and textured, the sort of flooring that looked like it belonged more in a shabby hotel than a modern home. But the sofa was modern and looked brand new. There was a large plasma-screen TV hanging in the alcove next to the fireplace. The only other items of furniture were a book-case stuffed full of books and a coffee table. There were no family photographs or ornaments, no pictures or plants or games or rugs. Functional, with a hint of grandma.

I went over to look at the bookcase. You can tell a lot about people from the books they read. There was the complete works of Shakespeare, and poetry by Ben John-son and John Donne. I noticed the usual nineteenth-century novelists: Austen, the Brontës, Thackeray, Dickens and Hardy. *The Rough Guide to Britain*. A range of cookbooks. A guide to popular culture in Britain. Late twentieth-century fashion. World atlases and basic science textbooks. Biographies of Darwin and Einstein. All the books were well thumbed. Nothing pretentious or phony about this book collection.

I sat on the couch. Ryan's backpack was on the floor, unzipped, a pile of books on the floor beside it. I glanced at the title on top. *A History of Twentieth-Century Britain*.

The door swung open and Ryan came in with two mugs of hot chocolate. He put them on the coffee table and sat next to me on the couch. I'd imagined Ryan as a strong-black-coffee kind of boy, not someone who would make hot chocolate with whipped cream and chocolate sprinkles.

Although he had left a few centimetres of space between us, I felt suddenly conscious of his closeness; it was as though little electrical currents were running between his skin and mine.

'Where's your dad?' I asked.

'Out. Cassie's out as well.' He raised an eyebrow. 'We have the whole place to ourselves.'

I giggled nervously.

'So what do you want to do?' he asked, just the tiniest hint of suggestion in his voice.

'You've been brushing up on your twentieth-century history this afternoon,' I said, indicating the books piled on the floor.

'That's my weakest subject, as you know.'

'I could test you,' I said, unzipping my backpack and taking out my books.

Ryan laughed. 'More studying. I'm not sure I can handle that much excitement in one day.'

I looked at the clock on the wall. 'Half an hour and then we'll do something fun.'

'Is that a promise?'

'Promise,' I said, wondering what Ryan's idea of fun would be.

He had clearly got to grips with his twentieth-century history. He had no difficulty answering questions about

Hitler or Mussolini or Churchill; he had informed opinions on the causes of the First World War; described the cold war right up to the fall of the Berlin Wall.

'You're not just a pretty face,' I said. 'If that's your weakest subject . . .'

'Pretty!' said Ryan. 'Thanks a lot! How about gorgeous or handsome. Even cute is better than pretty. Pretty makes me sound like a five-year-old girl.'

I laughed. 'You're definitely not a five-year-old girl.'

'Are we going to do something fun now?'

'Whatever you like,' I said, noticing that he had draped his arm along the back of the couch.

'Hmm,' he said, inching closer to me. 'I can think of something . . .'

He shifted his gaze from me to the window. I heard the crunch of tyres on gravel, saw the headlights of a car sweeping across the window like searchlights, then the slam of a car door.

Ryan sighed. 'We have company.'

'I should probably go,' I said.

'Don't go. I'll introduce you to my dad.'

'That's just the sort of fun I was hoping for,' I said.

'We can go up to my room,' he said.

The door to the sitting room swung open, but it was Cassie, not Ryan's father. 'You in here, Ry?' she said as she ran in. 'You'll never believe . . .'

Ryan turned towards her. 'Hi, Cass,' he said. 'What's up?'

Time slowed down. I saw Cassie look from me to Ryan

to me again. I saw her clock his arm along the back of the couch, how close to each other we were sitting.

'Well, this is a good idea,' she said after a pause. She turned and walked out.

Ryan leapt up off the couch and followed her into the hall. 'Cass,' I heard him hiss.

I strained my ears. 'How does this help anything?' she whispered. 'You're not supposed to bring anyone home.'

'I didn't invite her,' I heard him say. 'She just showed up at the door. But it's not a problem.'

'Get rid of her.'

I heard Ryan's voice again, but it was too soft to make out. I went back to the sofa and gathered up my books. I wanted to get out of the house as quickly as possible. Clumsily, I knocked Ryan's neat pile of books over. I straightened his pile and finished stuffing my things back into my backpack.

Ryan came back in. 'Sorry about her. She's socially inept.'

'It's OK,' I said, standing up. 'I should get home anyway. Miranda will be wondering where I am.'

'I'll drive you.'

'I can walk.'

'It's blowing a gale and the forecast isn't good. I'm not letting you walk.'

I didn't argue; I didn't much want to face the biting wind.

'I'll be back in five minutes,' he shouted, as we went out through the front door.

The wind whipped my hair in my face and despite the early hour, dusk was falling fast.

'Cassie's your sister?' I asked, once we were both inside the car. I was thinking about some of the rumours I had heard when they first arrived in town that he lived with his girlfriend, a beautiful blonde.

'Yes.'

'She seems . . .' I hesitated. I wanted to say jealous. 'Overprotective.'

'Don't take any notice of her,' he said, backing out of the driveway. He pointed to a brooding band of clouds on the horizon. 'Looks like there's a storm coming.'

I got the distinct impression he was trying to change the subject.

He parked around the corner from my house so that Miranda and Travis wouldn't see the car, and then he walked me to my door.

'Thanks for the lift,' I said, when we reached the front gate. 'Do you still want to do something tomorrow?'

'Definitely,' he said with a grin. 'We never got on to the fun stuff.'

After dinner, I left Travis and Miranda in the living room with the Sunday papers and a bottle of wine, and went up to my room. Ryan and I were going to hang out alone tomorrow.

I knew he liked me. He was always friendly and attentive. And I was pretty certain he had been about to kiss me just before Cassie arrived home.

I didn't care that his sister was weird and unfriendly or that Ryan and his family had possibly escaped from a cult. I didn't care that Connor hated his guts; he'd get over it. All I cared about was that exams would soon be over and spring would soon be summer and the most gorgeous boy in the universe was spending the day with me tomorrow. Alone.

I put on my happiest, most upbeat playlist and unpacked my backpack, stacking my books neatly on my desk. Right at the bottom was a book I didn't recognise. I must have taken one of Ryan's by mistake. The cover had a picture of a blue planet floating in black space, three small moons around it. *The Journey to Eden,* said the dust jacket. I smiled to myself. Ryan must have been reading up on the Eden Project. I was just about to put the book back, when I caught the name of the author on the spine. *Connor Penrose.* Connor would be amused by that. I turned the book over to read the blurb on the back.

As a teenager, I spent countless evenings gazing through my telescope into the black abyss of space. I never took much pleasure in the distant suns of our galaxy. Faraway galaxies left me cold. What captured my interest were the planets of my own solar system: Saturn with its weird rings, Jupiter with its many moons, Mars with its captivating red glow. I dreamed of one day finding a planet with conditions similar to those on Earth. And one day my dream came true. Serendipity led me to be in the right place at the right time and I managed to detect a small, elusive planet. A planet with

an atmosphere and water. A planet filled with life. The rest,
as we all know, is history.

Connor Penrose. 11th January, 2081

My heart rammed against my ribcage in a series of slow, hard thuds. *Eden. Connor. 2081.* None of this made sense.

Adrenalin coursing through my veins, I opened the book to the middle and looked at the photographs. The first was a picture of a baby. It looked like any baby. The next page showed a toddler. Cute but generic. Could be anyone. I turned the page.

There, smiling brightly at the camera was Connor. My Connor. I felt dizzy, like there wasn't enough oxygen in the room. The caption read *Perran School, 2012.* It was the photo I had taken two days ago. I remembered the photo perfectly. Connor in his scrawled upon school shirt, the sun in his eyes.

I jumped up and pulled my phone out of my pocket. Scrolling through my recent pictures, I found the three I'd taken on Friday. I held each of them up against the photo in the book. The last one was a match.

None of this made any sense. Either I was in a dream or I was having some sort of mental breakdown. Ryan owned a book called *The Journey To Eden* that was written by Connor Penrose, published in 2081 – sixty-nine years in the future – and contained a photograph that only existed on my phone. Was I losing my sanity, or . . .

I ran to my mirror. The wild-haired, bright-eyed girl in

the mirror was still me. For a moment there I had expected to see the reflection of a woman of eighty-five staring back. Just for an instant, I thought that I had lost sixty-nine years.

I opened my mobile and dialled Connor. He answered on the first ring.

'I'm sorry,' he said, before I had the chance to say a thing. 'It won't happen again.'

'What?' I asked. 'It's me. Eden.'

'I know it's you, Eden. I'm apologising for being an ass-hole this afternoon.'

'Connor, you remember the photos I took of you on the last day of school?'

'Yeah. When are you gonna send me copies?'

'I haven't done that already?'

'No. At least put them online so I can see them. I posted yours ages ago.'

'I'll do it later.'

So I hadn't posted the photos online or sent them to Connor. I knew that, but I was beginning to doubt my own memory.

'What do you think?' Connor was saying.

'I'm not sure.' I hadn't been listening.

'Oh.' He sounded glum. 'I suppose you have other plans.'

'What are we talking about Connor?'

'I asked if you wanted to get together on Tuesday to revise for French.'

'That would be great.'

'We could study in the morning and then go to the beach or the arcade in the afternoon.'

'Perfect. I have to go.'

I snapped my phone shut and picked up the book again, flicking through the pages until I wound up back at that photo.

I turned the page. The next photo was of a telescope. The caption read *My first telescope: a sixteenth birthday present.* Connor was fifteen. His birthday was exactly a week away.

My heart thumping wildly, I turned the page. The next picture was an older-looking Connor, aged about twenty perhaps, standing on the beach with a surfboard. Connor had been taking surfing lessons for weeks, which he really enjoyed, despite the fact he couldn't stand up on the board. The next plate showed him sitting behind a desk of books. The caption read *Studying for finals, University of Manchester, 2018.* I turned the page. Connor, now older, standing next to a good-looking young man identified as Nathaniel Westland. *Westland.* A relative of Ryan's? Connor looked middle-aged, though it was clearly him; Nathaniel looked as though he was in his early twenties.

There were only three photographs left. One was of a blue planet that looked just like Earth but had three moons in its sky. The caption simply stated *Eden from Mayflower II.* The next was of a middle-aged Connor beaming at the camera, surrounded by towering pink cliffs, a green river winding into the distance. *Zion Valley, Eden, 2053.* And the last one was of an old man with white hair and a party hat. *Connor Penrose at his eightieth birthday party, 2076.*

This was insane.

I turned to the front of the book and began to read. The chapter described a boy born in the late twentieth century, the first and only child of David and Rosa Penrose. David, an accountant, died from bowel cancer when Connor was six. His mother, a teaching assistant at a local primary school, raised him alone after that in a small fisherman's cottage near the harbour. All the facts added up. This was my Connor.

I needed the internet. The problem was Miranda had decided – on one of her overprotective whims – that the only computer with access to the internet should be in the living room.

I pushed the book under my pillow and ran down the stairs to the living room. Miranda and Travis were cuddled up on the sofa, the papers spread out between them.

'Here. See if you can finish this,' said Miranda, pushing the crossword across to me. 'There are only two clues to do.'

'What you been up to?' asked Travis.

'Science revision,' I said.

'You mustn't study too hard,' said Miranda. 'You need some down time too.'

'I'm having down time right now.' Privately I was calculating how long I would have to sit there and socialise before I could go online.

'Put the news on, Travis,' said Miranda.

He clicked the remote and the BBC News 24 channel appeared on the TV screen. I plastered a mildly interested expression on my face and tuned out. I needed answers.

'Do you mind if I use the computer?'

'More work?' asked Miranda.

'I got stuck on one of the science questions.'

'What was the question?' she asked.

'Is time travel possible? But I'm struggling with it. I thought I'd do some research.'

Travis shook his head. 'That's a complex topic for Year Eleven exams. Scientists themselves don't agree on that subject. Whose theories are you supposed to be considering? Einstein's?'

Einstein was supposed to be pretty smart. That seemed a good place to start.

'Yes. Einstein.'

Travis pressed the mute button. 'According to Einstein's Special Theory of Relativity, time travel would require faster than light travel and it would take an infinite amount of energy to accelerate an object to the speed of light.'

'So Einstein thinks time travel is impossible,' I said, feeling oddly disappointed.

'Yes. And no. General Relativity is a different matter,' said Travis. 'And then, when you bring quantum mechanics into the discussion . . .'

'Travis!' said Miranda. 'Where is all this geek-speak coming from?'

Travis grinned. 'Would you believe me if I told you that, before I decided to train as a chef, I briefly flirted with a career as a science teacher?'

'You're joking?' said Miranda, wide-eyed.

'Forget Einstein and quantum whatever,' I said. 'Do you believe in time travel?'

Travis caught my eye. 'No. Nor do most scientists. Just because something may be theoretically possible, doesn't mean it's likely.' He stood up and removed a packet of cigarettes from the back pocket of his jeans. Miranda pulled a face. Considering how much she loathed cigarette smoking, it surprised me that she was willing to overlook it in Travis. On the other hand, guys hadn't exactly been knocking down our door.

He pulled a cigarette out of the packet and tucked it behind his ear. 'I need to head home now. Early start tomorrow.'

'I'll see you out,' said Miranda.

As soon as I heard the sound of Miranda brushing her teeth, I booted up the computer.

The first thing I searched for was Connor. Connor Penrose. Not a common name, but on a planet with 7 billion people, there must be loads. Googling Connor Penrose brought up over a million results. I scanned through the first ten pages of results: Facebook profiles, boys who had won sporting tournaments or competitions, place names. But I didn't find any reference to an astronomer who had discovered a planet called Eden. I'm not sure I really expected to. Next I tried a web search for Eden, which brought up lots of pages about the Eden Project and an episode guide for Star Trek. It was a waste of time.

On a whim I searched for Wolfeboro, Ryan's home town. Like the previous searches, it brought up thousands of results. Wolfeboro was a small town of about six thousand people and claimed to be America's oldest summer resort. I scanned through images of the town, which was surrounded by blue lakes and huge forests of green trees. I remembered Ryan telling me that all the trees had died due to some sort of industrial accident. I added that to the search.

Nothing.

I tried again with a different search engine. I searched the news. There was no mention of an environmental disaster in or near Wolfeboro.

By the time I clambered into bed at eleven thirty, I had devised a theory. Although it seemed impossible, the evidence was staring me in the face. The book written sixty-nine years in the future. The fact that the book was written by Connor Penrose and my best friend was Connor Penrose. Ryan showing up at school just weeks before school ended. Ryan not recognising commonplace food such as pizza and burgers. Not knowing who Hitler was, or Gandhi or Mandela. Ryan telling me that an industrial accident had wiped out all the trees in Wolfeboro when that hadn't happened. Yet.

Only one thing could explain all these things.

Ryan Westland was from the future.

CHAPTER 9

The wind shrieked around the corners of the house, shook the windowpanes and howled down the chimney in my bedroom. I saw the clock strike midnight and one in the morning. After a few minutes of tossing and turning, I gave up trying to sleep. I took *The Journey to Eden* out from under my pillow and turned again to the photos in the middle. I half expected them to have changed.

I grabbed a pad of paper and a pen from my desk and began to list what I knew.

Ryan, Cassie and their father are from the future.
They have brought with them an autobiography of my friend Connor Penrose.
Connor will one day discover a planet that he will name Eden.
My name's Eden and I'm Connor's best friend.
Connor will get a telescope for his birthday next week.
Connor will go on to study at Manchester University.
Connor will visit the planet Eden.
Connor will write an autobiography called The Journey to Eden.
Connor will live to be more than eighty years old.

It wasn't a lot to go on. But one thing stood out brighter than the lightning that flashed across the night sky: the name Connor.

I might be overwhelmed, I might be confused, and I might not have all the pieces of the jigsaw puzzle. But it was obvious that Ryan was here because of Connor. The question was: why?

In the clear light of day everything seemed absurd, the product of an overactive imagination.

'You look terrible,' said Miranda, pouring milk on to her cornflakes.

'The storm kept me up.'

Miranda nodded. 'I was awake half the night myself. You should go back to bed and catch up on your sleep. Those bags under your eyes are huge.'

Miranda left for work at eight thirty. I waited ten minutes and then shoved *The Journey to Eden* into my backpack and headed down the lane to Ryan's house.

The wind bent the trees horizontal. Rain began to fall, stinging my skin. In my rush, I hadn't thought to grab a coat. The rain began to fall harder. I thought about heading back to get a coat, but I was halfway there. My tight black jeans were stuck to my legs and my white top was rapidly becoming transparent.

Three cars were parked in front of the large, detached double garage. Ryan's silver car, Cassie's red one and a metallic-blue one. Presumably Ryan, Cassie and their dad were all at home.

I knocked hard on the heavy front door, suddenly nervous. Yet I wasn't the one with a huge secret. I exhaled slowly, trying to keep my nerve as I listened to someone on the other side of the door fiddling with a bolt.

It was Cassie.

'Oh. It's you,' she said, her eyes running over me from head to toe and back again.

A raindrop ran down my forehead and into my eye. I wiped it away, conscious how I must seem to her with my rain-soaked hair and clothes.

Sheet lightning lit up the dark, shadowy sky and was quickly followed by a growl of thunder. The storm was back.

'You'd better come in,' she sighed.

I stood in the hallway, while water puddled around my feet.

'I need to see Ryan,' I said.

'Don't you own a coat?'

'It wasn't raining when I left the house.'

'Ryan's in the shower. Follow me.'

My heart lurched at the thought of Ryan in the shower, and for a moment I thought she was going to take me to him, but she took me into a large room on the left, a kitchen and dining room all in one with a massive farmhouse table in the middle. A man of about forty was sat at the table with a pile of newspapers and magazines in front of him. He appeared to be cutting articles from the papers.

'You must be Eden,' the man said, standing up and striding over to me with his hand outstretched.

'Pleased to meet you,' I said.

He pumped my hand vigorously. 'I'm Ben. I've heard a great deal about you.'

His hand was warm, his smile friendly. 'Cassie, get Eden a towel.'

Cassie flounced from the room.

'Take a seat. Ryan will be down in a few minutes. I'll make you a hot drink.'

I sat at the table and glanced at the articles Ben had cut from the newspaper. The headline on the topmost article read *Most Earth-like exoplanet gets major demotion*. The article had yesterday's date.

'What's an exoplanet?' I asked.

Ben carried two mugs of coffee across to the table. 'A planet outside our solar system.'

My body tensed. 'I didn't think there were any planets outside our solar system.'

'Careful, it's hot,' he said, passing me one of the mugs. 'There are probably millions of planets out there. New planets are being discovered almost every day.'

'Really? So why isn't it headline news?'

'They're usually gas giants like Jupiter. Uninhabitable. I don't think there will be headline news until we discover an Earth-like planet populated by little green men.'

I laughed. 'Is that your job then? Looking for planets.'

'Not exactly. I'm a science writer. I'm writing about the hunt for planets in our galaxy.'

Cassie flung the door open and threw me a white towel. I dabbed my face and squeezed the water out of my hair.

'There's fresh coffee in the pot,' Ben told her.

It suddenly occurred to me that I had interrupted their breakfast.

'I'm sorry to show up just like this,' I said. 'I just really need to speak to Ryan.'

'There's no need to apologise,' said Ben. 'It's not a problem.'

I heard the sound of Ryan barrelling down the stairs and into the kitchen.

'Hi,' he said, a big smile spread across his face. 'What happened? You missed me so much you couldn't bear to wait until this afternoon?'

He was dressed in jeans and a white shirt, his hair wet from the shower. Despite everything, I could feel myself blushing. This wasn't how I'd planned things at all. I'd run down the lane, hyped up and ready to confront him. Now, after all the waiting around, and Ben's friendly chatter, I was beginning to lose my nerve.

'I need to speak to you about something,' I said. 'It's important.'

He nodded and poured himself a mug of coffee. 'Let's go up to my room.'

I had never seen a bedroom so sparsely furnished. There was no colour. No mess. Nothing out of place. No posters on the wall, no dirty clothes on the floor, no empty glasses or mugs. The room of someone who hadn't been here long. And then I realised: the room of someone who didn't plan to stay.

'Take off your clothes,' he said.

'Excuse me?' I said, certain that I must have misheard him.

'Take off your clothes,' Ryan said with a smile. 'I'll find something of Cassie's for you to wear.'

'I'll be fine.'

Ryan insisted. 'You're drenched. Don't be ridiculous.'

When he left the room, I stripped down to my underwear and quickly wrapped myself in the towel Cassie had given me. His room was cold. Looking round, I could see no heater. There was a soft knock at the door.

'Is it OK to come in?'

'It's fine,' I said.

Ryan gave me a pair of black trousers and a black jumper. He left the room while I dressed. Cassie's trousers fitted OK, but her jumper clung very tightly to my body.

'OK, I'm decent.'

He came back in and smiled. 'What was so urgent you had to walk through a thunderstorm? I'm glad you did. I'm just wondering why.'

Watching him, I tried to sort out my feelings. Was he the same person? Did I still like him?

'I've been up all night thinking,' I began, sitting next to him on the bed.

'About what?'

'You,' I said.

He raised an eyebrow. 'I'm not sure whether to be flattered or alarmed.'

'When are you from, Ryan?' I asked, my voice shaking as the absurd question left my mouth.

'Wolfeboro,' he said looking at me with a bemused smile. 'I've told you before.'

'Not where,' I said, trying to keep my voice steady. 'When? What year?'

The smile faltered, just for a nanosecond, and then lit up even brighter than before. 'What are you talking about?'

'I know you're from the future. I just wondered how far in the future.'

Ryan laughed a short, hollow laugh. His pale skin went a shade whiter. 'You're not making sense.'

'Fine,' I said. 'We'll just pretend then. You're from the future and I know you're from the future and you know I know you're from the future. But we can just make out that I'm insane if that makes you more comfortable.'

Ryan swore. He stood up, opened the door and scanned the landing, before shutting the door again and sitting back on the bed. He leant forward, his elbows on his knees, head in his hands. I stayed where I was, awkwardly, wondering if I should speak or reach out to touch him or just stay as I was.

After what felt like for ever, he looked up at me. 'How do you know?' he whispered.

I felt a jolt through my whole body. Ryan had, effectively, just admitted that I was right.

'Lots of little things.'

He looked at me, his eyes strangely fearful. 'What sort of things?'

'You were clueless about ordinary food.'

He groaned.

'And you didn't know things that everyone knows, like who Hitler was.'

Ryan rubbed the space between his eyes. 'I looked him up after that history lesson.'

'And then there was the way you asked me lots of things about myself but you were really evasive when I asked questions about you.'

He nodded, as though making a mental list of how to improve his undercover persona.

'You told me that an environmental disaster wiped out all the trees in Wolfeboro, which isn't true. I Googled it. At first I thought you were a member of a cult or a strange religious sect that kept you sheltered from the world.'

Ryan looked sideways at me and smiled thinly. 'So what convinced you that wasn't the explanation?'

'*The Journey To Eden.*'

He swallowed hard. 'What are you talking about?'

'Connor's autobiography.'

'You've lost me,' he said, but the usual confidence had gone.

I unzipped my backpack and removed the book. 'I accidently took this home last night. I must have mixed it up with my own books.'

Ryan reached out, almost snatching the book. 'How much of this did you see?'

'I've seen all the photographs and read the first chapter,' I said. 'But really, even without the book, I knew there was something not quite right about you.'

'Is it really so obvious?' he asked. 'Do you think anyone else has figured me out?'

I shook my head. 'No one else suspects a thing. Just me.'

Ryan rubbed his fingers through his hair, frowning at the floor.

'So, now that I know your secret, are you going to have to kill me?' It was meant to be a joke and I attempted a laugh, but the sound came out all wrong.

'No. You're safe. I'm the one who's dead.'

'Why? It's hardly your fault I figured you out.'

'Ben and Cassie will kill me. I'm not supposed to bring anyone home. And I shouldn't have left the book out. I was reading it before you came yesterday and I just shoved it under a pile of school books. I panicked.'

'They can't blame you. You didn't invite me. I just turned up.'

'I shouldn't have let you in. I'm supposed to make an excuse if anyone shows up at the door. We have to keep a distance.'

'So why didn't you?'

He looked across at me. 'I couldn't. You'd walked down the lane in that gale with no coat to bring me my jacket. You looked so cold and I just couldn't . . .' He trailed off.

'I would have worked it out anyway,' I said. 'There were so many little things that didn't add up.'

Ryan looked at me and smiled. 'You know, for someone in your time, discovering that your friend is a time traveller from the future must be quite a big deal. How come you seem so unsurprised?'

I shrugged. 'It has been said that I'm hard to impress.'

'Along with beautiful, smart and completely unshock-able.'

I felt my face begin to heat up. I wished to God that I could learn to take compliments. 'So are you going to answer my question?'

'You'll have to remind me what it was.'

'What year are you from?'

He hesitated, as though considering for one last time the possibility of not telling me. A flash lit up the room and was quickly followed by a rumble of thunder. The overhead lamp flickered and then died.

'Hold on a sec.' Ryan rummaged around in his desk drawer.

He found a pack of twelve candles and a lighter. He put one half of the candles on the desk, the other half on the windowsill. As he moved the flame over the wicks, each of the candles flickered to life, casting a soft pool of wavering light.

Ryan sat back on the bed. 'I was born in February 2105. I travelled back in time from 2122.'

I tried to work it out in my head. I had been born in 1995. Ryan was a hundred and ten years younger than me.

'You're seventeen?' was all I said.

Ryan nodded. 'I just said I was sixteen so I could join your Year Eleven class.'

I glanced again at the pile of books on the floor beside his bed: *Of Mice and Men*, *Romeo and Juliet*, *Great Expectations*.

'You've already left school. No wonder you keep getting top marks in all your English assignments.'

Ryan laughed. 'Brilliant. I tell you I'm from the future and you're annoyed that I'm better than you at English.'

'You're not better than me,' I argued. 'You studied the course before.'

'I have studied *Romeo and Juliet* before. And *Macbeth*. But Dickens and Steinbeck weren't on my syllabus. We studied mostly late twenty-first century writers.'

'You studied writers who haven't even been born.'

He shrugged one shoulder. 'Yeah.'

'But Shakespeare is still on the syllabus?'

'We had to study pre-2050 literature.'

Outside, the wind changed direction and the rain started pelting against the window.

'Nice weather you have down here,' said Ryan. 'It's supposed to be summer.'

I shrugged. 'Good try, changing the subject. What's the weather like on Eden?'

Ryan smiled. 'Nice try. But I can't tell you about Eden. It's forbidden by the Laws of Temporal Integrity.'

'The laws of what?'

'Temporal Integrity. Laws of time. One of the most important laws is that nothing of the future is ever to be revealed to inhabitants of the past.'

I gave a short laugh. 'Bit late for that.'

Ryan sighed. 'I'm already in more trouble than you can possibly imagine.'

'I know you're from the future,' I said. 'And I know

you're here because of Connor. Connor discovers a planet.'

'Which he calls Eden after you.'

'Eden is an obvious name for a planet. It probably has nothing to do with me.'

Ryan laughed. 'Maybe I'm jumping to conclusions here, but Connor's best friend is called Eden. And Connor names his planet Eden. Of course it could be a coincidence.'

I rolled my eyes. 'It doesn't matter why he called the planet Eden. What matters is that you've travelled back in time and I want to know why. It's to do with Connor, isn't it?'

Ryan sipped his coffee. 'I can't tell you why I'm here.'

'Ryan, I don't care about your "Temporal Laws" or whatever they're called. Like I already said, it's a bit late for that.'

'Eden, this is serious. Backwards time travel is more or less prohibited. In the few instances it's allowed, the rules are clear. Do not communicate anything about the future to the inhabitants of the past. Knowing the future can change the future.'

'I already know the future.'

'You do. But I can't risk telling you anything else.'

'You don't trust me?'

'It has nothing to do with trust. Even in my own time, nobody will know the real reason for my mission. There will be a cover story.'

I sipped my coffee. 'How do I know you're a good guy and not a bad guy if you won't tell me why you're here?'

Ryan frowned. 'You think I might be a bad guy?'

'I know that Connor isn't.'

Ryan sighed deeply. 'Connor isn't a bad guy. But neither am I.'

'You expect me to just accept that because you said so?'

He hesitated. 'You're right. You do know too much already.' He looked into my eyes. 'But you have to promise me that you will never, ever repeat what I tell you.'

'I can keep a secret.'

'OK. This summer Connor discovers the existence of a planet.'

I thought back to what Ben had just said about planets being discovered all the time.

'Lots of planets are being discovered,' said Ryan, as if reading my mind. 'But they are almost all gas giants. Even those initially thought to be Earth-like, turn out not to be. But the one Connor discovers is a habitable, Earth-like planet. A planet with water and a breathable atmosphere.'

'I saw a photo in that book. Connor surrounded by pink cliffs and a river and what looked like jungle.'

'The planet he discovers has life,' said Ryan. 'Plants and animals. Even now, when I come from, Eden is the only planet we've discovered that has life.'

'It looked beautiful.'

'It is beautiful,' said Ryan, nodding. 'Very beautiful. And very deadly. It looks a lot like Earth; it has evolved like Earth in lots of ways.'

'Does it have humans?'

'No mammals. Just birds and insects and lots of plants.'

111

'How is it deadly?'

'A microscopic parasite lives on Eden. It's harmless to life on Eden. But back on Earth it's deadly. When trade ships moved between Eden and Earth, they inadvertently transported the parasite with them. It was so hard to identify that our quarantine procedures didn't detect it. Within months of transporting resources from Eden to Earth, entire habitats on Earth started dying off. It took decades before the parasite was discovered. By then, it was too late. Most of the globe had been infected. Many parts of the Earth are uninhabitable.'

I shook my head. 'That's terrible.'

Ryan shrugged. 'Earth is dying. Most of the trees have gone. So many plant species have died out.'

'What about people?'

'The parasite doesn't hurt animals directly. But by destroying plants, it destroyed the habitats of many animals. Including humans. Do you know how many people there are on Earth now?'

'About seven billion?'

'When I'm from, the population is less than one billion. The rapid reduction is due to global famine. Many people think the human race will be finished in less than fifty years.'

I stared into my coffee cup. 'Can't you find a way to destroy the parasite?'

'It's too widespread.'

'What about moving people to Eden? Can't the inhabitants of Earth relocate?'

Ryan shook his head. 'Eden only has a very small habitable region. Most of the planet is too hot or too cold. It's not an alternative to living on Earth.'

Suddenly everything was clear. 'So you're here to prevent Eden from ever being discovered.'

'That's right. Eden is beautiful, but it's lethal to life on Earth.'

My coffee was getting cold. I drained the mug and tried to take in the enormity of Ryan's purpose here. 'If Connor doesn't discover the planet this summer, won't someone else discover Eden? I mean, if it's there, surely someone will discover it eventually. You can't prevent that.'

'And you said you don't believe in Fate.'

'I don't. All I'm saying is that if Connor discovered it, it can't be that hard to find. No offence to Connor, but he's not exactly a genius.'

'Eden is actually very hard to detect from Earth. It's possible to detect for a few hours this summer and then not again for more than seven hundred years. Connor discovered it by chance. But if Connor doesn't discover it then, we're safe for centuries.'

'Why can you only see it once every seven hundred years? Surely it's either there or it's not.'

'Eden orbits a tertiary star system. That means three stars. From our vantage point here on Earth, Eden passes in front of one of those stars for just a few days every seven hundred and three years. It's hard to detect. The sky has to be clear, obviously. But it also has to be dark and it doesn't get that dark at this time of year. If Connor misses this opportunity, we're safe for a very long time.'

'No one will ever know the planet exists,' I said slowly. 'But you know, and Cassie and Ben know. And now I know.'

'And we must never tell.'

I let that sink in. 'If you're successful, only four people will know that there's a planet out there that has life on it.'

Ryan grimaced. 'Five, actually. There's one more person. Our clean-up agent.'

'What's that?'

'A clean-up agent, or cleaner, is an agent that accompanies a time trip to police the mission. They arrive before us and leave after us. It's their responsibility to ensure that nothing goes wrong. So, for instance, if we had crashed on arrival, our cleaner would have removed the evidence. Or if Ben went AWOL, our cleaner would find him and bring him back to his time. They also ensure the cover story, if needed, is watertight.'

'Who is your cleaner?'

'We're not allowed to know.'

I frowned. 'There are five of us that know about Eden. And three of you were sent back to change history. You're just a seventeen-year-old boy. How on earth did you end up on this mission?'

'Ben's not my real dad. My real dad is an admiral at the Space and Time Institute. He's very powerful. His father invented four-dimensional travel. And my mum's family are all environmental campaigners. My mother lobbied for this mission. They needed someone who could pass for a sixteen-year-old student, so I volunteered.'

'Slow down,' I said. 'Let's just back up to the part about four-dimensional travel.'

'Eden . . .'

'I don't want to hear any crap about Temporal Laws,' I interrupted.

'How did you know I was going to say that?'

'The look on your face.'

He laughed. 'So I'm guessing you want to know how four-dimensional travel works.'

'Exactly.'

'Many years ago, probably around the time you start getting a few grey hairs and crow's-feet around your eyes,' he began.

I shoved him and he fell back against the bed, laughing. 'I'm just trying to give you an idea of the timescale.'

'Fine. Give me a date. No more comments about wrinkles and grey hair.'

'OK, OK,' he said, holding his hands up. '2044. My grandfather, Nathaniel Westland, discovered how to create short cuts through space so that we can travel to distant stars in minutes instead of light years. The same technology allows you to travel through time.'

'Are there lots of people from the future living among us?' I whispered, suddenly wondering if all the people who claimed they'd seen flying saucers might actually be right.

Ryan sat up again. 'No. Just Ben, Cassie, me and our cleaner.'

'How can you be sure?'

'Like I said, time travel is owned exclusively by my father's company. And it is strictly regulated.'

'But why? It would be amazing to travel back in time and see Charles Dickens in Victorian London or Catherine Howard at her execution.'

'Gruesome choice.'

'Just an idea. I'd have thought people would be queuing up to take a journey into the past.'

'Imagine the terrible things people could do,' said Ryan. 'The neo-Nazis travelling back in time to help Hitler win the war, for instance. Altering the timeline. Time travel is the ultimate weapon of mass destruction.'

A dull pain began to throb at the back of my eyes. I rubbed my forehead. 'I have so many questions.'

'I've told you a lot this morning. And you can never tell anyone what you know. The more I tell you, the more difficult that's going to be for you. I've told you enough for you to understand why I'm here and what I have to do. Why our mission is so important.'

I nodded. 'I could help you.'

He smiled. 'I was hoping you'd say that.'

'What can I do?'

'You can help me get close to Connor. I've tried, but unfortunately he doesn't like me too much.'

'He does seem to have taken an irrational dislike to you. Almost as though part of him can tell that you're here to mess up his future.'

'I need to be close to him if I'm to stand any chance of controlling the events that lead to the discovery of the planet.'

'I can't make him like you, but I can make sure that you get to hang out with us after school and on weekends.'

'That's what I need. Especially around the date of the discovery.'

'Which is?'

'The twenty-third of June.'

'That's the day of the ball.'

'Exactly. But that's about all I have so far. He talks about a girl, the love of his life, breaking his heart. They have an argument and then, to blow off steam, he goes to look at the stars and discovers this planet.'

Ryan picked up Connor's autobiography and flicked through the pages, then began reading aloud.

'*We were at a party. I was upset. This girl was the love of my life. After she publicly humiliated me, I left the party and did what I always did when I was upset. I went stargazing. There's something about all those millions of stars out there in space that's so humbling. It makes a broken heart seem a trivial thing.*'

Ryan dropped the book back on the floor. 'The girl is obviously you.'

'How is that obvious?'

'You're his oldest friend and he names the planet Eden. I think that's pretty good evidence.'

'Circumstantial.'

Ryan shrugged. 'He doesn't say which party he was at, although I imagine it must be the leavers' ball or a party afterwards. Do people go to parties after the ball?'

I nodded. 'Most people go on to a party.'

'So this argument – this broken heart – happens at the

117

ball or right after. Then he goes to look at the stars. He would have to have used a telescope to detect Eden's transit in front of its sun. But he doesn't say which telescope or where he was. There are several amateur astronomy clubs in Cornwall, but Connor isn't a member of any of them. And only one has a scheduled viewing night for the twenty-third June and that's on the Lizard Peninsula.'

'Can I see his autobiography again?'

'No. You can't know Connor's future.'

'You do.'

'Yes, but I have to know. And once my mission is complete, I'll be heading back to my own time. All this will be history.'

I froze. For a moment it was as though my heart stopped beating. Ryan leaving. For ever. My body was washed with an all too familiar feeling. There was no word to describe it. Loss. Abandonment. The end of hope.

'Eden?' Ryan's forehead was creased with concern.

'Headache,' I said, shaking myself out of my miserable trance.

He pressed his thumb between my eyebrows. 'You've had a lot to take in. Lie back, put your head on the pillow.' I did as he said. 'Now shut your eyes.'

He sat beside me, gently running the tips of his fingers over my forehead, in a circular motion. I sighed softly and tried to imagine the tension leaving my body, but it was the opposite of relaxing; his touch made me tighten up and all I could think about was breathing.

'You're very tense.'

'I can't help it.'

Ryan pulled the duvet on top of me so that I was covered from my neck to my toes. Then he resumed rubbing my forehead gently.

'You'll get cold,' I said.

Ryan raised an eyebrow. 'Are you suggesting I get under the covers with you?'

I laughed, embarrassed, and secretly hoped he would.

Then the door opened. I sat up with a start. It was Cassie, a look of complete horror on her face. Within seconds the horror had been replaced by a condescending smile.

'Haven't you heard of knocking?' Ryan asked.

'I've never had to before,' she said, arching her eyebrows, her eyes running over the two of us.

From where she stood, it would be impossible for her to tell whether or not I was dressed beneath the duvet.

'Eden and I are in the middle of something,' Ryan said.

'So I see.' She stayed there, staring at us, clearly enjoying my discomfort.

'What do you want?'

'Dad needs your help with something. So, when you finish whatever it is you're in the middle of, perhaps you would come downstairs and lend him a hand.'

'Tell him I'll be down in a couple of minutes.'

'Really? Just a couple? You are quick.' She let the door slam shut behind her.

'Um, that was awkward,' I said.

He laughed. 'It could have been worse. We could have been naked.'

'Is Cassie really your sister?'

'No. We're not related. Just part of the same mission.'

I swallowed. 'Have you and Cassie ever . . .'

'No!' Ryan responded before I had the chance to finish the question. 'She's light years from the type of girl I like.'

'So what sort of girls do you like?' I asked.

'Are you flirting with me?' he grinned.

'No, why would I do that?' I asked, embarrassed. 'Please! You're young enough to be my great-grandson.'

CHAPTER 10

'Look at you!' said Mrs Penrose, opening the front door. She looked me up and down. 'Where's the party?'

Cringing, I realised maybe I had overdone it a bit. I usually just threw on jeans and a T-shirt when I went to Connor's house. Today I was in the shortest skirt I owned and knee-length boots. I had leave-in conditioner and shine serum on my hair, and had sprayed myself from head to toe with perfume. I was wearing practically every item of jewellery I owned. Ryan was meeting us later and I was all too aware that the last couple of times I'd seen him I'd either been windswept or drenched. I wanted him to see that I could scrub up well.

'Come in,' said Mrs Penrose. 'He's upstairs. There's a plate of cheese scones up there. You'd better hurry though if you don't want him to scoff the lot.'

I ran up the stairs.

'Knock knock,' I said, pushing the door open.

Connor was sprawled across his bed, a skywatching magazine opened at a page about telescopes. His eyes widened as I walked in.

'Whoa.'

He ran his eyes over my outfit, lingering just a fraction too long at my hemline. For a horrible moment I wondered if Ryan might be right about Connor's feelings for me.

'You look amazing,' he said, his eyes moving back up my body to meet mine.

'My jeans are all in the wash,' I lied.

'You should wash your jeans more often.'

Ryan was *definitely* right. Connor wasn't looking at me the way you look at a friend. A band tightened around my chest and I felt sick. 'Connor,' I began.

'Don't panic,' he interrupted, curling his top lip into a sneer. 'I know it's not for my benefit. I assume Westland is meeting us at the arcade later?'

'I've no idea,' I lied again.

I sat down on the floor and regretted wearing my short skirt, which made it almost impossible to sit with any dignity.

'So, I was thinking –' said Connor.

'Stop the press!'

'I don't suppose you've reconsidered going to the ball?' he asked, shutting his magazine.

Actually, I had. Now that I knew about Ryan's mission, I realised he would have to go to the ball. And as I was the only person who knew about his mission, surely I was the obvious choice for his date? I didn't want to open up that can of worms with Connor though.

I stood up again, pulled at the hem of my skirt and took a cheese scone from the plate on his desk. 'I'm not going to the ball and I don't want to discuss it any more.'

'You'll regret it if you don't go.'

'So I'll regret it,' I said, with a shrug. 'But don't let that stop you – you should definitely go. You should take Megan.'

'Nah,' he said. 'I'd go if you were going. But if you're not going, I won't bother.'

'You have to go,' I said. 'It's a rite of passage.'

Connor laughed.

'So, is it just me and you today?'

He nodded. 'Megan said she'll catch up with us later, at the arcade.'

'What do you want to do?' I asked, biting into the warm, crumbly scone.

'What's on the menu?' he asked, raising his eyebrows.

I made a mental note to never again dress up when going to his house.

I shrugged. 'French, as the exam is tomorrow.'

'French first,' he said. 'Then Scrabble.'

Connor and I spent an hour and a half testing each other on vocab and trying out our French conversation before ditching revision for a game of Scrabble.

'What are you going to do for your birthday?' I asked, as I grabbed seven tiles from the bag.

Connor was turning sixteen that weekend.

'Nothing.'

I stopped staring at my letters. 'Don't be ridiculous. It's your sixteenth. You have to do something.'

Connor snorted. 'I don't want a party if that's what you mean. I hate parties.'

'You don't have to have a party, but you have to do something.'

Connor laid down all of his tiles. 'Excited.'

'Oh, the irony,' I groaned. 'You just scored a huge amount and you're about the least excitable person I know.'

'Remind me what you did for your sixteenth.'

I sighed. 'Not my fault. Miranda wouldn't let me have a party. But you have to admit Amy's beach party was fun.'

'Remind me what you did for your sixteenth,' he repeated.

'Me, you, Megan and Matt at the pizza parlour. Probably the lamest sixteenth–birthday party in the history of the universe. But you have a choice.'

'I choose understated.'

I took my turn on the board. 'Here's the deal,' I explained. 'It's not just about you. Your friends will feel uncomfortable if they can't do something to acknowledge your birthday. You have to do something for their sake, if not your own.'

'Eden. I hate parties.'

'Why?'

He rolled his eyes and picked some more letters from the bag. 'Expectations always exceed outcomes. I don't want to celebrate my birthday by being disappointed.'

'Maybe you could try not having any expectations.'

'Maybe *you* could try that. Like, don't expect Connor to have a party on his birthday.' He took his turn on the board. 'Anyway, you're just looking for an opportunity to hook up with Westland.'

124

'Two days ago you apologised for being out of order about Ryan. Don't start again.'

He looked at me. 'You really like him, don't you?'

'Yes, I like him.' I moved my tiles around, searching for inspiration. 'Please let's do something for your birthday. Don't be stubborn. It doesn't have to be a party.'

Connor grabbed the bag of tiles. 'I'd quite like to go to Plymouth. I s'pose you guys could come along.'

'That would be perfect,' I said. 'Amy and Megan have been talking about going to Plymouth to buy our dresses for the ball. We could spend the day there and then maybe all have dinner somewhere. You choose a restaurant and I'll make reservations for us.'

A smile appeared briefly on Connor's face. 'Fine. Plymouth on Saturday.' He sighed. 'You can invite Westland if you like.'

I let Connor beat me. It was part of the plan I'd made with Ryan. Then we were to head to the arcade, where we would run into Ryan, who would let Connor beat him at pool. One thing I knew about Connor was that winning at something never failed to put him in a good mood.

Connor yawned and packed away the game. 'What time are we meeting the others?'

'Half two.'

He checked the clock on the wall above his desk. It was almost two o'clock.

'I think I've had enough studying for today,' he said.

'Shall we head down there and have a warm-up game of pool?'

'I'm rubbish at pool.'

'I know,' he smiled. 'And Matt always kicks my ass. So let me play you for a couple of games first to boost my ego.'

'When you put it like that, how can I refuse?' I said, with a smile.

Everything was going to plan.

The sky was overcast and the wind brutally cold. Definitely not a beach day. There were a few determined people wrapped up in thick jumpers on the harbour beach, but most of the Easter break tourists were ambling along the seafront road, window-shopping, eating chips and pasties and looking slightly bewildered by the sudden change in climate. The arcade was bustling. At the front of the arcade were life-size models of people who sprayed water at you or moved if you hit the target with your rifle. Further back were pinball machines and video games. I followed Connor through the throngs of teenagers hanging round the front of the arcade, towards the room at the back with the pool tables and the bowling alley. It was darker back there, and sweatier. Smoking had been banned a few years earlier, but the lingering smell of tobacco and spilt beer was ingrained in the carpet.

I saw Matt first. He was lining up a shot on one of the pool tables at the rear of the room. Then I noticed Ryan. He was chalking the end of his cue and watching Matt carefully. He didn't see me come in.

Connor groaned. 'Your boyfriend's here.'

'He's not my boyfriend.'

'But you wish he was.'

'No, I don't.'

Connor gave me a look that suggested he didn't believe a word I'd said.

'Whatever,' he said, rolling his eyes. 'You have to hand it to him. He's a real babe magnet.'

That was when I noticed Chloe Mason and her friend Melissa. Both of them were holding pool cues and giggling. Chloe was wearing a short, tight dress that clung to her curves, barely covering her underwear. I watched as she approached Ryan from behind and slipped her arms around his waist. She leant forward and whispered something in his ear. Over to the side, I saw Melissa, swigging from a Blueberry Juiska. Ryan turned to face Chloe and laughed at something that she said. She gave him some space as he leant over the table to line up a shot.

'I don't think this is going to be my scene,' I whispered to Connor.

'Is that because of Ryan and Chloe?'

The way he said it made it sound like Ryan and Chloe were an item. I wondered if he'd known she would be here.

'I don't like Chloe,' I said.

'You just said you don't want to go out with Ryan,' said Connor, his voice tinged with petulance, 'so why does it bother you that Chloe wants him?'

'I'm not in the slightest bit bothered that Chloe wants to

be with Ryan,' I said, aiming for a neutral tone. 'I just don't like Chloe Mason or her bitchy friend.'

'You're jealous!' said Connor.

Bruised would have been a much more accurate way to describe my feelings. Disappointed. Hurt. I thought that Ryan liked me. I was certain that there was something going on between us, that something was just about to happen. And I wanted it to happen, because, despite myself, I was starting to like him too. But here he was, not expecting to see me for another half an hour, playing pool with Chloe Mason and her friend. Laughing, while Chloe Mason slid her manipulative arms around his waist.

'I'm not jealous. I just don't feel like hanging out here this afternoon. I'm going to go home and do some more revision.'

'You're a terrible liar.'

'I'll see you tomorrow in the exam,' I said, trying to ignore Chloe's shriek of laughter.

She was responding to something Ryan had said in her usual exaggerated way. She moved close to him and whispered something in his ear. He laughed and blushed.

I walked out of the arcade and into the heartless wind, while my hopes and dreams turned to ash.

It hit me on the bus ride back home to Penpol Cove.

I was sitting at the back, my head resting against the grimy window. Outside, the gentle undulations of Perran golf course rolled by. The golf course where Ryan had shown me the stars the night of Amy's party. The night when he had lain on the ground so close to me I could smell his skin and feel his breath.

It was all about Connor. Ryan was here as part of a mission and everything he did and everything he said was part of that mission. Including me. He had joined our school because it was Connor's school. He had joined astronomy club because Connor went to astronomy club. He was friends with me because Connor was friends with me.

It hit me that every flirtation – every smile or accidental touch – was a calculated move on his part. And that when his guard was down – during the brief interludes in his mission – he chose to hang out at the arcade with Matt and flirt with Chloe Mason and her friends.

It made sense. Every boy at Perran School wanted to flirt with Chloe Mason and her friends. It was only natural that Ryan would too.

I felt like an idiot.

Ryan phoned me just as the bus left the bypass for the lane that ran into Penpol Cove.

'What happened to you?' he asked. 'We were supposed to meet at the arcade. You said you would help me.'

'You seemed to be doing a good job on your own.'

Which was true. Connor had cheered up immensely when he saw Ryan flirting with Chloe.

'I let him beat me at pool like you suggested,' Ryan said. 'I think it's working. He seems friendly this afternoon.'

'That's terrific.'

'Is something wrong? Did something happen at Connor's house?'

'Nothing's wrong. I'm just worried about my exam tomorrow.'

'Do you want to meet up with me later on? I could test you.'

He sounded concerned. Friendly. Which was right. He was my friend. Nothing more.

'No. I just want some time alone to study.'

'OK,' he said quietly. 'Shall I drive you to school in the morning?'

'No, I'll take the bus.'

'Oh. So, I'll see you at school then?' He sounded cautious, concerned that he might say the wrong thing. I was glad. I wanted him to suffer a little bit, to wonder if he'd misjudged his relationship with me.

I ended the call without saying goodbye.

CHAPTER 11

The air was still and filled with mist and drizzle. As I reached the cove, the thick vapour thinned for a moment revealing a woman throwing a stick for her dog and a boy perched on a rock, sketching. The boy turned towards me and smiled. Ryan.

I hadn't seen him for days. He'd offered me a lift home after the French exam on Wednesday, but I'd made up a lame excuse about needing to meet Miranda in town. He'd called me several times on Thursday morning, but I let the calls go to voicemail. He didn't try again. I'd heard from Connor that he'd spent Thursday afternoon at the arcade with Connor and Matt. Connor hadn't mentioned Chloe by name, but the glee in his voice and talk of 'some girls from school' allowed me to fill in the blanks.

The mist thickened and he disappeared again. Sketching seemed a strange occupation for someone sent back from the future. Didn't he have more important things to do?

For a few seconds I considered ignoring him and continuing on my run, but as usual, my desire to be near him outweighed my desire to forget him. Wishing that I was in the outfit I'd worn to Connor's on Tuesday, instead of my ratty running clothes, I strolled across the pebbles and sand to Ryan's rock.

'Hi, Eden,' he said, snapping his sketchbook shut and dropping it on the sand. 'Are you OK?'

'I'm great.'

'You haven't taken any of my calls. I was beginning to think you were avoiding me.'

'I *was* avoiding you.'

Ryan gazed out towards the sea. 'Oh.'

I sat down on a flat rock next to him. 'What are you drawing?'

'Nothing much. I like to sketch when I need time to think. It helps me relax.'

'Are you going to Plymouth tomorrow?'

Ryan nodded. 'I was planning to. Connor invited me. He said you wanted me to come. But now I'm not so sure.'

'Will Chloe be coming?'

He looked at me, a mystified expression on his face. 'Chloe Mason? To Plymouth?'

I just nodded, not trusting myself to speak.

'Why would she be coming with us?'

'The two of you seem pretty friendly now.' I couldn't keep the sulk out of my voice.

'Is that why you ignored my calls? Are you jealous of Chloe?'

He sounded more surprised than amused.

'Not jealous,' I said. 'It just helped me complete the puzzle.'

'What puzzle?'

132

'You.'

He raised an eyebrow.

'Look, when I saw you and Chloe fooling around together at the arcade, all the pieces fell into place. You don't travel through time to make friends with people. I get that. You're here to complete your mission and your mission is to prevent Connor from discovering a planet.'

'Yes,' Ryan nodded.

'So your friendship with me is a means to an end. I understand.'

'No.'

He left the comment hanging in the air.

'What is this anyway?' I asked, snatching his sketch pad from the sand.

'It's just my art project,' he said, reaching for the book. 'It's not interesting.'

I flipped to the first page. It was the sketch he'd made of me during our first art lesson together. I turned the page. Studies of leaves and trunks from our trip to the Eden Project. I continued to flick through the book. A sketch of me at the beach. Me lying back on the sand, my eyes closed. Another one of me, this time sitting on my bed, surrounded by books. My face in a half-smile. A full-length sketch of me standing by the school gate. Another sketch of me soaked through with rain. A close-up of my eyes, rain beading on my eyelashes, my mascara smudged below my eyes. A sketch of me sitting on Ryan's bed, dressed in Cassie's clothes.

'Why have you drawn so many pictures of me?'

133

Ryan kicked the jagged rock in front of him. 'I think about you a lot.'

'Why? Am I significant?'

Ryan laughed. 'To my mission? That's what you mean, right?'

I nodded.

'No. You're not remotely significant. I didn't even know you existed other than as the girl who broke Connor's heart.'

'So why do you have all these pictures?'

'Isn't it obvious?'

I shrugged. It wasn't obvious at all. I knew that he liked me. And he'd been flirting with me for weeks. But he'd made it clear that he wasn't looking for anything more.

'I can't allow myself to develop feelings for you,' he said softly. 'I leave for my own time on the twenty-third June.'

'The day of the ball?'

'That night. After the mission completes.'

I swallowed but a hard lump had lodged in my throat. 'Are you any further with finding out what Connor's plans are for that night?'

Ryan smiled. 'I don't suppose you'd consider going to the ball with him, would you? Then at least I would know where he is that night.'

I groaned. 'I just don't want him to get the wrong idea.'

Ryan punched my arm lightly. 'It's a small sacrifice, Eden. One night of wondering if Connor's going to try and kiss you versus the death of the planet.'

'When you put it like that, I don't really have a choice. You'll be there that night?'

'Of course.'

'Who are you going to take?'

He shrugged. 'I'd like to take you.'

I felt a surge of hope.

'But you'll be busy with Connor.'

I watched a trawler make its way across the horizon. 'Just promise me one thing.'

'Anything you like.'

'Don't take Chloe.'

Travis drove me to the railway station on Saturday.

'Who are you all dressed up for?' he asked, as we pulled into the station car park.

I shook my head, embarrassed. 'I'm not dressed up.'

Travis smirked. 'Eden, in the few months I've known you, you've lived in jeans and hoodies. Now you're in a very short skirt and – if I'm not mistaken – you're wearing make-up. So who's it for? Ryan or Connor?'

'It's none of your business.'

I glanced at the platform. The others were already there, laughing and chatting. Ryan was wearing his usual t-shirt, jeans and boots combo, but no jacket. He had a green canvas bag, the sort you see in army surplus stores, slung over his body. He was standing next to Connor, peering at something in a magazine.

'Thanks for the lift,' I said, slamming the door without looking back.

By the time I had bought my ticket, the train was gliding into the station. We scrambled aboard and jostled through the carriages until we found two tables for four.

Connor looked at my short skirt and winked at me. 'Jeans in the wash?'

'Happy birthday, Connor,' I said passing his card and present across the table. I had bought him a couple of books he'd mentioned the week before. 'You'll have to carry them around Plymouth, but I wanted you to have them today.'

'Not a problem,' he said, pointing to his large red backpack.

Megan gave him a T-shirt with a logo that I didn't recognise.

'How did you know I love that film?' asked Connor.

Megan threw back her head and laughed. 'I found it on a website called T-shirts for nerds. I immediately thought of you.'

The others promised to find something in Plymouth.

'What did you get from your mum?' I asked.

Connor flashed me a thick wad of twenty pound notes. 'Cash to spend as I wish.'

'What you gonna buy?' asked Matt. 'An Xbox?'

'A telescope,' he said.

Ryan and I looked at each other.

'But you don't have any kind of games console,' said Matt.

Connor smiled. 'That's why I spend so much time at yours.'

As the train made its way up the line, we all settled into various distractions. Amy and Matt both plugged into an iPod, an earpiece each. Megan had a celebrity magazine. Connor took out a printout about telescopes and binoculars and started talking to Ryan about the one he planned to buy.

'It's going to be heavy,' Ryan said. 'Why don't you just order it online and have it delivered?'

'I don't want to wait. I've got the money today and I want the telescope today. If I order it online, it might be next weekend before I get it, and there'll be the shipping cost. And Mr Chinn recommended this shop called Stellar Optics. The guy who owns the shop is a friend of his. He'll give me a ten per cent discount if I show him my school astronomy club card.'

This was it. I thought back to the photo of the telescope in *The Journey to Eden*. By the end of the day, Connor would have that telescope. And on the twenty-third of June he would probably use it to discover Eden. It felt like Fate was winning after all. What if Ryan's mission really was just part of a bigger unstoppable scheme?

The gentle rocking of the train combined with the sun shining through the window made me feel sleepy. It wasn't until we'd just pulled out of St Austell that I had an idea.

'So, Connor,' I said, trying to sound enthusiastic. 'What's the name of this telescope?'

He pushed the printout across the table and pointed at a photograph. 'That's the one,' he said. 'It's big enough to see the planets in some detail but not so big that it'll be too heavy to carry around and set up. And it's just within my budget.'

'What will you be able to see?' I asked.

'Saturn's rings should be clear,' he said. 'And the red spot on Jupiter.'

'Will we be able to see the rings around Uranus?' said Matt, sniggering.

Connor ignored him and carried on talking about binary stars and nebulae and other objects that meant little to me, and I nodded and smiled and committed the make and model of the telescope to memory.

'It sounds amazing,' I said, pushing the printout back across the table to Connor.

Ryan caught my eye and frowned.

'Right,' I said. 'Drinks are on me. What's everybody having?'

'Coffee,' said Amy and Matt at the same time.

'I'll have a cappuccino with cinnamon and chocolate,' said Megan.

I rolled my eyes. 'Not on this train, you won't. You'll have coffee, tea or a soft drink.'

Megan groaned. 'I'll have a Coke then. And a Kit Kat.'

'Me too,' said Connor.

'Megan, do you have a pen and paper so I can make a list?'

Megan laughed. 'It's a pretty simple order, Eden. Two coffees, two Cokes and two Kit Kats.'

'I know. I think my short-term memory is full. Too much studying.'

She passed me a piece of paper and a pen and I scribbled down the make and model of Connor's telescope.

'Ryan, can you help me carry the drinks?'

We both got out of our seats and swayed our way along the carriage to the doors. I stopped in the space between the carriages.

'You look nice today,' Ryan said. He smirked. 'And I love it when you blush.'

'How much money do you have?' I asked.

'Enough to buy the drinks.'

'Do you have a credit card or anything?'

Ryan pressed a button and the door to the toilet slid open. 'Inside,' he said.

We both walked inside and Ryan hit the lock button. He pulled a black wallet out of his back pocket and flicked it open. 'I have dozens of cards,' he said. 'We were given one for every bank in the UK. My credit limit is huge by your standards.'

'What do you mean, by my standards?'

He shook his head. 'Not yours personally. Huge for this time. But that's irrelevant. How much money do you want?'

'Enough to buy out the entire stock of telescopes in Connor's price range.'

Slowly, as my plan dawned on him, a grin appeared on Ryan's face. 'I think I can handle that,' he said.

'Does your phone have a web browser?' I asked. My phone was a basic, cheap model that did nothing more than call, text and take photos.

He nodded.

'Find the phone number for Stellar Optics in Plymouth. Then we'll call and you can buy up all the telescopes Connor wanted. I have the make and model here on this piece of paper.'

By the time we emerged from the train toilet, ten minutes later, Ryan had called the shop and bought all five of the telescopes in stock that Connor wanted. Then, just to make sure, he had bought all the telescopes in the next price bracket, as well as the model just below, and arranged for them to be shipped to his house in Penpol Cove.

'That was brilliant,' Ryan said, laughing as the door slid open.

Outside, a woman with a toddler glared at us. 'Kids these days,' she muttered.

Ryan looked bemused. 'She didn't think we were making out in a toilet, did she? Ugh!'

'That or doing drugs,' I said. 'Come on, let's get the drinks.'

Shopping had never been a favourite pastime of mine, but that Saturday in Plymouth was the worst. By the time I arrived at the Monsoon Palace late that afternoon, I was exhausted. Everyone else was there before me. They were sitting at a table by the window.

Tealights in tiny red vases flickered on the table, which was already covered with plates of poppadoms, dishes of chutney and bottles of beer. Connor swigged from a bottle just as one of the waiters showed me to the table.

'You're late!' Connor said, a little too loudly.

'Sorry. I got caught up in the bookshop,' I said.

I'd gone to the bookshop to get away from Amy and Megan. Dress shopping had been horrible. It wasn't the dresses themselves or the fact it took Amy nearly three hours to choose one. It was Megan.

First, she'd refused to buy a dress because she didn't want to waste money on one if she didn't have a date. Then she'd confessed that the person she really wanted to go with was Connor. Finally, she decided she was going to ask him and wanted all sorts of advice from me. Did he prefer long dresses or short? Hair up or down? What was his favourite colour?

'I didn't want to say before,' she'd told me. 'Not when there was a chance that you might go with him.'

I couldn't tell her. She was smiling and trying on dresses and Amy was encouraging her. And all the time I knew that I'd promised Ryan I would go with Connor.

I ordered a Coke. Connor swigged from his bottle again and then burped. Amy, Matt and Megan were also halfway through their large bottles of Kingfisher beer, but Ryan's was untouched.

'How was your day?' I asked Connor.

'Awesome,' he said, pausing to burp again. 'Stellar Optics had sold out of the telescope I wanted, but I bought an Xbox instead. And Matt and Ryan both bought me a game for it. And guess what?' Connor lowered his voice to a stage whisper. 'Ryan has fake ID. He bought us beers.'

'That sounds great,' I said, catching Ryan's eye.

141

The flicker of a smile crossed his face.

'So what did you buy?' Connor asked. 'Megan and Amy already showed us their dresses and stuff.'

'I bought a dress and a couple of other things,' I said.

Connor swigged his beer and eyed me thoughtfully. 'Why did you buy a dress?'

'For the ball.'

'You said you weren't going.'

'And you told me I would regret it for the rest of my life. Miranda said the same thing this morning. So I changed my mind.'

Connor drained his beer. 'Who are you going with?'

'I don't know.'

There was a silence around the table. I could feel everyone looking at me.

'Don't look at me,' said Connor. 'I'm not taking you. I already have a date.'

'You do?'

Connor beamed across the table at Megan. 'I'm going with Megan.'

I looked at Megan. She gave me a tiny, uncertain smile.

'That's great,' I said brightly.

Connor was still beaming at her.

'Ryan,' said Matt. 'You're gonna have to go to the ball, mate. Eden has a dress and no Prince Charming.'

'I don't need a pity date, thanks,' I said.

Ryan smiled at me. 'So how about it, Eden,' he said. 'Will you go to the ball with me?'

Everyone fell silent again.

'OK,' I said.

Ryan grinned. 'Control your enthusiasm, Eden. Or I might start to think you have a crush on me.'

Connor banged his empty bottle on the table just a little too heavily. 'Perfect,' he said.

Ryan drove me home that evening. Connor was too nauseous to notice what anyone else was doing. Matt had promised to take him around the block a few times to walk it off.

'That was a successful day's work.'

Ryan nodded. 'I wish I could have enlisted your help earlier.'

'You should have. But you didn't trust me.'

'It wasn't that I didn't trust you. It's forbidden by the Temporal Laws for me to tell anyone. You shouldn't know any of this.'

'S'pose not.'

He glanced at me. 'I do trust you, Eden. I've told you lots of things I shouldn't have.'

'Not really. You just confirmed things I'd figured out for myself. You don't trust me enough to tell me something you don't have to.'

He sighed and shifted down to take the sharp bend in the road above Lucky Cove.

'I owe you,' he said. 'Not only have we successfully prevented Connor from buying a telescope, but we have him going to the ball with Megan. Now I know where he'll be the night of the twenty-third. If there's anything I can do for you . . .'

'You already have,' I said. 'You're taking me to the ball. One minute I didn't have a date, the next minute you stepped in and saved the day. My hero.'

My tone was much more sarcastic than I'd intended. But my feelings were such a jumble – I was both thrilled and mortified by the turn of events – that I had no idea how to express myself.

Ryan glanced at me. 'I hope you don't mind. It was a bit awkward. I felt that I had to ask you.'

I ignored the slight contraction of my heart and shrugged. 'Don't worry. I won't hold you to it. Although I have to admit, I was rather looking forward to going to the ball with some freak from the future.'

Ryan whistled through his teeth. 'I do understand if the whole time travel thing is too weird for you.'

'It has nothing to do with that,' I said. 'Strangely enough, I've got used to the whole idea. And it is weird, but not too weird, not like it would be if you turned out to be an alien or something.'

'So that would be too weird,' Ryan said slowly, looking sidelong at me through his long dark lashes.

'Ryan?'

He slowed down as we approached the street next to my house. 'How would you define "alien"?'

I backed up against the car door, not exactly scared, but definitely anxious. 'You have got to be kidding me.'

'Don't panic,' he said with a grin. 'I'm human. Completely human.'

'So what are you saying?'

He pulled the car to the kerb and switched off the engine. 'I wasn't born on Earth. I was born on Eden. Which means I'm technically an alien. But both my parents were born on Earth. I'm as human as you are.'

I looked at him carefully, wondering if he was holding back information he ought to be sharing. 'So you don't have two hearts or a tail?'

He shook his head. 'Unfortunately not. No special powers. Just a regular human with a regular human body. I could take off my clothes and show you if you want.'

'Don't ask me again,' I said, reaching for the door handle. 'I might not be able to answer responsibly.'

Ryan insisted on walking me the thirty-second walk between his car and my house. The air was cold and the sky clear and brightly starlit.

'Seriously,' he said. 'You were a big help today. I wish I could repay you in some way.'

'You can,' I said, stopping.

'How?'

'By trusting me.'

'I do trust you.' He ran his hand through his hair and gazed up at the sky. 'Do you remember any of the constellations I showed you after Amy's party?'

I stopped and craned my neck skyward. 'That's Cassiopeia,' I said, pointing at the w-shaped constellation high in the sky.

'You remember.'

'Of course I remember.' I searched the sky for Orion.

'It's the wrong time of year for Orion,' he said. 'Winter

is the best season. But now I'm going to show you another constellation.'

He turned me towards a different section of the sky and held out my hand as a pointer. High in the sky, he traced the shape of a letter 'y'.

'The constellation is Perseus,' he said. 'And that bright star is called Mirfak.'

'It's beautiful.'

'It is beautiful. But there's another star in Perseus I want to show you.'

Ryan moved my hand slightly. 'Algol. The demon star. It's also known as the evil eye.'

'Why?'

'Algol looks like a single star, but actually it's a triple star system. One of the stars is small. But two of the stars regularly eclipse each other, affecting the brightness of the star to the naked eye. It's almost as if the star makes a slow wink. If you watch it over a period of three days, you'll see its brightness wax and wane.'

'That's cool,' I said.

'Isn't it? But you know what's really cool about it?'

I shook my head.

'Algol has a planetary system. Five planets orbit the three stars.' He paused. 'Three are gas giants. One is too close to the main star for life to exist. But one of those planets is in the habitable zone. That planet is called Eden.'

Gazing out across the black sky at this brilliant, white star twinkling brightly above me, I considered how incredible it was that this star had a planet orbiting it; a planet that sustained life. Human life. Earth life. I knew about it before Connor discovered it.

'You need to forget that now,' Ryan whispered in my ear, his breath warm against my neck.

Goosebumps prickled my skin. The night air was cold and I hadn't brought a jacket, but I didn't care. Ryan had just told me that he was born on a different planet and told me where in the sky that planet was. And I was the only person from my timeline to know this. He shouldn't have told me. But he trusted me.

And I trusted him.

The curtains to the front room were shut, but I could tell from the blue flicker that Miranda was watching the television. She would be alone, waiting for me to come inside and tell her about my day while helping her finish the crossword. The enormous gulf between her life and the one I was beginning lay there between us, between the world inside the house, where everything followed the laws of physics as we understood them, and the one outside, where stars were really suns to other planets and people could travel through time.

'I'll call you,' he said.

I nodded and opened the door. I turned just as Ryan closed the gate.

'Goodnight, alien boy,' I said.

'Night, Earthling,' he said, laughing, and then he was walking back to his car.

CHAPTER 12

Dust motes floated in a shaft of sunlight. Outside, the sun blazed. The invigilators had opened the windows as far as they could, but the room was still stifling.

Physics. The last exam. The clock at the front of the hall read ten minutes to twelve. Ten minutes. Ten minutes until we were all told to put our pens down. Ten minutes until the end of exams. I should have been checking through my answers to make sure I hadn't made any silly errors, but I couldn't concentrate any longer.

All around me, heads were bent over the question papers. Ryan's seat remained empty. Although he had gone through the motions of sitting the exams over the past three weeks, he had decided to skip this one so he could help Ben and Cassie prepare for their departure in two days' time, after the leavers' ball. I wondered what sort of preparations you had to make for travelling through time. Was it complicated or dangerous like the old shuttle missions to the International Space Station or was it a more mundane journey, like a train ride to Plymouth?

'Pens down,' said the invigilator.

* * *

The sun beat down on us as we ambled towards the gate. Matt and Connor removed their ties and began whipping each other with them, laughing and saying that they would never ever wear a tie again for the rest of their lives.

Ryan was leaning against the gate, dressed in a white T-shirt and khaki shorts, a pair of very dark sunglasses hiding his eyes.

'Did I miss anything interesting?'

'Hell yeah,' said Matt. 'That was officially the most fun I've ever had in school.'

Students were spilling out of the school gates, laughing and yelling, tying their ties around their foreheads like thin bandannas.

'Everyone's going to the park,' said Chloe Mason, walking over to Ryan.

She had unbuttoned her school shirt halfway, exposing just the edge of her hot-pink bra. 'I hope you're coming. I have a going-away present for you.' She swaggered back to her group of friends, laughing and spiralling her tie above her head like a lasso.

'What's the plan then?' asked Ryan.

'Looks like we're going to the park,' said Connor.

Ryan groaned. 'Really?'

'What's the matter, Westland?' asked Connor. 'Scared?'

Ryan laughed. 'Terrified.'

Ryan's car was discreetly parked a couple of streets away from school. He opened the passenger door for me and told the others to squeeze in together in the back.

Connor pulled a face. 'Why don't we walk? It's not far.'

'I picked up the booze you wanted,' said Ryan. 'It's in the boot. It'll be easier if we take the car.'

'Come on, Connor,' said Megan. 'It's only a five-minute drive.'

Connor said nothing, but he got in the back of the car.

Ryan pulled away from the kerb and on to the street that led across town to Perran Park. I turned around. Amy was half sitting on Matt's lap, his hands resting on her thighs. With four of them in the back seat, it was inevitable that they would be squashed together. But Connor's arm was resting along the back of the seat, behind Megan's shoulders, and his body was angled close towards hers. He was laughing at something she had just said. Ryan took a corner sharply and Megan rolled against Connor, resting her head on his shoulder.

'Sorry,' she giggled.

'Don't be,' he said with a smile.

I turned away, whatever it was I'd been about to say forgotten. Until now I'd assumed that Connor had asked Megan to the ball because I'd said no, or even as a way to try and make me jealous. Could it be that he really did like her?

Even before we entered the gates to the park, we could hear squeals and laughter and the babble of voices. Over in the bandstand, two boys and a girl were drumming on overturned buckets while another boy strummed on his guitar. The whole park had the feel of an impromptu party.

'Let's sit by the fountain,' I said, imagining the cool spray on my hot, sticky skin.

We found a shady spot beneath a thicket of trees, close to the fountain. I lay back on the grass, my face in the shade of a gnarled apple tree, my legs and body in the warmth of the sun. I kicked off my school shoes. The lightest spray from the fountain reached my shins and feet.

Ryan lay beside me. 'I think apple trees are my favourite tree in the whole world,' he said.

'Why's that?'

'I like their shape. The blossom in the spring. The apples in the autumn. The smell of their fruit. They're perfect.'

'You're really into trees and plants,' I said with a laugh.

'You know why.'

'What are you drinking, Eden?' Megan asked.

'Raspberry Juiska.'

She passed me an open bottle and I propped myself up on my elbow. I didn't usually drink, but this was the last day of exams. I swigged from the bottle. A mouthful of slightly warm, sweet liquid left a trail of fire as it ran down my throat. I squeezed my eyes shut and winced.

Megan took a cherry-flavoured bottle and clinked hers against mine. 'Cheers!'

'Beer or cider, Ryan?' asked Matt.

Ryan shook his head. 'Not for me. I'm driving.'

Matt passed him a bottle. 'You can have one beer.'

Ryan passed it back. 'Maybe later.'

I swigged again from my bottle, trying not to screw up my eyes as the liquid burned my throat. Ryan was sitting next to me, propped up against the tree trunk. I looked around. It was as if we were all paired up. Connor and Megan were sitting next to each other, tasting each other's drinks. Amy was sitting in the shade, ensuring her milk-white skin didn't curdle, while Matt ran his fingers through her blue-black hair.

'I'm so glad it's all over,' said Connor.

'This is only the beginning,' Megan sighed. 'It is going to be the best summer ever.'

The first bottle of Juiska was sweet, sour and sickly. The second one was sweet and sour. By the time I had reached the bottom of the third bottle, it was just sweet and I realised I liked the taste.

I stood up and wobbled. I could sense the edge of a headache floating in from somewhere in the distance. 'The strange thing is,' I said, 'it doesn't matter how much I drink, I'm still thirsty.'

'Sit down and drink this,' said Ryan. He twisted the top off a bottle of sparkling water.

'I'm fine,' I said. 'I think I've acquired a taste for it.'

I stretched across for another bottle, but Ryan moved the bag out of reach.

'You need to slow down.' He put one hand on the back of my head. 'Open your mouth.' Gently, he spilled water on to my tongue.

Although afternoon was blending into evening, the air felt ever hotter and thicker. I padded across the soft cool grass to the fountain, a concrete construction of Poseidon holding a trident. I sat on the edge and swung my legs over. Dangling my legs in the pool, I shut my eyes, letting the spray shower over my face and body.

'Come over here!' I yelled to the others. 'This feels so good.'

Ryan joined me at the edge of the fountain.

'I've always liked the way you look in your school uniform,' he said, a light smirk on his face. 'But it's never looked as great as it does right now.'

Looking down, I saw the hem of my skirt was soaked, and my white school shirt soaked through and transparent. I waited for my habitual blush, but it never came.

Megan and Amy jumped in next to me, closing their eyes against the spray.

'Make a wish! Make a wish!' Megan yelled.

'It's not a wishing well,' said Amy, giggling.

'I don't care. I feel lucky. Make a wish.'

Connor climbed the fountain and straddled Poseidon's shoulders and grabbed the trident with one hand while the other held a bottle of beer in a triumphant salute.

'Here's to the best days of our lives!' he yelled. 'Make a wish!'

'I wish for a summer of hot, sunny days at the beach,' said Megan.

'I wish I had a cooler summer job than washing dishes at the Fisherman's Arms,' said Amy.

'I wish I could lose ten pounds without dieting,' said Megan.

'I wish I hadn't dyed my hair black,' said Amy. She hiccupped.

153

'I wish that Megan would . . . oh shit!' Connor yelled with a nervous laugh, as he swayed dangerously atop Poseidon's shoulders.

I squeezed my eyes shut and wished that Connor would get down from the statue before he fell and hurt himself. I wished that time would stand still and Ryan could stay with us for ever. And I wished that the world would stop spinning.

Ryan drove me back to the farmhouse with the windows down all the way. I rested my head on the door frame, gulping lungfuls of fresh air. Ryan had insisted that I go back to his house and sober up before heading home to Miranda.

We left town and drove along the coastal road, passing the sand dunes that lay between the road and Perran Towans, the golf course, and the fields of cauliflowers and potatoes. Overhead, the moon was a ghostly crescent in the bright blue sky.

'It must be strange having three moons,' I said.

'Not when you've grown up with them,' said Ryan 'None of Eden's moons are as big as Earth's moon, but when all the moons are up, it is beautiful. And then there are the three suns. From Eden, the universe seems less lonely somehow.'

As we pulled into Ryan's place, I noticed that Ben and Cassie's cars were parked in the driveway.

'I think I need to splash some cold water over my face,' I said. 'I'm burning up.'

Ryan smiled and ran one finger across my nose. 'You've caught the sun. Your nose is all pink.'

'Fantastic. That will look great in all the ball photographs.'

Ryan opened the door and ushered me inside. 'I'll make some strong coffee. The bathroom is the second door at the top of the stairs. I'll meet you in the living room.'

I gripped the banister and dragged myself up the stairs. The fresh air had helped me feel better and I no longer felt sick, just hot and dehydrated. Just as I reached the door to the bathroom, it swung open and Cassie came out. She was dressed in green combats and a white T-shirt, her long blonde hair tumbling over her chest. Just below the sleeve of her T-shirt I could see the edge of a tattoo. It looked like the same tattoo I'd seen on Ryan a few weeks earlier at the beach.

'Oh,' she said, apparently surprised. 'It's you again.'

I said nothing. I refused to show how much she intimidated me.

Her eyes slid down to my school shoes and slowly back up to my eyes. 'Apparently some guys like that look,' she said. 'I wouldn't have thought it was Ry's thing.'

'Maybe you don't know him as well as you think,' I said.

'I think I know him pretty well.' She raised her chin as if averting her face from a bad smell.

A surge of anger coursed through me. 'What's your problem with me?'

'I don't have a problem with you.'

'You obviously don't like me.'

She shrugged. 'I don't get why Ryan spends so much time with you.'

I leant against the door frame, wishing the squishy churning in my stomach would stop. 'He likes me. And I like him.'

Cassie clutched her heart and batted her eyelashes at me. 'That's so touching. You like each other. Did you spend the afternoon at the beach making out? Has Ryan convinced you to sleep with him yet? Are you in love with him?'

'It's not like that with us,' I said. 'We're just good friends.'

'I'm sure you're a fascinating person,' she said, her tone serious again. 'But I doubt he's interested in you for your mind.'

I had a sudden moment of clarity.

'We weren't alone. We spent the afternoon with Connor and our other friends in the park. You see, Connor is my best friend. If it wasn't for me, Ryan and Connor wouldn't even be friends at all.'

Cassie nodded slowly. She opened her mouth as if to speak and then snapped it shut again. I smiled to myself. She had no comeback for that one.

'So you see,' I said. 'He's not wasting his time with me. I'm helping him.'

'I understand,' she said quietly.

I smiled smugly.

Cassie galloped down the stairs, leaving me free to freshen up in the bathroom.

Like the rest of the house, the bathroom was a peculiar

mixture of old-fashioned floral wallpaper and simple functionality. As well as pink flowers blooming all over the walls, there was a neat pile of white towels stacked on a stool.

I filled the basin with water and dunked my face into it. The water was cold against my burning skin. Gasping for breath, I pulled my head out of the water. Cold droplets ran down my face and on to my neck. Blinking, I grabbed a clean white towel and gently dabbed my face dry. My skin felt raw. I opened the medicine cabinet to see if Cassie had some moisturiser and foundation I could use to soothe my skin and cover up the redness. But there was nothing more than a tube of toothpaste, a comb and a couple of bottles of cologne. Of course. Cassie was a natural beauty. No need for make-up or straighteners or hair serum or any of the other items I relied on. I dragged the comb through my tangled hair until it was smooth, rubbed some toothpaste across my teeth and headed back downstairs.

Ryan was at the bottom of the stairs, a mug of steaming black coffee in each hand. He nudged the door to the living room open with his shoulder.

'You're looking better,' he said.

'I feel better.'

We sat on the sofa, close, but with several centimetres separating us. I longed to close the gap, to feel the brush of his skin against mine.

'That was a bad combination of too much alcohol and too much sun,' he said, passing me one of the mugs.

I bit my lip. 'Did I make a complete idiot out of myself?'

He smiled. 'No. You danced around in the fountain, which was kind of cute. And you stumbled around a bit on the way to my car, which gave me an excuse to put my arm around you.'

I sipped my coffee. It was scalding hot and I felt it burn the roof of my mouth. 'You don't need an excuse to put your arm around me.'

Ryan leant closer to me and gently placed an arm around my shoulders. I lay my head on his chest.

'I was thinking,' said Ryan. 'We've only got two days left. Connor will be at the ball on Saturday and we'll be there to keep tabs on him. Why don't we spend the day together tomorrow? Just you and me.'

I nodded, unable to trust myself to speak without choking up. We had just two days left before he returned to his time.

'How would you like to spend the day?' he asked.

'I don't mind.'

'Come here to the farmhouse tomorrow morning. There's something I want to give you.'

I lifted my head and raised both my eyebrows.

Ryan laughed. 'Not the sort of going-away gift Chloe was talking about. I'm not that much of a creep.'

'You're not even remotely a creep,' I said softly, the words falling out of my mouth with more courage than I felt. 'You're perfect.'

'That's the alcohol talking,' he said, tucking a loose strand of hair behind my ear.

The door to the living room swung open, hitting the wall. Cassie stood in the doorway, her arms folded across her chest.

'Sorry to interrupt you lovebirds,' she said, her voice dripping with sarcasm. 'But Ben and I need to talk to you.'

'Both of us?' said Ryan, frowning.

'Both of you,' she repeated.

CHAPTER 13

Ben was standing in the middle of the kitchen.

'Take a seat, Eden,' he said, gesturing towards the kitchen table.

I had the uncomfortable feeling I was about to be lectured on under-age drinking.

Ryan pulled out two chairs. We each took one.

'You've told her,' Cassie said simply.

Ryan caught my eye. I tried to tell him with my eyes that I hadn't confessed to anything, but all three of them were looking at me.

'I don't know what she's talking about,' I said. 'I'm not sure what it is that I'm supposed to know.'

'She told me that she's been helping you with your mission.'

'I didn't say that.'

Cassie narrowed her eyes and looked at me appraisingly. 'Not in so many words perhaps. But you told me.'

'I have no idea what you mean,' I said as I raced through my recent memory, trying to remember what I might have said.

There was a jug of water and a stack of glasses in the middle of the table. Ryan filled two glasses and pushed one across to me. My hand shook as I lifted it to my mouth. What would happen if Ben and Cassie found out that I knew why they were here? Ryan had said things about laws, and about how much trouble he would be in if anyone found out.

Ben turned to Ryan. 'You may as well tell me the truth.'

Ryan swirled the water in his glass. He didn't look up. 'She worked it out herself.'

Ben was calm. 'What exactly does she know?'

Ryan looked up. Up until now he'd always seemed mature, confident, in control, but now he looked like a boy who was in big trouble with his dad. 'She knows why we're here and where we're from.' His voice was barely more than a whisper.

Cassie swore and sat down. 'We should never have agreed to let him come with us. I knew he'd be a liability.'

'Be quiet,' Ben told Cassie. He looked back at Ryan. 'Explain how this happened.'

'Eden worked most of it out for herself.'

Ben turned to look at me. 'What did you work out, Eden?'

I shrugged. 'Lots of little things didn't seem right. There were strange gaps in Ryan's knowledge. He hadn't heard of some really famous people and he didn't recognise pizza. I knew there was something not right about him the first time I met him.'

'That doesn't explain how you figured out where we're from,' said Ben. I noticed that he had made no mention yet of them being from a different time.

I looked at Ryan. He gave me a faint smile. 'You can't get me in any more trouble than I'm already in.'

'I saw Connor's autobiography. It was on the floor in the living room.'

Cassie laughed sarcastically. 'Which is why we don't bring people back to the house, Ry.'

'So I screwed up!' he said to her. 'Just like you screwed up when you didn't tell me about pizza. You're supposed to be the researcher, but you forgot to mention one of the most popular dishes in twenty-first century Britain. And you weren't so great on twenty-first century fashion either! I should've been wearing one of those sweater things with a hood!'

'Quit squabbling,' said Ben calmly. He looked at me. 'Tell me everything you know.'

I glanced at Ryan.

'Don't look at him,' said Ben. 'Ryan doesn't expect you to lie for him. He knows we have to know how much you know so we can figure out how to make this right.'

I swallowed hard, trying to calculate how much or how little I should say. I didn't want to get Ryan into any more trouble than necessary. Nor did I want to put myself in harm's way. 'I know that you are from the future and that you are here to alter history,' I said. 'I know that you don't want Connor to discover Eden.'

Ben nodded, his expression unreadable. 'What else do you know?'

'Nothing really. Ryan wouldn't give me details. I do know that a parasite from Eden destroys Earth's ecosystem. I know it's important that your mission is a success.'

'Do you know what will happen if we're not successful?'

I glanced at Ryan again.

'Look at me,' said Ben.

'Billions of people will die. The planet might die.'

Ben nodded thoughtfully. 'Is there anything else he's told you?'

I shook my head.

'Ry?' Ben asked.

'I think that's everything,' he said quietly.

Ben turned back to me. 'How long have you known?'

I concentrated. It seemed a long time ago now. 'About six or seven weeks,' I said.

'And how long have you known that she knows?' he asked Ryan.

'About six weeks.'

'Six weeks!' said Ben, raising his voice for the first time. 'You've known we have a serious problem for six weeks and you didn't tell me.'

'She won't say anything. You can trust her.'

'Maybe I can. But can I trust you? This isn't a game, Ryan. This isn't a little vacation to the past where you get to meet a celebrity and pick up a pretty girl before heading home to your old life. This is everything. This is the past and the present and the future.'

'I know I screwed up.'

'You're so immature,' Cassie said. 'You couldn't keep your eye on the prize. You allowed yourself to become infatuated by a twenty-first century girl and then spent half your days hanging out with her instead of working on Connor, which is what you should have been doing.'

163

'It's not like that,' Ryan said, his voice rising. 'I know I messed up! I shouldn't have brought her home and let her find the book. But I did and she did. I'm not wasting my time with her. She's important.'

'Is that right?' said Cassie. 'I thought your brief was rather straightforward: make friends with Connor Penrose and make sure he doesn't discover Eden. I don't remember the part that instructed you to fool around with a high-school girl.'

'I'm not fooling around with her.'

Cassie's laugh was razor-sharp. I could sense a pounding on the periphery of my senses. It pulsed to the beat of my heart. Bang-bang thump. Bang-bang thump. I gulped a mouthful of cold water.

'What would you call it, Ryan?' asked Cassie. 'Falling in love?'

'Eden isn't just some random high-school girl. She's the girl Connor falls in love with. His best friend. The one who breaks his heart. The one he argues with just before he discovers Eden.'

Cassie looked at me and then back to Ryan. 'And how exactly does you falling in love with her help us?'

Ryan's jaw clenched and he glanced at me. I was waiting for him to announce that he wasn't in love with me. 'She's helping me.' He went on to explain how we had plotted together to get Connor to the ball and to spend his money on a games console.

'And you never thought to include this information in your daily debrief?' asked Ben.

Ryan frowned. 'Of course I thought about it. But I worried that if I said anything she'd be vulnerable in the clean-up mission.'

Cassie and Ben looked at each other.

'He's broken the First Law of Temporal Integrity,' she said. 'You know what that means.'

The clock on the wall chimed eight.

'Could we finish this conversation another time?' I asked, standing up. 'I really should get going.'

'Sit down again, Eden,' said Ben. 'I think you're going to need the whole story.'

Ben made a fresh pot of coffee and ordered in pizza. The headache that had been sprouting deep within my skull for a couple of hours was now beginning to bloom. Privately I promised myself I would never again touch raspberry Juiska – or any alcohol – if the pain would go away now and let me think. Ryan poured me glasses of cold water and encouraged me to eat lots of pizza.

Ben began by going over the stuff that Ryan had already told me. Connor would discover a habitable planet on the twenty-third of June. Thirty-two years later Nathaniel Westland would discover a method of travelling great distances through space and time. One of the first places was Eden. But I knew this already. I knew from the pictures in Connor's autobiography that it was a pink-rock planet with a lush jungle of green plants under a clear blue sky. By the time he had reached the part about Earth's habitats dying out and billions of people dying, the dusk was deepening from blue into purple and the shimmering moon was a hard, white scar in the sky.

'Fast forward to 2122,' said Ben, 'and you get to our timeline. Do you know the population of Earth today?'

'Over six and a half billion?' I offered.

'That's close enough. In our timeline there's less than one billion. Some people think that's a good thing. No overpopulation, more space and resources for everyone. Of course, they're not the people who watched their own children dying from starvation.'

'It's even more serious than the deaths of billions of people,' said Cassie. 'The way things are going, many scientists believe the human race won't survive another fifty years. So you see, we can't fail.'

'So you had to travel back in time,' I said.

'Not everyone saw it that way,' said Ben. 'Some people felt strongly that there is never a good enough reason for backwards time travel.'

'But surely, if the human race is dying out, if the planet is dying, you have to? How could anyone oppose that?'

'It's gone terribly wrong before,' said Ben. He hesitated. 'Do you know why the dinosaurs died out sixty-five million years ago?'

'A meteor in Mexico?'

Ben laughed. 'Is that the current theory?'

'I think so.'

'There will be many theories. But it was time travellers from the late twenty-first century. One of the travellers had influenza. He was symptom-free when he left his timeline, but began to get sick after returning. The flu virus wiped out the dinosaurs.'

'I need a moment,' I said, pouring myself a mug of coffee. 'You mean to tell me that there was no meteor?'

'There were several, actually,' said Ben. 'But the dinosaurs were already dying out long before any meteors crashed to Earth.'

'The dinosaurs died of flu,' I said to myself. I began to laugh. More in disbelief than anything.

'I know it's a lot to grasp,' said Ben gently. 'And because you've always been told something else, this must seem absurd. But it's important for you to understand why our mission protocols are so strict. The extinction of the dinosaurs isn't the only massive disaster caused by time travel.'

'What else?' I whispered.

'The Black Death which wiped out one third of the population of Europe,' Ben continued.

'The bubonic plague,' I said.

Ben shook his head. 'A different bacteria altogether. A bacteria that is well tolerated in humans in the twenty-second century, but was deadly in the fourteenth.'

'How many of these disastrous missions have taken place?' I asked.

'Those two are the worst,' said Ben. 'They happened in the early days of four-dimensional travel. Very few time missions have been approved since then. But this one was allowed because so much is at stake.'

'I understand,' I said. 'But if it's so important that Connor doesn't discover Eden, why not kill him? Surely that would be a safer bet.'

'We're not assassins,' said Cassie. 'We're here to do a job, which is to prevent Connor discovering Eden. We don't have to kill him to do that.'

'But wouldn't it be easier?'

'It would be easier,' said Ben. 'And perhaps if Connor went on to become a nobody who did nothing with his life, our mission would be to eliminate him. But Connor's descendants are very influential.' He glanced at Cassie. 'They only approved this time mission provided Connor's timeline was left largely intact.'

'I see.'

'The only person around here in danger of being killed is you,' said Cassie.

'Cassie,' said Ben. 'Cut it out.'

'It's true. She knows about the planet, she knows about time travel. If our cleaner gets wind of what she knows, she's history. And Eden needs to know that.'

'Our cleaner isn't going to know,' said Ryan. 'Eden can keep a secret.'

'For the rest of her life?' said Cassie.

'Be quiet!' said Ben. He turned to me. 'Did Ryan tell you about cleaners?'

I vaguely recalled him saying something about them all those weeks ago when I first found out he was from the future, but I didn't think it would be a good idea to admit it. I shook my head.

'Every time mission has a cleaner,' said Ben. 'Someone

who arrives in the timeline before the rest of us and leaves after we have gone. They make sure we follow the mission directive and don't stray from it. They also make sure we obey the Laws of Temporal Integrity. One of those laws is that we don't alter the timeline by revealing the future to inhabitants of the past.'

'Which is exactly what Ryan has done,' said Cassie, her voice loud in frustration.

'If our cleaner discovered what you know, your life would be in danger,' said Ben.

'What's so bad about me knowing your mission?' I asked. 'I'm on your side.'

'The thing is,' said Ben, 'you know there's a planet out there somewhere that harbours life. You know that humans can live on it. You also know that one day it will be possible for humans to travel there. In many ways, even if we stop Connor from discovering the planet, our mission has failed because you know about Eden. You could choose to discover it. Or you could mention it to someone else in a throwaway remark one day.' He sighed. 'I hope to God Ryan wasn't foolish enough to tell you which star the planet orbits.'

'No. He didn't,' I said quickly.

'That's one blessing, I suppose,' said Ben. 'But you still know about things that haven't been invented yet and events that haven't happened yet. That's dangerous for the timeline.'

'But I won't say anything.'

'I believe you. But our cleaner won't.'

'What will happen to me if your cleaner does find out?'

'He'll kill you,' said Ben.

My hand trembled as I poured myself another glass of water. 'Why is it OK to kill me but not Connor?'

'As I said, Connor's family in 2122 is powerful and influential. You, however, are just a regular person. There's no one here to look out for you. Our cleaner would consider you collateral damage. He would take a risk that your death wouldn't significantly affect the timeline. Not as much as your revealing the truth about the planet Eden.'

'What do I do?' I asked.

'We have two options,' said Ben. 'The first is that we do nothing.'

'How is that an option?' asked Cassie, her voice rising again.

'Our options are few,' said Ben. 'Doing nothing may be the best thing. Eden keeps her mouth shut for the next hundred years.'

'I can do that,' I said.

'And the second option?' asked Ryan.

'She comes with us when we leave. Any knowledge of the future comes with us. The cleaner won't have anything to clean up.' Ben looked at me. 'Travel to the future is perfectly legal. It doesn't affect the timeline too much.'

'What about her descendants?' asked Ryan.

'Again, collateral damage,' said Ben. 'A risk worth taking, given the circumstances.'

'Shouldn't I be the one to decide if I go to the future?' I asked.

'No,' snapped Cassie.

'It will affect our fuel supplies,' said Ben. 'We're only equipped to transport three people. We might not be able to stabilise the portal for long enough. It's not without risk.'

'So we put all our lives in danger,' said Cassie.

Ben nodded. 'I'm leaning towards option one. Less lives in danger.'

'Just mine,' I whispered.

Ryan squeezed my hand. 'You know how important it is never to reveal what you know. So long as you do that, everything will be OK.'

'So what happens now?' I asked.

Ben smiled at me. 'We'll finish our mission, save the planet and go home. Everything will work out.'

'What happens if you fail?' I asked.

'We fail,' said Ben. 'That's it. End of story. This is our only chance to get it right.'

'Couldn't you just come back and try again?'

Ben shook his head. 'No. We distort four-dimensional space when we travel through time. It becomes dangerous and unstable. The more times you travel the same route, the more likely the portal will collapse in on itself.'

'Like a black hole,' Cassie explained.

'You don't go back to the same place twice,' said Ben. 'It would be like playing Russian roulette. You might get there safely. But probably not.'

'It's down to us to get it right this time,' said Ryan.

*   *   *

Ryan drove me up the lane in silence. There was no parking space left at our usual hidden away spot around the corner from my house, so he parked up at the end of my street. He switched off the ignition, unbuckled his seat belt and turned to face me.

'I'm so sorry,' he said.

'It's not your fault.'

'It's entirely my fault. I should never have dragged you into my life.'

'I wasn't exactly kicking and screaming.'

He laughed. 'There was a bit of kicking and screaming when you thought I was using you to complete my mission. Actually, it was more like sulking and the silent treatment.'

I gave him a playful shove. 'Well, I think this afternoon put any lingering doubts to rest,' I said, smiling at him. 'It's clear to me that Cassie and Ben wish you'd never met me.'

Ryan reached across for my hand and squeezed it tight. 'I'm glad I've met you.'

I felt the now familiar blush sweep across my cheeks. Except that now our time was running out, every moment of pleasure was accompanied by an aching anticipation of loss.

'Are we still going to spend the day together tomorrow?' I asked.

'Definitely. Come down to the farmhouse at noon and I'll make lunch.'

He was still holding my hand, still looking deep into my eyes. Feeling self-conscious suddenly, I lowered my eyes and turned towards the door.

'Oh, crap,' I said, recognising the couple ambling along the pavement hand in hand in the dusky twilight. Miranda and Travis. They hadn't seen us yet.

And then she locked eyes with me.

'Incoming,' I said.

Ryan squeezed my hand and then released me. 'It can't be worse than the Cassie and Ben interrogation.'

'Miranda does guilt really well,' I replied, watching her slow march towards me.

'Shall I speak to her?' he whispered.

I shook my head. The last thing I needed was an audience when Miranda tore me to shreds. 'It's OK. I'd prefer to face this one alone.'

'How gallant of him,' Miranda said stonily as Ryan pulled away from the kerb.

'He offered to stay,' I said, rising to his defence. 'I told him to leave.'

'Wise advice,' she said. 'If I get my hands on that boy . . .'

'Miranda,' I began.

'Home!' she said. 'I'm not having this conversation out on the street.'

We walked in silence down the street to the house. Travis stood by the front door holding a carrier bag of beer from the corner shop. He gave me a sympathetic shrug behind her back.

Miranda slammed the front door and marched into the kitchen. 'I don't even know how to begin,' she said.

'I'm sorry I let you down,' I said. Usually the best way of handling Miranda was to fess up and apologise. Repeatedly.

'Let's hear it,' she said.

'What?'

'Your account.'

'Ryan's dad invited me to stay to dinner,' I said. 'And then, since it was getting dark, Ryan offered to drive me home.'

'Let's hear the rest of it.'

I took a deep breath. 'That's all there is to tell.'

Miranda shook her head. 'So you didn't spend the afternoon in Perran Park drinking vodka with your friends?'

'Oh,' I said flatly.

'Oh,' she repeated sarcastically. 'Connor's mother called me a couple of hours ago. Apparently Connor was really sick when he got home this afternoon. He confessed to his mother that he'd spent the afternoon in the park with you and your friends drinking vodka.'

'I didn't drink vodka,' I said.

Miranda put a hand on one hip and looked me up and down. 'I never thought you'd lie to me, Eden. I thought we were closer than that.'

'I had a raspberry-flavoured drink. It might have had vodka in it. I only drank one.'

'According to Mrs Penrose, Connor was concerned because he saw you staggering out of the park, barely able to walk, and he believed you were going to accept a lift home from Ryan.'

I was going to kill Connor.

'Why would you, of all people, get in a car with an under-age driver who's been drinking?'

174

'Ryan doesn't drink.'

'You expect me to believe that?'

I nodded. 'He doesn't drink because he drives.'

She sighed dramatically. 'Let's talk about the car. Where did he get that from? Was it stolen?'

'It's his dad's. He borrowed it.'

'He borrowed it? Are you suggesting his father gave him permission to use his car?'

If I said no, Ryan had stolen it. If I said yes, Ben was irresponsible too. I couldn't win.

'No,' I said eventually. 'But he has his licence back in the States.'

'Does he have his licence here?'

'No. But it was just along the coast road from Perran to Penpol Cove.'

'Your parents *died* just driving along that same stretch of road. They nearly killed you too.'

I shut my eyes. We never talked about how my parents died. Or how close to dying I'd been.

'I've spent the last ten years trying to keep you safe from boys like him.'

I said nothing. The rest of the conversation remained unspoken, but the message was loud and clear. Miranda had tried to keep me safe. Miranda had taken care of me even though she was only twenty herself when my parents died. Miranda had abandoned her law degree and dream of becoming a lawyer to take care of her six-year-old niece. Miranda had a string of failed relationships and no children of her own because she had sacrificed her own

175

future so that she could take care of mine. And I had let her down.

'I'm sorry I upset you,' I said quietly. 'I'm sorry I let you down.'

'I'm disappointed,' she said quietly. 'I'm going to have to think about Saturday night.'

'What do you mean?' My voice shook.

'I'm not sure I can trust you to go to the ball with your friends. I'm not so old that I don't remember what happens at the leavers' ball. I know there's alcohol and parties afterwards.'

'I won't drink anything,' I said. 'And Megan's parents are paying for a limo to drive us.'

'I'll have to think about it.'

I poured myself a large glass of water and went out of the kitchen door into the back garden. The purple sky from earlier was now a deep, endless black and the faint stars were turning on and slowly brightening, like a chain of fairy lights. I went over to the picnic table in the middle of the lawn and lay down on it so that the whole black canvas of night was stretched above me. Instinctively I scanned the sky for Cassiopeia, the reassuring w-shape that reminded me the universe was not an empty swirling mass of chaos. I scanned my eyes across the sky to Perseus and Algol, the winking star that was a sun – three suns – to Eden. Home. Ryan's home. About to become the best-kept secret in the universe.

'It's beautiful, isn't it?' said a quiet voice.

Travis. I sat up on the table. He flicked open his lighter and held the flame to the end of his cigarette.

'Spectacular,' I said. 'Do you know any of the constellations?'

'The Big Dipper,' he said, pointing up at the sky. 'Everyone knows that one. And there's Polaris, the North Star. That's about it though. What about you?'

'I only know a couple. You see that w? That's Cassiopeia. And that over there is Algol, the demon star.'

Travis chuckled. 'Between us we know half the sky.'

'Did you know that Algol looks like one star, but actually it's three?' I asked.

'How do you know that?' Travis inhaled deeply on his cigarette.

'Someone told me,' I said. I gazed at the sky. Sea mist was heading swiftly inland. In a few minutes the stars would be hidden from view. 'I wonder if there's anyone out there, lying in the garden and looking up at the stars and maybe looking at our sun, wondering if there's anyone out there looking up at the sky and wondering . . .'

'How much did you drink?' Travis interrupted. 'Or are you high?'

I giggled. 'Stone cold sober. Although from Miranda's response you'd think I'd spent the afternoon turning tricks on the high street so I could get my next fix.'

'Did she rip you a new one?' he asked.

I smiled. 'You could say that.'

He perched himself on the seat. 'She'll calm down. She'll let you go. I'll speak to her.'

'I have to go. Ryan is leaving on Saturday night after the ball. He's going home and this is my last chance to see him.'

'You really like this boy.'

It wasn't a question.

'I like him more than I can put into words.' Somehow the darkness made it easier to say.

'He's from New Hampshire, right?'

'Right.'

'The world is not so big, Eden. You'll stay in touch.'

'No,' I said. 'It's complicated. I can't explain why. But I know I'll never see him again after Saturday.'

'Oh, Eden,' he said sadly. 'I really am sorry to hear you say that.'

CHAPTER 14

As I made my way down the lane to Ryan's house with my hair caught in the branches of the sapling in my arms, I began to regret choosing a tree as my gift to Ryan. Earlier that morning it had seemed a perfect choice – something that would last as long as the distance between us. Now it just seemed designed to ensure that I looked a mess. My hair was tangled, my arms covered in dirt and I could feel a trickle of sweat run down my back.

'Wow, a walking forest!' Ryan laughed as I approached. 'What's this? Birnam wood approaching Dunsinane? Have you come to defeat me? To prove once and for all that you can't escape your fate?'

'Umm, help?' I replied, attempting to untwist a length of hair from one of the branches.

The smell of lemons filled the air around me as Ryan gently untwisted my hair and took the tree from my arms.

'So what's this all about?' he asked, a smile making his eyes twinkle.

'A gift,' I said. 'The gardener at the nursery promised me that this tree will last over a hundred years and produce a healthy crop of juicy apples each year. I thought we could plant it today and then when you get back home . . .' I swallowed as my words threatened to catch in my throat. 'When you get home it will still be there, an old, crabby tree, full of apples. You can see what's become of it.'

'Is it indigenous?' he said, placing the tree on the ground. He smiled up at me, a big, happy smile that contained none of the barely concealed grief behind my shaky smile.

'What do you think? Come on, let's choose a spot.'

Now I was no longer trapped in a splay of branches, I could see that the only car in the driveway was Ryan's.

'They're meeting with a lawyer in town,' he said, following my eyes. 'They won't be back for a while.'

He winked ironically, but I was used to his flirtations by now and knew they were entirely innocent.

Ryan carried the sapling over one shoulder as we strolled across their vast lawn.

'How was Miranda?' he asked.

'As expected. Disappointed in me.'

Ryan laughed.

'She didn't have anything good to say about you either.'

'But she let you come and spend the day with me?'

'She's at work. She doesn't know I'm here.' I held up my phone. 'And I've switched my phone off so she can't reach me.'

Ryan fetched a shovel and began digging a deep hole in the middle of the lawn. His muscles bunched and lengthened as he effortlessly scooped out the earth and piled it to one side. He was just about to lower the roots of the apple tree into the hole, when I stopped him.

'Why don't we bury something underneath the apple tree?'

'Like what? A body?'

'How about a time capsule?' I said.

'What do we put in a time capsule?'

'We did one at school once,' I said. 'To celebrate one hundred years of Perran School. It's supposed to be buried for another hundred years. We put all sorts of things in it. Headlines from newspapers, a photo of the school staff, another one of the student body. A school tie, the school newspaper.'

'So we could bury things about us,' he said. 'What it's like to be you and me in 2012.'

'A time-crossed friendship capsule,' I said. 'Things that represent our friendship here in 2012.'

'Any ideas?'

'Do you have a printer?'

He nodded.

'Then let's start with a photo.'

I held my phone at arm's length, put my arm around Ryan's shoulder and grinned into the camera. *Snap.*

In the kitchen, we printed out two copies of the photo – one for me to keep and one to bury in our time capsule. It was one of those lucky strikes, a quick snap in which we both looked good. My grin was crinkle-eyed and genuine, quite unlike the careful face I usually composed for a photo. Ryan was smiling at me, not the camera.

Ryan got a Tupperware container from the cupboard under the sink. 'We can use this.'

I put one of the photos in it.

'What else?' he said.

I checked my jacket pocket. My fingers touched a letter I had written for Ryan the night before. I planned to give it to him the night he left.

'Have you got anything?' he asked.

I shook my head and then I felt a smaller piece of paper. 'Train ticket to Plymouth.'

'Ah, the romantic train journey to Plymouth where I pulled you into the loos and showed you my credit cards.'

'Do you have anything?'

'My ticket to the Eden Project.'

'I think we should include a page from Connor's autobiography,' I said. 'If it wasn't for that book, I wouldn't know who you really are.'

'Too risky. We mustn't include anything that's from the future. How about I put in one of my sketches of you?

He ran upstairs to fetch it.

My fingers closed again over the letter in my pocket. I took it out and reread it.

Dear Ryan

By the time you read this, I will be long dead. Although my life will be over, only a day or two will have passed for you. It's strange to think of you out there, still young and pretty when I am dead and gone.

Meeting you has changed my life. I hadn't thought much

about what I wanted to do, but now I know I want to do
something good with my life, something that helps take care
of the planet maybe.

I wish I'd had the courage to tell you to your face how
much you mean to me. But it's so much easier to write your
feelings than it is to say them. I wish you could have stayed.
I know why you couldn't. But I will never forget you.

Thank you for three wonderful months.

I love you.

Eden.

I wasn't sure I would have the courage to give it to him. I'd never told anyone I loved them before. Not even in writing.

'I'm going to miss this picture of you,' Ryan was saying as he came back into the kitchen.

Impulsively I pushed the letter into the container, hiding it under the photo.

'It's the first picture I drew of you,' he said. 'Back before I knew you were the evil girl who broke poor Connor's heart.'

I smacked him jokingly. 'If you miss it that much, you can dig it up when you get back to your own time.'

We carried the container back outside.

Just as Ryan lowered the time capsule into the ground, a car came slowly up the drive. Ryan stood up straight and wiped his dirty hands on his jeans.

'That's not Ben or Cassie,' he said squinting into the sunshine.

The car stopped and a man got out. Travis.

'I thought I might find you here,' he said, strolling over to us. 'Why aren't you answering your phone, Eden?'

'I switched it off.'

'Miranda was worried about you. She asked me to go home and check you're OK. I managed to persuade her to let you go to the ball tomorrow, but if you're not careful she's going to change her mind.'

'I'll call her now.'

'You need to be more careful,' he said.

I knew he was right, but all I could think of right now was that Ryan and I had only a few hours left together.

'Um, Travis?'

'Yeah?'

'Do you think you could tell her I'm at home? In the garden?'

'You want me to lie for you?'

'You know how she overreacts. And it's not like I'm doing anything wrong.'

'What are you doing?' Travis peered into the hole.

'It's a time capsule,' said Ryan.

'What's in it?'

'Nothing,' I said.

'Right. A time capsule with nothing in it.' He looked at us both. 'Fine. Don't tell me.'

'So will you cover for me?'

Travis scratched his neck. 'I haven't seen you. Don't get drunk. Don't let him drive you anywhere. And don't get caught.'

We waited until Travis had driven away before saying anything.

'Travis is cool,' said Ryan.

'He's growing on me.'

Ryan covered the time capsule with dirt while I called Miranda.

She answered on the first ring. 'Where are you?'

'In the garden.'

Technically that was true.

'Why didn't you answer the house phone?'

'I couldn't hear it from here.' Also true. 'And I didn't realise I'd turned my mobile off. Sorry.'

'Just keep your phone switched on, OK? I need to be able to reach you. I have to work late tonight. You'll need to make your own dinner. I'll see you around ten.'

'See you tonight,' I said.

Ryan had finished planting the tree. 'You hungry?' he asked.

'Starving.'

'I made a picnic.' He looked up at the sky. 'It looks like the sun is going to shine for a few more hours. Shall we eat outside?'

'Are you expecting the weather to change?'

'It will cloud over later on. But tomorrow will be clear again.'

'You're becoming quite British you know – this unhealthy obsession with the weather.'

Ryan stood up. 'When the sky is cloudy, you can't see the stars. Most of the last two weeks have been too cloudy for stargazing. But tomorrow night will be clear all night.'

Of course. He would be tuned into things like that. I was suddenly reminded of the fact that Ryan was here for a reason and that he'd only shared with me the big picture, the things I needed to know. By tomorrow evening, he would be gone and it would be too late to ask any more questions.

He came back with a blue check picnic blanket that was still in its protective plastic wrap and a traditional wicker picnic basket, crammed with food. He tore the plastic off the blanket and spread it across the grass.

'When did you get all this?'

'This morning.' He gestured to the blanket. 'Make yourself comfortable.'

He took out a green bottle and two crystal champagne flutes.

'I was going to buy champagne, but decided that you'd probably had enough alcohol for one weekend.'

'You thought right. I will never, ever, drink alcohol again.'

'So we have sparkling water with a slice of lemon.' He pulled a couple of lemons out of the basket.

'What else is in the basket?'

Ryan pulled out several different packages. 'Sandwiches,' he said. 'Roasted vegetables and hummus. And I made a salad.' He pulled the lid off a glass container. Inside was a salad made from cherry tomatoes, cucumber, pumpkin seeds, walnuts, black olives and tiny grains I didn't recognise. 'And we have cherries and strawberries.'

'Wow. That looks really good,' I said, stunned. I would have expected Ryan to be the sort of boy who'd buy prepared food from the supermarket.

Ryan rolled his eyes. 'What? You didn't think I could make a picnic?'

'It's not that. I'm just surprised at how much trouble you've gone to.'

He smiled. 'It was no trouble. I wanted today to be special. Tomorrow will be stressful. I'll be working. We both will be.'

The sun was warm on our backs. We ate the sandwiches and drank the cold water and talked about trivial things: the pink and silver theme of the ball, our favourite music, Connor and Megan going to the ball together.

'It's hard to believe that Connor is such an important person in the future,' I said. 'He's so ordinary. He's just Connor. He's good academically, but he's not exceptional. I know at least a dozen people in Year Eleven who are cleverer than him.'

Ryan laughed quietly. 'A few weeks ago you asked me who my hero was. When I was younger, Connor was one of my heroes. For becoming such a big hero with so little effort.'

'How do you mean?'

'He discovered a temperate planet, quite by chance. Serendipity. It could have been anyone or no one. It wasn't as though he'd been searching the skies for a habitable planet. He just happened to have a big argument with someone – you – and go outside and look up at the sky.'

Ryan smiled and shook his head. 'The discovery wasn't a big deal at the time. Planets were being discovered every week. There was just a small article in the daily paper and that was that. He didn't go on to become a famous astronomer or anything like that. He just bummed around for a few years being spectacularly unexceptional.'

'What did he do?'

'You can probably guess.'

'From the pictures in his autobiography, I'm guessing he finally learns to surf. If I had to predict Connor's future, it would probably be underachieving beach bum. Am I close?'

'Don't ask me to confirm or deny,' said Ryan. 'You're going to grow up with the guy. How would you like it if he knew everything you were going to do before you did it?'

'But you haven't explained why he was your hero. Why do you admire him if he did so little?'

'For seizing opportunities when they arose. Eden didn't matter when we couldn't get there. But then my grandfather discovered a means of travelling across the galaxy, and suddenly Connor Penrose was famous. He was everywhere. He was on one of the first voyages to Eden. He was interviewed on every chat show. He was everyone's favourite dinner-party guest. He dined out on that one opportune discovery for the rest of his life. To achieve so much success with so little effort is quite admirable.'

I grinned. 'There's no such thing as a work ethic in the twenty-second century then?'

'Work for work's sake? No.'

I sighed. 'Poor Connor. To think he would have had a lifetime of cool parties and easy money ahead of him and now he doesn't.'

'We're not there yet.'

'I hope he finds something else. I would hate to be responsible for robbing him of a lifetime of fame and fortune.'

Ryan raised an eyebrow. 'I'm not sure Connor cares too much about fame. And I bet he'll have a good life whatever lies ahead of him. He has the knack of seizing opportunities when they arise. You may be helping him achieve even greater things.'

'Or not. It feels so unethical to be helping you ensure he doesn't achieve the one thing he was known for.'

'Well, remind yourself that you're helping save the lives of billions of people. I bet, if he knew, Connor would be willing to sacrifice a little celebrity for that.'

When the food was gone, I lay back down and shut my eyes against the sun, wondering what sort of magic it would take to keep Ryan here in my time. I tensed as I felt his fingers in my hair.

'I love your hair,' he said, taking a strand and bringing it up to his face. 'It smells like apples. Whenever I see apples, I think of you.'

'With you it's lemons,' I said, squinting up through the sun at him. 'Lemons and metal.'

Ryan crinkled his nose. 'Metal?'

I shrugged. 'I like the smell. No one else smells anything like you.'

He smiled and lay back on the blanket next to me. I could feel the warmth of his skin radiating across the small divide between us.

'Tell me about your life in the twenty-second century,' I said. 'I bet it's loads different to life here. What is it like? How did you grow up?'

'We had two homes. One in New Hampshire on Earth and one in Zion on Eden.'

'What is Zion like? Is it a big city?'

In my head I pictured cities I'd seen in futuristic films: large polluted cities with hover cars and neon signs everywhere.

'Not really. Zion is in a valley. It's almost completely enclosed by mountains, so it can't grow very big. The only way in or out of the city is by river. The city itself is built from pink stone, but the surrounding mountains are covered in green jungle so it's pink and green.'

I remembered the photograph in Connor's book.

'I was conceived on Earth, but my parents moved to Zion just before I was born. I spent most of my childhood there. Then Dad decided we needed to be on Earth, to monitor the political mood. So just after I turned twelve, we moved back.'

'Did you have a best friend?'

'I hope I still do. His name is Peg. We were in school together.'

'A boy called Peg? Peg's a girl's name. Peggy. Short for Margaret.'

'How is Peggy short for Margaret?'

I shrugged. 'I'm not sure.'

'Peg's a boy's name,' he said. 'Short for Pegasus.'

'Pegasus!' I couldn't help but giggle.

'Maybe I shouldn't tell you my real name then.'

I rolled on to my side so I could look at him. 'Ryan's not your real name?'

He tilted his head in a half-nod, half-shake. 'Yes and no. My full name is Orion, after the constellation.'

'Orion,' I said, staring at him. 'I like it.'

'No one calls me Orion, except my mother when she's cross with me. It's usually Ry. In the second half of the twenty-first century, naming children after stars and constellations is very popular.'

'Orion and Pegasus,' I said smiling. 'What about Cassie?'

'Cassiopeia.'

I sat up and reached for my glass of water. 'And Ben?'

He laughed. 'Short for Benjamin. Not everyone is named after a constellation or a star.'

Ryan sat up. He reached out a hand and touched my cheekbone, his warm fingers running slowly down the side of my face. My skin burned beneath his touch.

'But you're unique,' he said. 'You're not named after a star or a constellation. You have a planet named after you.'

He looked into my eyes. His brown eyes were dark; I could see my reflection in his pupils. His hand cupped my chin. I held my breath.

'Orion,' I said. It felt strange calling him by his real name.

I could feel his warm breath on my face. Then, abruptly, he turned away. Something dawned on me. 'Is there a girl back in the twenty-second century?'

He shook his head. 'There's no girl.'

'So . . .'

'I'm not going to make this harder than it already is.'

'What's that supposed to mean?'

'I'm not going to kiss you. How much harder will it be for me to leave tomorrow night if . . . ?'

'I understand,' I said softly. And I did understand, but it was still hard not to feel rejected. Surely if he really liked me – if he wanted to kiss me as much as I wanted to kiss him – he would kiss me anyway and to hell with the consequences. In fact, I knew that if I was the one who had to leave, I wouldn't be able to do it. I couldn't leave him behind. And the only thing stopping me from begging him to kiss me and then begging him to stay, was knowing that he would say no.

'You know, when I signed up for this mission,' he said quietly, 'I thought it would be the biggest thrill-ride. I thought I could be a hero, save the planet, meet some cool people and then go home. I thought it would be easy. I never expected to develop feelings for the people I met. It never occurred to me that I wouldn't want to go back.'

'Is there no way?'

'You know the answer to that.'

I remembered, miserably, what he had said about clean-up agents ensuring that the laws of time travel were followed.

Ryan jumped quickly to his feet and took out a small silver box from the pocket of his jeans.

'It's time for your gift,' he said.

I took the box from him and lifted off the lid, wondering what on earth he would give me. Lying on a bed of white cotton was a key.

'Um, thanks?' I said, confused.

'It's the key to my car,' he said. 'Or perhaps I should say, your car.'

'Oh my God!' I yelled. 'Thank you!'

He shrugged. 'I can't take it with me.'

'I'm not seventeen for three months.'

'Let's be honest, it hasn't stopped me!'

'Are you suggesting . . .'

'Look, you've often said how isolated you are out here at Penpol Cove. One of the first times I spoke to you, you were walking home alone on a dark and windy night. I figure, if I teach you to drive now, you can get a bit of prac- tice in here, and then by the time of your birthday, you'll be ready to get your licence.'

I tried not to run like an excited little girl as we headed over towards Ryan's silver car. I unlocked the door and slid into the driver's seat. Ryan sat in the passenger seat.

'Let's belt up,' he said. 'This could be a bumpy ride.'

'I don't want to hear any crap about female drivers,' I said.

Ryan laughed and showed me how to check the gear- stick was in neutral before turning the ignition. The car purred into life.

He rested his hand on my left knee. 'This is your clutch foot,' he explained.

If he kept his hand on my knee, there was no way I would be able to focus on learning to drive.

'The only thing you do with it is dip and release the clutch pedal. Your other foot controls the gas and brake.'

He held my left hand and placed it on the gearstick. 'I want you to press down on the clutch and I'll help you find first gear.'

I pushed down on the clutch, the way he'd described, and he moved my hand into first gear.

'Gently release,' he told me, 'and step down lightly on the gas.'

I did as he said. The car lurched forward and stalled.

'It's getting hot in here,' I said, feeling my face flush with embarrassment. I rolled down my window.

'Cassie, Ben and I all had to teach ourselves,' he said, laughing. 'We had the cars delivered here to the house. We kept stalling too. In fact, we nearly sent them back to the manufacturer because we thought they were faulty.'

'What am I doing wrong?'

'Nothing. It takes a while to get a feel for how to release the clutch. Just keep trying.'

By the third attempt, I managed to get the car moving. Within seconds the engine was screaming.

'Take your right foot off the gas pedal, dip the clutch and we'll move up into second,' Ryan shouted above the noise of the engine.

I lurched forward again.

By the time I had driven to the end of the driveway and reversed back ten times, I was feeling pretty confident.

'I think it's time for you to take us out on the road,' said Ryan.

'What if someone sees me?' I said.

'I've been driving along the coast road for months without anyone noticing,' said Ryan. 'I've never seen a cop car. Miranda and Travis will both be at work.'

'OK,' I said shakily.

I drove up the lane from the farmhouse to the village in second gear, leaning forward over the steering wheel, terrified that I would meet a car coming in the opposite direction and have to brake suddenly, or worse, reverse. Once in the village, Ryan directed me round the roundabout. Several roads radiated off the roundabout like the spokes of a wheel. I took the last exit, the coast road. The road my parents had driven along the night they died.

'Maybe it's time to try third,' Ryan suggested, when the engine started roaring again.

He helped me ease the car up through the gears until we were cruising along the coast road in fifth gear, at a leisurely thirty miles per hour. He was right. It was empty. Most people used the bypass these days, unless they were visiting one of the few farms or cottages along the road.

My internal organs rearranged themselves and my knuckles whitened as we approached the cliff top above Lucky Cove. The road turned back on itself in a sharp hairpin bend. I changed down to third and took the corner slowly.

'You're doing great,' said Ryan. 'You're really good at this.'

I could feel him looking at me, but I was concentrating too hard on the road ahead to meet his eyes. The road snaked wildly, following the curve of every hill, rising and dipping with the contours of the land. It wasn't difficult to imagine a driver losing control. I couldn't fail to notice the cheery yellow gorse flowers lining the road, or the glimmering blue sky above us.

As we approached Perran, I began to panic. I hadn't passed a single vehicle on the coast road, but Perran would be busy.

'I can't drive through town,' I said.

'Yes, you can. Don't lose control. Just drive. I'll talk you through it.'

'What if Miranda sees me? Or Travis?'

'They won't expect to see you driving a car. Just relax and keep doing what you've been doing.'

I slowed down to twenty miles an hour and tried to avoid hitting the brake every time a car approached me.

'Shift down to second,' said Ryan, as we came close to the harbour car park.

He talked me through the gear changes, indicating and pulling into a parking space. It wasn't until I switched off the engine that I realised my hands were shaking.

'That was fun!' I said, secretly pleased with myself.

'You deserve an ice cream. You did great.'

Ryan reached for my hand. I wanted to squeeze it tight, but I knew that my hand was sweaty with nerves and I didn't want to gross him out.

'It doesn't look like there are any clouds coming our way,' I said, as we sat on the edge of the wall with our 99 flakes.

'It will cloud over,' he said. 'Tomorrow night will be the only clear night during the transit of Eden.'

'What's the first thing you're going to do when you get home?' I asked.

'I don't know. Check out our apple tree and our time capsule?'

'And then what?'

'See my family. Find out what has changed. Things could be very different when I get back. Our time here in the past will have changed the future. Who knows what I'll find when I get home.' He smiled at me. 'A healthy planet with lots of trees, I hope.'

'I wish I could come with you. I would love to meet your family and friends.'

'I wish you could too.' He squinted out to sea. 'I'll tell them all about you.' He sighed. 'Not everything of course. In the old timeline they'd be fascinated to hear about the girl who Eden was named for. But they can't know that now.'

'What will you tell them? Won't they wonder why you travelled to the past? Won't they wonder what your mission was?'

'We have a cover story. About preventing the extinction of the chicken.'

I giggled. 'You're kidding?'

He shook his head. 'No.'

'Why chickens?'

'If we went back and told them the real reason for our mission, it would defeat the whole purpose of the mission! Most time missions have to have cover stories. I'm not sure you can understand the value of a chicken's egg in my time. You have more than enough protein and farm-raised animals are plentiful. When I come from, chicken eggs are considered the ultimate luxury protein food.' He shrugged. 'It seemed like a good idea at the time.'

'I can't imagine you living your life in the future.'

Ryan looked at me. 'I can't either. Being so distant from you. One of the first things I'm going to do when I get home is find out how you've lived your life. I'll be checking into everything. I want to find out you've led a brilliant, exciting life. Learnt to drive, gone to university, travelled the world. Gotten out of Penpol Cove.'

'What's wrong with Penpol Cove?'

'Nothing. It's wonderful. But you need to experience the rest of the world as well. Get out there and explore the possibilities.'

'I have to consider Miranda. I'm all she's got.'

'But you still have your own lives to live. Maybe when you leave home she'll go back to college and train as a lawyer. You can't hold each other back. You're made for more than Penpol Cove.'

I bit my lip. He was right. 'How will you find out about my life?'

'We all leave a trail behind us,' he said. 'Marriage

certificate, children, social-networking pages, newspaper articles. Maybe I'll visit your descendants.'

'That thought makes me feel so sad,' I said.

Out on the horizon, a thick band of sea fog was rolling slowly towards the shore.

As soon as I pulled into the driveway, I knew that Ben and Cassie were home. Their cars were parked side by side on the block paving by the house.

'Did they give you a hard time last night?' I asked.

Ryan shrugged and unclicked his seat belt. 'They freaked out a bit. Reminded me of my mission objectives. Lectured me on the Temporal Laws. The most frustrating thing is they don't believe that we're just friends. The number of times Cass went on about too much testosterone and me having poor self-control.'

'I wish you'd exercised a little less self-control,' I said, because time was running out for us and anything that was to be said needed to be said now.

'So do I. Sometimes,' he said. He reached out and cupped my face in his hand. 'Maybe I'll fall in love with your great-granddaughter.'

I knew he was trying to make a joke, but his words just left me with a gaping emptiness. To be born in the wrong time, always wondering if one of my descendants would be the girl who finally felt those arms wrapped around her, those lips on hers, was too tragic to laugh at.

'What a lucky great-granddaughter,' I said, attempting a light-hearted tone.

We went inside. Cassie and Ben were sitting at the dining room table, frowning at a large sheet of paper. Cassie covered the paper as soon as I entered the room.

'How was your driving lesson?' she asked.

'Good,' I nodded.

'She's a natural driver,' said Ryan.

'Eden, I would like you to stay for dinner again tonight,' said Ben. 'We'll be going over the final preparations for the ball.'

'I'd love that,' I said. I wanted as much time with Ryan as possible, even if that meant enduring Cassie's sarcasm.

'Ben wants to go over the flight plans with you, Ryan,' said Cassie. 'Eden, come with me.'

Cassie took me shopping. I looked at her side on as she put the car into reverse and backed out of the driveway. Her shiny, tightly coiled blonde ringlets snaked down her back. Her skin was clear and, although it seemed she never cracked a smile, she was undeniably beautiful. She caught my eye as she slipped the car into first and I looked away, embarrassed to have been caught staring.

'What are you going to do when Ryan leaves?' she asked expressionlessly.

She moved up through the gears rapidly.

'What do you mean?'

'You're in love with him, aren't you?'

I felt my face flush pink. This was not a conversation I wanted to be having with Cassie.

'Yes,' I said quietly. 'But I've known for a while that we only have a short time together.'

'So you're not going to try and persuade him to stay here?'

'No.'

'And you're not going to try and come with us when we leave?'

'No.'

She glanced at me, the slightest smile crossing her lips. 'Ryan is right. You're practical. Strong. You're coping with some weird stuff very well.' She hesitated. 'It will be difficult when you're left behind. You might want to tell someone about what you've been through.'

'I won't say anything.'

'Good.'

We were on the main road now, heading towards Tesco. She drove in silence until we reached the turn-off.

'Just remember that you must never speak of this. The Guardians of Time will eliminate you if they ever get wind of the fact that you know.'

'Guardians of Time? I thought it was cleaners I had to worry about.'

'They are the organisation set up to ensure the integrity of the timeline. A bit like the United Nations, I suppose, but with considerably more power. They monitor energy signatures that time travel leaves behind, approve and decline missions and organise clean-up agents.'

I shuddered. 'They sound scary.'

'They're powerful. They do what needs to be done to protect the future. Which is as it should be.'

We pulled into the car park and parked close to the shop.

Cassie locked the car and walked towards the trolley stand. I followed.

'What's Connor really like?' she asked, as she pushed the trolley into the shop. 'I've read the books and I know the official story and the gossip, but what is he like as a friend?'

'He's a good friend. Kind, funny, thoughtful.'

'That's generic,' she said impatiently. She picked up some chicken wings and dropped them in the trolley. 'I think we'll have a barbeque.'

'Don't you mind about the meat?' I asked.

She gave me a funny look. 'We don't eat meat because there aren't any animals left. Not many anyway. But you have plenty.'

'But Ryan acts like it's a crime to eat meat.'

'Yeah, well Ryan has strong feelings about things. He tends to overreact.'

I felt like I should defend him, but I didn't want to get into an argument with Cassie. I suspected she would win and leave me feeling stupid.

'So tell me how you and Connor met.' Cassie grabbed a couple of boxes of vegetarian sausages and threw them in the trolley.

'We met on the first day of primary school, but we didn't become best friends until a couple of years later. Everyone else was making cards for Father's Day, but the teaching assistant took us on to the school field to paint landscapes. We both knew why we'd been removed from the lesson. We would have been six.'

'His father died from cancer, didn't he?'

'That's right. His father died a few months before mine. A few years later his mother moved them into Perran and I didn't see him for a couple of years, not until we both started at the secondary school. But it was like no time had passed at all. We were so pleased to see each other again.'

She tossed packets of tortilla chips and dips into the trolley. 'What else should I get?' she asked.

'Some sort of dessert. And some bread.'

Cassie grabbed a strawberry cheesecake and a baguette.

'Is he popular?' she asked, pushing the trolley towards the checkout.

'I wouldn't say he was popular, but he's not unpopular either. He's got friends in astronomy club and in surf club. He's hard not to like.'

'I wish I could meet him.'

I helped her unload the food on to the conveyor belt.

'You should have said something before. It could easily have been arranged.' I smiled to myself. 'I'm sure he would have loved to meet you too. You're just his type.'

Her eyes flashed. 'What do you mean?'

'Connor likes blondes. That's why I never really accepted Ryan's idea that he is into me. I mean, look at the evidence. Megan is the girl he's taking to the ball. She's a voluptuous blonde. His favourite movie stars and singers are blonde. You're right up his street.'

'Why would you say something like that?' she said. 'That's not funny. It's disgusting.'

I bit my lip, confused. 'I'm sorry. I know that technically

he's old enough to be your grandfather, but right now he's sixteen and . . .'

'My grandfather?' she interrupted. 'Ryan hasn't told you, has he?'

I shrugged. 'I'm not sure what you mean.'

She glanced at the cashier, then leant in close to me and whispered in my ear. 'Your friend Connor Penrose is my *great*-grandfather.'

It was too cold to have a barbeque. The sea fog had rolled inland, chilling the air and obscuring the sky, just as Ryan had predicted. Ben cooked the chicken and the sausages in the oven and we ate at the kitchen table instead.

'You didn't tell her who I am,' Cassie said to Ryan.

'I'm not supposed to tell her anything.'

'But she knows when we're from and why we're here. Why did you fail to mention my relationship to Connor?'

'It didn't seem important. And you're always reminding me not to reveal any more than necessary.'

Cassie turned to me. 'I'm here to ensure there is no Plan B.'

'What do you mean?'

'We're here to prevent Connor from discovering Eden. But, like you said, in many ways it would be simpler to kill him. Strangely enough, I'm quite strongly opposed to the thought of my great-grandfather being killed. It might cause all sorts of problems for me, such as the non-existence of my parents and grandparents. So, you see, Ryan is here to make sure Connor doesn't discover Eden and I'm here to make sure that, if he fails, there is no Plan B.'

'And I'm the mission leader,' said Ben. 'So let's clear away the dinner things and go over the plans for tomorrow.'

Once we'd cleared away the dirty plates and empty serving dishes, Cassie brewed a pot of coffee and the four of us sat back at the table.

'The limo picks me up at seven thirty,' said Ryan. 'And Matt and Connor will be picked up ten minutes later. Then we get Amy, Megan and Eden. All six of us should be at the school by eight.'

Cassie glanced at her notes. 'The ball begins at eight and ends at eleven. Sunset is at nine twenty-two, but it will be at least another hour before it begins to get dark.'

'We're going to be able to enjoy the first couple of hours,' said Ryan, smiling at me.

'From sunset until the end of the ball, you will not let Connor out of your sight,' said Ben.

'Eden will be detectable between ten thirty and eleven o'clock,' said Cassie. 'That's a very small window. Will you stay at the ball all evening?'

'I think so,' I said. 'There are usually a few after-parties to choose from. Some people leave early for the parties, but most people stay till the end of the ball.'

'It's those after-parties I'm worried about,' said Ben. 'When you're at the ball, you're inside. I can't see Connor discovering Eden at the ball. But if you leave early for a party, all bets are off. Maybe he'll find a telescope. Maybe someone's dad will be looking through a telescope. The possibilities are endless.'

'Haven't you discussed your plans for after the party?' said Cassie.

'Yes,' I said. 'A couple of people are holding parties. But a lot of people just head down to the beach for an hour.'

'It's what happens after the ball that really concerns me,' said Ben. 'We don't know where you'll be.'

'Eden and I will be wherever Connor is. I'll call you as soon as I know the after-party location,' said Ryan. 'And you guys can drop off my car somewhere nearby.'

'Try to keep Connor at the ball until the end,' said Cassie.

'And keep him away from telescopes at all costs,' said Ben.

I giggled suddenly. That was what it all came down to: this mission from the future had the simple directive of keeping Connor away from telescopes.

Everyone stared at me.

'What's the joke?' asked Cassie.

I shrugged. 'Sorry. It just seemed so . . .'

'This is not a joke,' said Cassie.

'Of course not,' I said, trying to sound serious.

'In many ways, it's good to have you on board,' said Ben. 'Because you can help enormously by not arguing with Connor. In the first timeline, it was an argument with you that caused him to storm off and end up discovering the planet. So bite your tongue. Agree to anything he asks.'

'Within reason,' said Ryan.

'I'll try not to upset him,' I said.

Cassie turned back to her notes. 'We have a viewing night out on the Lizard tomorrow evening with the South Cornwall Amateur Astronomy Group. That's about twenty-five miles from Perran.'

'Connor doesn't drive,' I said. 'The only friend he has who does is Ryan.'

'I think we can safely assume that he won't be hitching a ride out to the Lizard,' she said. 'Which is confusing. He doesn't own a telescope himself, the school astronomy club doesn't have a viewing night for two weeks and I'm not aware of any other active clubs locally.'

'It has to be someone else's telescope at one of the parties after the ball,' said Ben. 'He says in his autobiography that he discovered the planet while he was at a party.'

'Maybe we changed the future enough when we stopped him buying the telescope for his birthday,' I said.

'That's quite possible. But we can't assume anything,' said Ben. 'We discussed this before. Listen in on his conversations.'

'Finally,' said Cassie, running her finger down the page of notes in front of her. 'We'll set the coordinates for mid-night tomorrow. That gives you an hour to make your way back here, Ryan. It's only a ten-minute drive, so you shouldn't be pushed for time.'

'Midnight,' he repeated, catching my eye across the table. 'Why not a few hours later?'

'It's safer to travel at night,' said Cassie. 'And frankly, once the viewing window has passed, there's no reason to wait.'

CHAPTER 15

Amy, Megan and I dressed at Megan's. When we had applied the finishing touches to our hair and make-up, Megan's mum took photos of the three of us in the back garden. She photographed us alone and together, then humoured us for a while as we goofed around, pulling faces and posing for silly shots. Megan and Amy were giddy with excitement – the evening still lay ahead of us, long anticipated, ripe with possibilities. I smiled and laughed along with the others, reminding myself that this should be one of the happiest nights of my life, trying to forget that I would have to spend the whole evening making sure I didn't argue with Connor and inadvertently help to bring about the end of life on Earth.

We viewed the photos on Megan's laptop while we waited for the limo to arrive. There was a photo of Megan alone by a blue ceanothus tree: her lilac dress, floor-length, shimmering satin, like the sky at dawn; her hair curled and pinned up on top of her head with small curls framing her face; her smile hopeful and innocent.

There was one of Amy standing next to a bench by a rosebush. She had one foot up on the bench and she'd pushed her skirt up high enough to reveal a black garter snug around her thigh. She was winking at the camera. Megan's mum appeared to think she was just being mischievous and ironic. We knew better.

There was one of me in my vintage, beaded sea-green dress. It was shorter than the others' – flapper style – and I'd pinned up my hair so that it resembled a nineteen-twenties bob. It was very different to everyone else's dresses, but it suited my lean shape perfectly. My smile, however, was more sad than hopeful. Like my dress, I seemed nostalgic. Out of time.

There were other photos too. Megan and I with our arms around each other, grinning stupidly at the camera. The three of us with exaggerated pouts. Megan with her parents.

We were still viewing them when the limo pulled up outside and the driver sounded the horn.

'Bye, Mum!' Megan yelled, hiking up her dress and almost running out of the door.

The limousine was silver with white leather seats. Ryan, Connor and Matt were already inside, each dressed in tuxedos with bow ties and cummerbunds to match our dresses. Matt was holding a half-empty bottle of vodka. He passed the bottle to me.

'Not for me, thanks,' I said, passing the bottle on to Megan.

'Someone still hung-over?' said Connor.

That was when I remembered that I was angry with Connor for ratting on me to Miranda.

'About that,' I said, trying to control my voice. 'Why did you tell your mother that I spent Thursday afternoon drinking vodka in Perran Park?'

'I thought you might have alcohol poisoning,' he said, his expression wide-eyed and earnest. 'You don't normally drink and you downed a lot of bottles in a short amount of time.'

'Oh, please,' I said. 'Ryan was with me. He drove me home.'

'Which – no offence, Ryan – was also a bad idea.'

'Connor!' I began. 'If you were concerned about me, you could have called Ryan. Or me, for that matter.'

'I was too busy throwing up myself. All I was able to do was tell my mum that I thought you might be sick.'

'You know what Miranda's like!'

Ryan kicked me gently from across the limousine. I looked up and caught his eye. Almost imperceptibly, he shook his head.

'I wanted to make sure you didn't pass out in your room and choke on your own vomit.'

I literally bit down on my tongue and counted for ten seconds. Then I composed my face into a grateful smile. 'That was very thoughtful of you, Connor. Thank you.'

'Where's the other bottle?' asked Amy.

Matt removed a medium-sized bottle of vodka from the inner pocket of his tux. Amy reached out for the bottle, but he pushed her hand away gently.

'Let me,' he said.

Amy laughed and hiked up her dress, revealing her lacy, black garter.

'Close your eyes, boys,' said Matt.

They didn't.

Matt slid the bottle of vodka under Amy's garter and checked that it was snug against her thigh.

'How does that feel?' he asked.

'Fine,' she said, pulling her dress back down.

'Why are you wearing a bottle of vodka under your dress?' asked Ryan.

Amy raised her eyebrows. 'How else are we going to smuggle alcohol into the ball? They'll check your jackets and our bags. But there's no way they're going to check my thighs!'

Mr Peterson, the deputy head, was standing at the entrance to the school canteen, flanked on either side by Mrs Link and Mr Chinn. The two men were dressed in the same suits they wore to school every day. Mrs Link, however, was dressed in a pink cocktail dress that showed rather too much of her ample bosom and the crêpy skin of her neckline.

'Link is looking rather glamorous tonight,' Ryan murmured, raising an eyebrow.

Matt laughed. 'I think I might have to ask her to dance. Imagine being pressed up close against those.'

Connor made a puking sound. 'Enough.'

The canteen had been transformed from the usual yellow plastic tables with moulded white chairs and harsh fluorescent lighting to something actually quite striking. If you had a good imagination – or had had a few drinks – you might be able to make believe you were in a restaurant in a

211

luxury hotel rather than a glammed-up school canteen. The tables were covered with heavy, white linen table-cloths, and each table had a simple glass vase with a single pink rose. Pink and white confetti was sprinkled across the table like cherry blossom. Shadows flickered on the walls and the ceiling; hundreds of white tealights placed in pink holders were dotted around the room, giving the whole place a rosy glow.

'This looks amazing,' I said to Amy, who was part of the leavers' ball committee.

'Doesn't it?'

Out of habit and nostalgia, we chose our usual lunch spot by the exit. A table for six. I looked around. The tables were mostly full. Year Ten prefects were our wait-ers, coming around to take our orders. Ryan and I both ordered the only vegetarian option on the menu – some sort of pasta dish. The meat-eaters had a choice of fish, chicken or beef. As I watched my friends order their meals, I leant back in my chair feeling utterly content. This was perfect. School and exams were behind me, I was sitting in a pink and white dream with all of my class-mates, sharing a table with my best friends, sitting across the table from the best-looking boy in the universe. Later on, I hoped, we would dance. I glanced up at Ryan, who was smiling at me with his big, happy grin. I didn't allow myself to think any further forward than that night. I wanted to enjoy the feeling of contentment, the thrill of the here and now.

'I can't believe that this is the last time all of us will be together,' Megan was saying. 'In September Matt and Amy will be going to college in Truro and . . .'

'Stop,' I said. 'No nostalgic comments. That can come later. Let's enjoy being here all together tonight.'

'Hear, hear,' said Connor, raising his glass of fruit punch. 'Here's to the end of school, the best friends a guy could wish for, and a brilliant future ahead.'

'Aww,' said Matt, leaning in to hug Connor. 'You're so sweet.'

One of the Year Ten prefects arrived back at our table with a tray of bread and soup. Our first course. Surprisingly, it looked nothing like the watery gruel served up at lunchtime on a daily basis. The bread rolls were different shapes: some were round wheat rolls, others were star-shaped with walnuts, and others had little pieces of tomato and olive in them.

'If they can produce food like this, why have we eaten crap for the last five years?' moaned Megan. 'It's the same cooks.'

'They had a way bigger budget,' said Amy. 'Like ten times what they get to spend per head on a school day. And the menu had to be approved by the leavers' ball committee.'

'Well, they did a good job,' said Ryan. 'This actually looks edible.'

Amy smiled happily. She and her drama-club friends had spent hours organising the ball.

'But the big question is where do we go after the ball?' said Matt.

*   *   *

213

The dance was in the drama hall. Like the canteen it was decorated in pink and white, but rather than candles, the room had been rigged up with disco lights and a strobe. A cover band was supplying the music for the first hour and then a DJ for the rest of the evening. Amy and Matt went straight on to the dance floor. Out of the corner of my eye I saw Chloe Mason heading our way. I tensed up. With only a few hours left, I did not want to have to share my time with Ryan. But then she slipped her arms around Tyler Cook and dragged him out on to the dance floor.

'Come on,' said Ryan, reaching for my hand.

His hand felt warm and strong. The band was playing an upbeat rock song, too fast for slow dancing, so we just danced next to Amy and Matt. Connor didn't dance. Ever. Ryan kept repositioning himself so that he was facing Connor.

'It's not nine thirty yet!' I yelled in his ear. 'You're not on duty. You can enjoy yourself for a bit longer.'

'Sorry. Force of habit. And I am enjoying myself.'

The cover band started playing a song I recognised from the radio and pretty much everyone came on to the dance floor. The door to the corridor was open, but the drama hall was hot and stuffy. Megan pushed her way through the crowd to join the rest of us.

'I can't persuade Connor to dance,' she said. 'I don't know what he's afraid of. All he has to do is shuffle from foot to foot. That's all Matt is doing.'

'I am not shuffling from foot to foot,' said Matt.

'Silly me. You're also making infinitesimal movements with your arms. So while it looks like they're merely hanging by your sides, they're actually dancing along with the rest of your body.'

'OK, so show me how it's done,' he said with a laugh.

Megan liked to put on a show. She gyrated her hips, wound her arms into the air and sang along with the music. Matt started copying her.

'Let's get some fresh air,' I said to Ryan. 'It's too hot in here.'

We walked through the lobby and out into the cool, night air.

'And where are you two going?' Mr Chinn asked, startling us.

'It's hot inside,' said Ryan. 'We just need some fresh air to revitalise ourselves.'

He gave us a look that suggested he didn't believe a word of it. 'I hope you're not thinking of revitalising yourselves with contraband refreshments?'

'Certainly not, sir,' said Ryan, his expression wide-eyed and innocent. 'I don't use alcohol or tobacco if that's what you're implying.'

'That's exactly what I'm implying,' said Mr Chinn. He made a big show of looking at his watch. 'Five minutes. That should be plenty of time to *revitalise* yourselves.'

Ryan reached for my hand and we walked around the corner to the small memorial garden. The sun was now low in the violet sky. We sat on one of the two benches in the garden. The other was taken by a group of girls who were swigging from a shared bottle.

'How long till sunset?' I asked.

Ryan glanced at his phone. 'Twenty minutes.'

He slipped an arm around my shoulders and pulled me close to him. Even through his tux, I could feel the warmth of his body. I breathed in the smell of him and reminded myself to live in the moment. This moment right now which was beautiful and perfect.

'Eden,' Ryan said softly.

I turned to him.

His fingertips lightly traced the outline of my face. 'You are so beautiful,' he said.

I held his gaze, drinking in the sight of his gorgeous eyes, even as I felt my own face begin to redden. He'd said he wouldn't kiss me because that would make it harder to leave, but I didn't want it to be easy for him to leave. And I didn't want to face a future of regretting not doing the one thing I wanted more than everything else in the world. A mixture of desire and desperation rushing through my veins, I leant in and gently pressed my lips to his. At first he just received the kiss, his lips hard and unyielding. I pulled away, but before I had the chance to feel embarrassed or hurt or any of the other emotions beginning to emerge from deep within me, he slipped his arms around my neck, pulling me closer to him, and then he kissed me. His lips were warm and gentle and sweet. I ran one hand through his soft, brown hair and he kissed me harder, more urgently, as though we had a couple of minutes to cram in a lifetime's worth of kisses.

When we came up for air, we just gazed at each other.

'I don't want this day to end,' I said.

Ryan pulled me against him tightly. 'If I had the power to stop time, I would stop it now and spend the rest of eternity with you here.'

'That's the most romantic thing I've ever heard,' I said with a nervous laugh.

And then he kissed me again.

I shivered. Despite being a clear evening, the wind was cold. Ryan put his arm around me and we walked slowly back to the hall.

Mr Chinn checked his watch as we approached the entrance. 'Just in time,' he said. 'I was about to send out a search party.'

'We're quite revitalised, thank you, sir,' said Ryan.

I checked my watch: nine fifteen. 'Seven minutes till sunset,' I said.

'The sky is still quite light. Twilight lasts for about sixty minutes at this latitude. I don't think we have to worry too much for the next hour at least.'

Connor and Megan were slow dancing. Megan caught my eye and waved.

'Connor's dancing,' I said.

'Is that dancing? It looks to me like Megan is trying to keep him upright.'

'This is a breakthrough for Connor. I have never seen him dance, ever.'

'Shall we?' asked Ryan.

I let him lead me out to the dance floor. He wrapped his arms around my waist and I slid mine around his neck and we danced. For a few minutes I just closed my eyes and moved to the music, enjoying the feel of Ryan's body pushed up against me, remembering the feel of his lips on mine.

'Connor's headed our way,' Ryan whispered into my ear. 'Remember your promise. No falling out.'

'What if he tries to grope me?'

'Just smile sweetly and tell him to keep his hands to himself. Anyway, from the way he's been gazing at Megan all evening, I don't think you're the person he'd like to grope.'

'Dance with me, Eden?' Connor asked.

I laughed. 'Now I know you're an impostor. There's no way the real Connor would dance with one girl, let alone two.'

'You don't want to miss this opportunity. This may never happen again. Tonight the stars are aligned just so and I have enough vodka in my blood and enough sentimentality in my heart, to break with tradition and . . .'

'Fine, yes,' I said. 'Just stop talking.'

I didn't know what to do with my hands. His waist seemed too intimate, his neck too romantic. In the end I settled for his shoulders while he rested his hands on my waist.

'Are you having a good time?' he yelled in my ear.

'Great!' I yelled back.

'Where did you and Ryan disappear to?'

'We just went to catch some fresh air.'

'Is that what it's called these days?'

I felt myself stiffen. Surely he wasn't going to make an issue out of me and Ryan disappearing for five minutes.

'So where did you stash your liquid refreshments?' he asked. 'Are you holding out on us?'

'I don't have any.'

'You mean you really were just getting some air?'

'Honestly. It was getting hot in here.'

I spotted Megan and Ryan dancing across the other side of the room.

'Amy still has a full bottle under her dress if you want some,' he said.

'Maybe later,' I said.

I didn't want anything to drink. I didn't want anything to interfere with my ability to remember this evening in every little detail.

'I've been meaning to say thank you,' said Connor. 'For turning me down when I asked you to the ball.'

I wasn't sure how to respond. Every time Connor spoke to me, I worried that it would turn into an argument.

'Why is that?'

'I never would have asked Megan if you'd said yes.'

'Are you going out together?'

'Not officially. But she's my date tonight.'

'Are you going to ask her out again?'

'I want to. Do you think she likes me?'

'I know she does.'

When the song ended, I danced with Matt and then I was back with Ryan again. The band finished and the DJ started and we all carried on dancing. It must have been ten thirty when we stopped to get drinks.

'This is turning out easier than expected,' Ryan whispered in my ear as we queued up for fruit punch. 'Let's see if we can keep him dancing until eleven.'

I took a plastic cup of the red punch and gulped it down.

Ryan took his mobile out of his jacket pocket and tapped in a number.

'If you'd like a little punch to your punch, follow us,' Matt murmured with a sly wink.

'I'm just going to step outside to phone Cass and tell her to leave my car by the harbour beach,' Ryan whispered in my ear. 'There's no reception in here. Stay with him. In fact, encourage him to drink. Then he won't be able to focus.'

Connor, Megan and I followed Matt and Amy down the corridor and behind a bank of lockers by the dance studio. The high slit in Amy's dress was a practical as well as stylish choice: she opened the slit to reveal the garter and bottle of vodka. Hurriedly, she unscrewed the cap and poured a large splash in everyone's cups, except mine.

'Still recovering from Thursday?' asked Matt.

I shrugged.

Amy pushed the half-empty bottle back in its hiding place. 'Right, back to the dance.'

'Actually,' said Connor. 'Megan and I will join you in a few minutes. We're just going to get some air.'

'I could do with some air myself,' I said. 'I'll come with you.'

Connor shook his head. 'Why don't you go and get some air with Ryan?'

'He's making a phone call,' I said. 'I'll just tag along with you guys.'

Connor slipped his arm around Megan's waist. 'I don't want you to tag along with us.'

'Connor, don't be mean,' said Megan, looking embarrassed.

Connor continued to glare at me. I remembered what Ryan had said about not falling into an argument with Connor. I was going to have to follow him, out of sight.

'Oh, I get it,' I said. 'I'll see you in a few minutes.'

I stood and watched as Megan and Connor walked along the corridor, away from the drama hall. As soon as they turned the corner, I followed them. I started to run, but my shoes made a loud clip-clop on the tiled flooring and they would have heard me a mile away. I pulled off my shoes and ran along the corridor, reaching the corner just as they got to the end of the next corridor and began to go up the stairs. I waited a few seconds and then ran along the next corridor to the stairwell. Above me I could hear Megan's high-pitched giggle. Connor said something in a low voice and then she giggled again. Although the classrooms and corridors away from the drama studio were in darkness, the stairwell was brightly lit. Probably some health and safety thing. Keeping close to the wall, I crept up the stairs behind them, praying that they wouldn't look down and see me creeping up behind them like some perverted stalker.

There were four floors to the building. The ground floor held the drama hall and the dance studio. The first floor held the maths classrooms and the two floors above them held the science labs. Why on earth would Connor want to take Megan to one of the classrooms? Unless he really did like her and bringing her to the ball had nothing to do with making me jealous or making do. Ryan had convinced me of my importance in Connor's life to the extent that I had begun to believe that he'd never be able to get over me and move on. Yet here he was, at the ball, dancing with Megan, stealing off to a classroom for some alone-time with her. Her giggle echoed down to me. I cringed. I really didn't want to spy on Connor and Megan making out in one of the classrooms.

They reached the top of the stairwell and began walking along the third-floor corridor. I crept along behind them, working out where I could hide if either of them turned around. There was nothing much to hide behind, but the corridor was dark and shadowy and I could duck into a doorway if I needed. Far below us I could hear the bass of some song throbbing up through the building.

When they reached the lab at the end, Connor took a key out of his jacket pocket and unlocked the door. I waited until they had both gone inside and then padded along the corridor in my bare feet as quickly as I could. They had closed the door behind them, but every door in the school had a narrow glass panel running down the middle of it. I crouched down in front of the door and lifted my eyes high enough to peer through the panel. At first I could see nothing. And then the overhead fluorescent light flickered on. There were rows of high desks with stools tucked under them. A table of microscopes. Bunsen burners. A life-size human skeleton.

And a telescope.

How had we overlooked the possibility of Connor coming up to the science lab? Of course, the classrooms were always locked outside of lessons. But somehow he had obtained a key. I wished I had brought my phone so I could call Ryan, but it had been too bulky to fit inside my tiny clutch bag. I glanced at my watch: ten forty-five. The ball wouldn't end for another fifteen minutes. Eden was still visible.

Connor unlocked the glass door that led from the classroom to the flat roof outside. It was where the school astronomy club held its viewing nights. My heart pounding, I crossed my fingers and hoped that Connor had brought Megan up to the roof because he wanted to kiss her away from the rest of us. The presence of a key made it look like he had planned this. I watched through the glass panel as he took Megan by the hand and switched off the light. The room plunged back into darkness.

I waited a few seconds and pushed open the door to the lab. The door swung shut behind me with a bang. I crouched behind one of the lab tables, holding my breath. Connor and Megan didn't come back inside. Either they hadn't heard or they didn't care. I stood up and tiptoed towards the glass door. They were standing on the edge of the roof terrace, gazing down at the garden below. Connor was standing very close to Megan, their shoulders brushed, but he hadn't touched her. He said something and she threw her head back with laughter. Above them, all around them, a million stars were twinkling. But the telescope was still inside.

I fixed my eyes on the sky, trying to locate a familiar constellation. I quickly found the w-shape of Cassiopeia. From there, I located Perseus, just as Ryan had taught me a few weeks earlier. Looking back down, my eyes reached Connor just as he spun around, facing the classroom. I pulled back from the window, but the shock in his expression told me that he'd seen me.

I stayed where I was, flat against the wall, my heart thudding in my chest. Perhaps he couldn't tell that it was me. He might think it was a teacher. After all, the lab was in darkness. I didn't move.

The glass door slid open and Connor stepped inside.

'Eden,' he said, his voice grim. 'What are you doing here?'

Megan joined him in the doorway.

'I came up here to get some air,' I said.

'You followed us.'

'I had no idea you were here. I just needed some air and thought I would head up to the roof terrace.'

'What an odd coincidence,' said Connor. 'You must have known the classroom and the door to the roof terrace would be locked, but you decided to come here anyway.'

I shrugged helplessly.

'I don't get you, Eden. You don't want me. But you don't want Megan to be with me either?'

'That's not true.'

'This is weird, Eden,' said Megan.

'Were you spying on us?' asked Connor, his voice rising in irritation.

'No.'

The door banged open and the overhead lights flickered on. I blinked and rubbed my eyes. Mr Chinn.

'OK, kids, hand over your booze and don't make a fuss.'

'We don't have any booze,' said Connor.

'Connor? Is that you? What are you doing up here? Dare I ask?'

'I was just showing my friend Megan the view of the night sky from up here,' said Connor.

Mr Chinn walked out on to the roof terrace and gazed up at the sky. 'It is a beautiful night. How about it, Connor? One last look?'

'We should head back down and find our friends,' I said. 'The ball is nearly over.'

'You go down and find our friends,' said Connor. 'We'll be down in a minute. I want to show Megan my favourite star in the universe.'

Mr Chinn was already carrying the telescope out on to the roof terrace. I ran to the door and looked down the corridor. Surely Ryan would have finished his phone call with Cassie by now. He would have realised we were missing. He would be looking for us. 'I would love to see the Pleiades through a telescope,' I said, running back into the classroom.

'Good luck,' said Connor. 'It's the wrong time of year for the Pleiades.'

'And I'd love to see a galaxy,' I said. 'Could you show me a galaxy, Mr Chinn?'

'Certainly we can take a look,' said Mr Chinn. 'There are several galaxies we could take a look at tonight.'

I got the impression that he had completely forgotten about the ball downstairs.

'Eden!' said Connor, his voice heavy with disgust.

'Oh, come on, Connor,' I said cheerily. 'You get to look through the telescope all the time. It's my turn tonight.'

'Because you've always held such an interest in astronomy, haven't you?' said Connor, his voice rising.

'Hey, Connor, it doesn't matter,' said Megan, reaching for his arm. 'We can do this another time.'

I glanced back at the door. Where was Ryan? This was the most important part of his mission and he was nowhere to be seen.

'Whereabouts in the sky do we need to aim this thing?' I asked Mr Chinn.

Connor sighed loudly. 'Move away from the telescope, Eden. I want to show Megan my favourite variable star. You can have a look too, OK?'

'What's your favourite variable star?' I asked, although I already knew the answer.

'Algol. The Demon Star.'

I checked my watch. Ten fifty-five. Five minutes until the end of the ball; five minutes until Eden had finished its transit of Algol.

'The ball ends in a few minutes,' I said. 'They'll be playing the slow, romantic songs now. We should leave stargazing for another night and go down for the last dance.'

'You're right,' he said. 'You should go down and dance with Ryan. Megan and I will be down in a minute.'

I took a quick look at the door again. Nothing.

'OK, folks, I've lined up Algol,' said Mr Chinn, seemingly oblivious to the tension between us. 'If I remember correctly, it should eclipse in the early hours of this morning.'

I gripped the railing at the edge of the terrace and watched, cold adrenalin coursing through my body, as Connor made his way to the telescope. It was as if I was up against Fate. Connor was going to discover this planet and the world was going to die. And the only way any of this could be prevented was if I did something. I wasn't equipped for this. I wasn't the sort of person who saved the day. Connor was seconds away from the eyepiece. My heart pounding in my ears, I shoved past Mr Chinn and repositioned the telescope until it was pointing at a completely different section of the sky.

'What the hell is your problem?' asked Connor.

I ignored him and put my eye to the eyepiece. The next thing I knew, his hands were pushing against my ribs and I staggered sideways.

'Calm down, Connor,' said Mr Chinn. 'There's no need for that. We can all take turns looking through the telescope. Let Eden see what she wants to see and then we can check out your star.'

There was no way I could keep Connor away from the telescope for a full five minutes. He was already moving the telescope back towards Algol. Cringing inwardly at what I was about to do, I launched myself at him with all my strength. I pushed him away from the telescope so that he staggered and fell on to the concrete roof.

Connor just lay there, blinking up at me, his face shocked and horrified. Megan knelt beside him, glancing up at me with confusion.

And then I picked up the telescope and hurled it off the roof. Everyone stared at me as it crashed to the ground.

For a moment, the world appeared to freeze. No one spoke and no one moved. And then everyone came back to life. Connor picked himself off the ground and peered over the edge of the terrace.

'It doesn't look as if anyone will be looking at the stars tonight,' said Mr Chinn.

'It's in pieces,' said Connor.

'Of course it's in pieces,' said Mr Chinn. He narrowed his eyes at me. 'I hope you have plenty of money. Because that is a very expensive telescope.' He turned to Connor. 'I'm going to give you two minutes to lock this room and get out of here.'

The door banged against the jamb as Mr Chinn slammed it behind him.

'You need help,' said Connor. The disgust on his face broke my heart.

'It was a misunderstanding,' I said, my mind racing, grappling for an excuse that might explain my bizarre behaviour. I glanced at my watch. Eleven o'clock. We were safe. Eden was gone.

'There was no misunderstanding.'

The door flung open and Ryan burst in. 'There you are!' he said breathlessly. His eyes moved wildly from me to Connor to the open door to the roof terrace. 'What's going on?'

'Why don't you ask your psycho girlfriend?' said Connor, tossing the keys to Ryan. 'Because I have no idea.'

He wrapped an arm tightly around Megan's waist and left the room, slamming the door behind him.

'What happened?' asked Ryan.

'I did it,' I said. I laughed, a harsh sound, faintly hysterical. 'I stopped him from discovering Eden.'

Ryan stared at me. Exhaustion rippled through my body, and then my knees buckled and I slid to the cold, hard floor of the lab.

'He had a telescope out on the roof terrace,' I said, my voice cracking. 'He was going to show Megan his favourite star. It was happening. Just like you said it would.'

Ryan slid on to the floor beside me and reached for my hand. I told him everything.

'You saved a lot of people's lives just now, Eden,' said Ryan.

'And earned myself a reputation as a violent pervert who likes to spy on her friends when they make out,' I said, covering my eyes with my palms. 'As well as a destroyer of telescopes. How am I ever going to explain my behaviour?'

He touched my arm. 'If it had been down to me, Connor would have discovered the planet tonight and it would be game over for us all. What you did was brave.'

'What I did was an act of desperation. I wish I could have found a less dramatic way of keeping him from that telescope. Now they all think I'm weird.'

'They'll get over it eventually. They've been friends with you for too long to hold it against you.'

'I hope you're right.'

Ryan stood up and helped me to my feet. We walked out on to the terrace and looked down. Below us, our friends were weaving their way across the school campus towards the harbour beach. Laughter and shouting carried through the air.

'What shall we do now?' I asked.

Ryan checked his phone. 'It's time for me to head back.'

'Already?'

He nodded. 'It's quarter past eleven. Connor can't detect Eden now.'

Time was slipping away from us.

'I want to come with you.'

'To the farmhouse?'

To the farmhouse. To the future. Anywhere he was going, I wanted to be there.

'Yes.'

'It might be easier to say goodbye here.'

'Ryan, in less than an hour you'll be gone for ever and I

will never, ever see you again. Please let me come back to the farmhouse with you.'

He nodded. 'Course you can. It's not that I don't want you to. It's just that saying goodbye doesn't get any easier.'

'We've already said goodbye. I just want to be with you for a few minutes longer.'

'Come on then. Let's go.' He reached for my hand.

Cassie had left the car in the car park next to the harbour beach. We paused by the car for a minute and watched everyone on the beach. The tide was high, leaving just a bright crescent of silver sand. There were groups of people around a small fire. Others had shed most of their clothing and were paddling or swimming. A little further along the beach, couples found quiet places to be together.

'Are you going to say goodbye to the others?'

Ryan looked across the beach to the water's edge. 'They're all having a good time. And everybody hates goodbyes. I'd sooner just disappear quietly.'

I followed his gaze. Connor and Megan were at the water's edge. The bottom of Megan's dress was floating in the water and her arms were twisted around Connor's neck. He wrapped his arms around her waist and leant towards her. I held my breath as she lifted her lips to his and they kissed.

Ryan squeezed my hand. 'Let's hit the road.'

'How will you get back?' I asked, as we pulled out of the car park.

'In a flying saucer.'

'You're not serious?'

He laughed. 'I'm not serious.'

'Do you have, like, a spaceship hidden somewhere? Where would you even hide a spaceship?'

'Yes, we have a spaceship. Although I doubt it's anything like you're imagining.'

'I don't know what I'm imagining. I guess I'm thinking of a huge battleship-grey ship shaped like a disc.'

'Like a military style flying saucer.'

I laughed. 'I don't really have any idea.'

Ryan pulled on to the coast road as usual. 'Our ship is small. It can carry five people maximum. We only have enough fuel to transport three people safely.'

'It must be tiny.'

'It's just a bit bigger than an average size car.'

'You travelled through space and time in a car?'

Ryan grinned. 'Yeah. Although spaceships come in all sizes. You can get large ships and small ships. Those that travel through time are usually smaller because it's easier to distort space-time for a small ship than a large one.'

'How long does it take to travel back to your time?'

In my head I imagined years, but Ryan was only seventeen so I knew that couldn't be true.

'Two minutes exactly.'

'Two minutes,' I repeated. 'How is that even possible?'

Ryan shifted down as we took the dangerous bend above Lucky Cove. 'It's hard to explain. We create a short cut. You probably think of it as a wormhole.'

'I can assure you I don't think of it as anything.'

232

'Well, it uses a ridiculous amount of energy, but our ship distorts space and time allowing us to travel from one time and place to another quickly. To reach most times and places takes only minutes.'

'That certainly beats driving or flying. No queues, no waiting around. Travel in the future must be incredible.'

'You can't use it for short journeys. It's much too dangerous.'

'What's dangerous about it?'

'Portals – that's what we call these short cuts – are unstable. If they collapse when you're travelling through them, you've had it. Distorting small sections of time and space is too difficult. You need some distance. So you can use them to travel to distant parts of our solar system or to other star systems or through time, but not from one place on Earth to another.'

'Will I be allowed to see you leave?' I asked.

'No,' he said softly. 'Ben didn't want me telling you anything about our technology. He'd be furious with me if he knew what I'd just told you.'

'Where will you do it from?'

'The ship has been stored in the garage. By the time we get home, Ben will have moved it into the back garden, behind the garage where it isn't overlooked.'

All the lights in the farmhouse were blazing and Ben stood in the open doorway, a halo of light around him.

'Mission accomplished!' yelled Ryan as we approached.

Ben hugged Ryan and slapped his back. 'Was it difficult?'

'Eden took care of everything. Connor went on to the

roof of the school with the telescope from the science lab! Eden tackled him and destroyed the telescope in the process.'

Ben laughed and shook his head. 'Despite everything we've changed, he was still planning on looking up at the stars through a telescope tonight of all nights. It makes you wonder if there's any such thing as free will.'

Cassie appeared alongside Ben. 'Everything is ready to go.' She checked her watch. 'Ten minutes till departure.'

'Then we'd better say our goodbyes,' said Ben. He pulled me in for a big bear hug. 'You're an amazing girl,' he said. 'I still can't believe how you've taken so much in your stride. Thank you for being such a good friend to all of us.'

'Thank you for letting me,' I said. 'I know that my finding out about everything left you with some tough decisions. Thank you for trusting me.'

'Ryan didn't exactly give us a choice,' he said, laughing. 'But he was right to trust you.'

Ben released me from his grip and held me at arm's length. 'I know I don't need to ask you this,' he said, looking deep into my eyes. 'But don't forget to keep all this secret, will you?'

'Of course not,' I said.

'Have a good life.'

'You too,' I said. 'Look up my grandchildren. Or my great-grandchildren.'

'I intend to.'

I tensed at the thought that my future was out there somewhere, lying ahead of me, unlived, unknown, unimagined, but that in a few minutes' time Ben and Ryan would be able to find out exactly what I had done with my life, exactly what I would do.

Cassie shook my hand. 'Take care of my great-grandfather.'

'I will.'

Ryan took my hand and pulled me to him, so that the full length of our bodies was pressed together. He looped his arms around my waist and pulled me tight. I could feel the warmth of his arms against my own cooler skin, the warmth of his body through his shirt and my dress. He kissed me hard, with the urgency and passion I realised meant goodbye. For ever. I felt myself flush. Ryan seemed oblivious to anyone else, but I was acutely aware that we had an audience.

Cassie cleared her throat loudly. 'How long is this good-bye going to take? Should we sit down with a cup of coffee and come back later?'

Ryan ignored her and looked at me. 'I'm going to miss you so much.'

'I'm going to miss you too.' I put my lips to his ear. 'When you get back, dig up the time capsule. I wrote you a letter.'

'You did?' He looked surprised.

Cassie sighed loudly. 'Five minutes to go, Ry. Have you finished your goodbyes or are you planning to go back for an encore?'

He kissed me lightly on the lips. 'Goodbye, Eden.'

'Goodbye,' I said, swallowing hard, determined not to spoil our last moments with tears.

He looked at the watch on my wrist. 'It's four minutes to midnight,' he said. 'It will take us about twenty seconds to leave. Go inside and sit down. Wait until two minutes after midnight.' He smiled apologetically. 'Temporal Laws and all that.'

I nodded, no longer trusting myself to speak.

'Ry!' shouted Cassie.

He released me and followed her behind the garage to the back garden.

I went inside the house and sat at the kitchen table. If I was in a film, if I was a different person, I would have raced outside and around the back of the garage yelling at them to stop, wait, and take me with them. I would have told Ryan that I didn't want to live without him. And I would have told him that I loved him.

But I wasn't like that. I was practical and sensible. I knew that I had obligations here in Penpol Cove in my own time. So I sat at the kitchen table as I'd been told and stared at my watch as it ticked away the minutes till midnight, while Ryan, Cassie and Ben prepared to travel forward in time.

I did quite well. I watched the second hand make three complete revolutions before I went outside. I didn't run. I walked calmly through the garden and around the back of the garage.

Directly in front of me, a huge translucent disc vibrated and shimmered. Through it I could see a blurry vision of a grey vehicle. The disc vibrated faster and the image beyond it blurred further. After a few seconds the disc appeared to stop vibrating and the blurry image disappeared. A flash of light blinded me. And then the disc collapsed inwards until it vanished. All that remained in front of me was the lawn.

I walked back to the front garden and our apple tree and sat beside it. My watch told me that it was thirty seconds after midnight. In another ninety seconds he would be back in his own time. I watched the second hand of my watch tick away. At precisely two minutes past midnight I gazed up at the clear night sky. High above me was the constellation Perseus with its demon star Algol. Out there somewhere was Eden, the birthplace of the most perfect boy in the universe. Ryan was gone. And it would be months before I would once again see the constellation Orion, his name written across the sky in stars. I shut my eyes and breathed in deeply. Where was he now? Was he thinking about me? I liked to imagine him sitting in the garden beside me, separated only by time.

CHAPTER 16

I woke early, the cheery sunshine bringing me back to the depressing reality of the rest of my life. I was sixteen. I wouldn't live for another hundred and ten years, no matter how well I took care of myself. And if, by some miracle, I did live for a hundred and ten years, I would be the crinkliest, most wrinkled old woman on the planet. I would be one hundred and twenty-six. He would be seventeen.

I made another calculation. If I lived until one hundred and nine, I would be around when he was born. I could see him as a baby. Of course the chances of living to a hundred and nine were not much better than living to one hundred and twenty-six. And the whole idea was, frankly, sick.

There would be no happy ending for Ryan and me.

Tears pricked the back of my eyes and I knew that if I didn't take steps to pull myself together now, I would end up wallowing in a full-on pity-fest.

I heaved myself out of bed. My green dress was in a heap on the floor. I draped it on a hanger and hung it on my wardrobe door. At some point I would take it to the dry-cleaners.

I threw open my curtains. The rising sun was like a wound, staining the clouds a deep red and slowly spreading across the horizon. *Red sky in the morning, shepherds' warning*. That meant bad weather would be arriving later. It didn't look like bad weather. In fact, it looked sunny and hot – perfect beach weather. After breakfast I would call Connor and make plans for the day. Then with a shudder I remembered the night before. Perhaps he wouldn't want to talk to me. I put on a short blue beach dress and then, as Cornish weather typically changes direction several times a day, tied a warm hoodie round my shoulders.

The smell of grilled bacon was drifting up the stairs, the only smell that could still tempt my vegetarian taste buds after six years of abstaining. Travis. He had started staying over at the weekends recently and he loved a full English on Sunday mornings.

I dragged myself downstairs into the kitchen. I wasn't hungry. I wasn't in the mood for Travis's sarcasm and I didn't think I could stomach Miranda's cheery questions about the ball.

Miranda was standing at the stove, pushing food around a hot, oily frying pan. Travis was standing just outside the back door, a half-smoked cigarette dangling between his lips. He removed it when he saw me and smirked.

'I've been led to understand that a greasy fry-up is the perfect hangover cure,' he said.

'That's not funny, Travis,' said Miranda. 'You know she doesn't drink.'

Travis winked at me, as if to suggest that he didn't believe that for a second, but was willing to keep it just between the two of us.

He stubbed out his cigarette on the doorstep. 'I was merely offering you a fried breakfast. Miranda's cooked enough for a family of ten.'

I shook my head. 'I'm sure it will involve too many slaughtered pigs for my taste.'

'Why don't you make an exception?' he said. 'You can't deny that this smells good.'

'I don't want to feast on the misery of another being.'

'You don't know how to enjoy yourself,' said Travis. 'That's your problem.'

I grabbed a cereal bowl and a box of muesli and plonked myself down at the table.

'So tell us all about it,' said Miranda. 'Was it wonderful?'

'It was a lovely evening,' I said as I splashed milk into the bowl.

'Did you take lots of photos?'

'I didn't take my phone, but Megan's mum took some before we left her place and Connor took loads. I'll get copies.'

Miranda served up two steaming plates of bacon, eggs, sausage, mushroom and fried bread. The smell of hot grease made me feel queasy.

'Did your boyfriend leave last night?' asked Travis. 'He was due to leave after the ball, wasn't he?'

'Yes, he left,' I said. 'But he isn't – wasn't – my boyfriend.'

Miranda and Travis smiled at each other over the table.

'You said you were in love with him.' Travis dipped the end of a sausage into the runny yolk of his egg.

I groaned to myself. It was one thing to confess to being in love when it was dark and I was still a little drunk. It was quite another to talk about it now in front of Miranda and Travis. Especially when I was doing everything I could to not think about him.

'Yes, I did. But that didn't make him my boyfriend. We were just friends.'

Travis looked at me. I had the vague recollection of telling him that I had no plans to stay in touch with Ryan. That must have sounded weird.

'We can keep in touch via email,' I said. 'But I doubt we will. You know what they say: out of sight, out of mind.'

Miranda laughed. 'You have no heart.'

'What are your plans today, Eden?' asked Travis.

'I'll probably meet my friends at the beach. It looks like a hot one.'

'There's a storm coming in later,' he said. 'Late afternoon according to the forecast.'

'We'll probably spend a couple of hours at the beach and if it gets cold we'll go to the arcade or somewhere like that.'

'Who's going to be there?' he asked.

'Why do you care?'

Miranda glared at me. 'Don't be rude.'

'Just making conversation,' said Travis.

'Connor and Megan and probably Amy and Matt.'

'Do you want a lift into Perran?' asked Travis. 'I need to pop home this morning.'

'No thanks. I probably won't go in until later.' I pretended to be interested in Miranda's fashion magazine and hoped they'd just leave me alone.

With some trepidation, I dialled Connor's mobile. I knew he would still be cross with me, but Ryan was right. We'd been friends for too long for him to hate me for ever. It went straight to voicemail. He was probably still sleeping. While I'd gone to the farmhouse with Ryan, they had probably partied into the early hours. I would have to wait a couple of hours before I got to talk to anybody.

'Hey, Connor, it's me,' I said to his mailbox. 'Call me when you wake up. Please.'

I threw the phone on my bed and looked around my room. Miranda hadn't picked up the Sunday papers yet so there was no crossword to do. But I could play Scrabble against the computer or do a jigsaw or read a book.

I went down to the living room and chose a jigsaw from the games box. I cleared the coffee table and began to sort through the box looking for corner pieces and edges. I heard Travis slam the front door and then the deep growl of his car engine rumbling to life. In the kitchen I could hear the crashing of plates as Miranda washed up the breakfast dishes.

At ten o'clock Miranda popped her head round the door to tell me she was going to Marks & Spencer.

'Do you want to come along?' she asked. 'We could get elevenses.'

I shook my head. 'I'll just stay here. I'll go to the beach later.'

Miranda shuffled around with her jacket and keys in the hall and then I heard the door slam.

Silence.

Our house in Penpol Cove was only a half mile from the sea, but it was just far enough inland not to be plagued with the shriek of seagulls. The only cars that ever drove past our house were our neighbours on their way to work on weekday mornings and on their way home on weekday afternoons. I hadn't realised how quiet the days could be in Penpol Cove. Outside, just the hum of a distant lawnmower. Inside, just the quiet, rhythmic ticking of the clock.

I tried Connor again. Straight to voicemail. Surely he was awake by now. I left another message asking him to call.

I looked back at my half-completed jigsaw and with a sweep of my arm, flung the pieces to the floor. Why the hell was I doing a jigsaw?

Until Ryan came along, my life had been timid, like a mouse scurrying amid the long grass. I'd hidden safely in the quiet routines of school and home, filling the empty hours with jigsaws and chess and crossword puzzles. My dreams had been small – studying A levels at the local college, learning to drive – and my expectations low. Falling in love had changed everything. The ground had been torn up from under my feet and I felt like I had been grabbed from the sanctuary of a summer lawn and hurled into the jungle. My old life seemed like a whisper in the face of a roar.

I couldn't live my old life any more. I picked up the pieces and shoved them back in the box.

I called Connor's house phone. Mrs Penrose picked up.

'Hello, Eden, did you have a lovely time at the ball?' She didn't give me a chance to answer. 'What time did you get home? Connor rolled in around three in the morning.'

'I was home just after midnight.'

'Very sensible. I'm just taking the phone up to him now. Connor?' I heard her knock on his door. 'It's Eden.'

I heard Connor grunt something at his mother. 'What?'

'Hey, Connor. I tried you on your mobile but I guess the battery's dead.'

'Hmm.'

'Look, I'm sorry about last night. I don't know why I behaved that way.'

'Whatever.'

'So, what's the plan? Are we going to the beach?'

'I dunno.'

'Shall I come to yours? We can decide when I get there.'

Connor said nothing for a few seconds. I could hear him breathing down the phone.

'Connor?'

'Look, Eden. I'm busy today. I'll call you later in the week, OK?'

'Connor,' I began, but he'd already hung up.

So he hadn't forgiven me yet. I knew he'd be mad with me, but I'd expected him to give me the chance to explain. I called Megan.

'Hi, Eden,' she said wearily.

'Did I wake you up?'

'No, I've been awake for a while.'

I lay back on the living room carpet. 'Did you have a good time last night?'

'Brilliant. The best night of my life.'

I shut my eyes. At least Megan wasn't holding a grudge. 'I'm so glad. Look, I'm sorry about my meltdown last night.'

'You were really strange,' said Megan.

'Too much vodka combined with a mixture of excitement and sadness,' I said. 'It's well known to cause bizarre behaviour in susceptible individuals.'

'I didn't know you were drinking.'

'Oh, yeah. I had quite a bit. I think I must have made a fool of myself.'

'To be honest, I was worried that you didn't like me and Connor hooking up. I thought perhaps it might be an issue?'

'It's not remotely an issue,' I said. 'I think it's great the two of you got together.'

'What time did Ryan leave?'

'Midnight. They wanted to take advantage of the empty roads.'

'Are they flying out of Heathrow?'

'I think so.'

'Has he called you today?'

'No. We're not going to stay in touch. Neither of us believes in long-distance relationships. They never work out.'

'Really? Why? The world is getting smaller all the time, Eden.'

'This is for the best.'

She sighed. 'You're probably right. You were never more than friends, were you?'

'No,' I said. There was no point in telling her we had kissed. She would probably try to persuade me that we must keep in touch.

'I'd better go,' said Megan. 'I'll call you tomorrow, OK?'

'Don't you want to do anything today?'

'Well, the thing is,' she said. 'I'm kind of spending the day with Connor.'

'Right. I see,' I said. 'I'll call you tomorrow.'

I hit the end call button. So this was the way things were going to be now that Megan and Connor were a couple. I didn't think I could stand it. Not only was Ryan gone, but I was stuck in a silent house on my own while my best friends hung out together without me.

Dusk was still several hours away, but the sky was already darkening. The wind blew wildly and the sun was obscured behind the low, glowering storm clouds gathering in the west. I pulled my hoodie over my dress, slipped the key to my car and the key to the farmhouse in my pocket, and headed down the lane.

I'd hoped being with Connor and Megan would help take my mind off Ryan; with neither of them available, Ryan was all I could think about. His name was like a charm. Ryan. Two syllables, like a heartbeat. Orion. Three syllables, like 'I love you.'

I paused at the entrance to the farmhouse. I'd promised

myself I wouldn't come down here yet, but I needed to link with Ryan in some way. This was the only place I knew for sure he would visit, the only place where we might be separated, not by space, but just by time. I wanted to sit under our apple tree and feel him nearby, in the future.

My sandals crunched over the gravel. The lawn was still neatly cut. The silver car was parked in the driveway. Maybe I would give myself a driving lesson later. I walked across the lawn to the apple tree and sat beside it. We had planted it well. Although its trunk bent in the wind, it was going nowhere. I hugged myself. It was too cold to enjoy sitting outside.

It was strange, unlocking the door to the farmhouse and just going inside. Walking into the kitchen, I could still smell the coffee from the night before. The table and chair were just as I'd left them. The floor had been swept clean. I opened the cupboard where they kept the mugs. All of them were still there, stacked higgledy-piggledy on top of each other. I'm not sure what I expected. When Ryan said they'd cleaned out the farmhouse, I'd assumed they'd have got rid of everything. I checked the fridge. It had been cleaned out and turned off, but there were a few bottles of beer left inside.

I went across to the living room. All the books that had been on the bookshelf were gone. So was the television. The coffee table and the sofa remained. I tried the light switch. Nothing. So they'd had the electricity disconnected.

I ran up the stairs and into the bathroom. A small pile of towels was still neatly stacked inside and a half-used bar of soap sat by the basin. I checked the tap. Water flowed. It seemed they'd cleared out most of the furnishings and thrown away most of their personal stuff, but a few pieces remained behind.

I went into Ryan's bedroom. The bed had been stripped and the bedding was neatly folded at the foot of the bed. There was nothing of his in the room. No sketch pad or book or dirty mug. No trace of him whatsoever. I was just about to head back downstairs when I heard a car approaching. I looked out of the window and saw a black car pulling into the drive. It hadn't occurred to me that anyone else would visit the farmhouse. But it made perfect sense. The house was empty. Presumably, Ben would have arranged for it to be sold. My heart ached at the thought of another family moving in. Of not being able to visit our apple tree. How long would I have? Days? Weeks? Months?

I didn't like the thought of an estate agent or solicitor finding me inside the house. The problem was, the back door just led into the back garden. There was no way back on to the lane without coming round to the front and heading down the driveway. There was nothing for it: I would have to face them.

I headed back down the stairs and up to the front door. A man was facing away from me. He was bent over, pulling hard at something in the ground. Our apple tree. Why anyone would wish to destroy a tree was completely mystifying. But what was even more confusing was the person pulling it out of the ground. Because even though he had his back to me, I could tell immediately who it was: Travis.

I was just on the verge of running outside and yelling at him, when I stopped. Something wasn't right. I backed away from the door and gently pushed it to. My blood had turned to ice. I went back into the kitchen and stood near the window. He tossed the sapling on to the ground and continued digging. If he went any deeper, he would find our time capsule. The tree and the time capsule were the only permanent reminders of me and Ryan, the only mark we had left on the Earth.

And that was when I realised what was happening.

Travis pulled the time capsule out of the ground and tossed it on to the lawn next to the tree. He dropped the shovel and wiped his forehead with his sleeve. He turned to face the house. His face was pink from exertion and mud was smeared across his arms. I stepped back from the window.

I wasn't sure if he had seen me or not. I'd only been there for about a second and it was much harder to see in through a window than out. I could run to the car, but he would probably intercept me on the way. Run out of the back door. That could work, but there was nowhere to hide. Hide in one of the rooms upstairs. But then if he found me, I'd be trapped. I had to face him.

I went to the front door and opened it. Travis was standing right in front of me.

'Hey, Travis!' I said, as though there was nothing that could have pleased me more than to bump into Travis at the farmhouse. 'Did Miranda send you here to fetch me?'

'We need to talk,' he said.

'Can we talk at home? I was just leaving.'

Travis put one hand in the small of my back and pushed me gently, but firmly, inside.

'What's going on, Travis?' I asked, trying to keep the fear out of my voice.

'I'm cleaning up your mess.'

'I don't know what you're talking about.'

'I think you do.'

'Who are you?' I whispered.

'I'm sure you've worked that out by now. He told you everything else. He must have told you about the clean-up agents.'

I swallowed. Travis was Miranda's boyfriend. They'd been together for months. He was a part of the family. When Ryan had mentioned cleaners, I'd imagined some sort of arch-villain from a James Bond movie. Not Travis.

'We need to do some damage limitation,' he said, steering me into the living room. 'We can start with this.'

He held a piece of paper in front of my face. My letter to Ryan. I grabbed for it, but Travis held it out of reach.

'Imagine if somebody else had found this. *By the time you read this, I will be long dead. Although my life will be over, only a day or two will have passed for you. It's strange to think of you out there, still young and pretty when I am dead and gone.*'

'Stop!' I said, my face burning.

Travis flicked open his lighter and held the flame to the end of the letter. I watched the paper char and then burn. He dropped the paper in the fire grate.

'How did you know about that?'

'I didn't till I dug it up. I had to check, to make sure the two of you hadn't done something stupid. I can't believe he let you put that in there.'

'He didn't know about it.'

'Sit down, Eden,' said Travis, gesturing towards the sofa.

'I'd prefer to stand.'

'Don't worry. I'm not going to hurt you.'

I couldn't imagine Travis hurting me. We'd shared so many meals together; we'd flaked out on the sofa with Miranda. He'd given me lifts into town. Maybe he wouldn't hurt me. Perhaps he would trust me with their secrets, as Ben, Cassie and Ryan had chosen to do. Perhaps not.

I sat down. 'How did you know?'

'That you knew?'

I nodded.

'It's my job to know these things. But truthfully, you made it easy. You started asking questions about time travel around the same time you became friendly with Orion Westland. It was obvious you had sussed him out. And then, the other night, of all the stars in the night sky, you chose Algol. You wouldn't know this, but Algol is still considered to be a binary star system in 2012. It's not until 2045 that a third star was confirmed.'

'Are you going to kill me?'

He laughed. 'I'm not going to hurt you. Like I said, we need to talk. I need to know just how much Westland told you. Wait here. I'll get us a drink.'

He left the room. I could make a run for it. Try to get to the car. But I wouldn't have much time and he might cut me off at the front door. I decided to stay put and wait for a better opportunity. Travis didn't know I had learnt to drive and he didn't know I had the car key with me. I needed to sit tight and hope that he didn't do something before I had the chance to put my plan into action.

'They haven't left much behind, have they?' said Travis, coming back into the living room. 'Very inconsiderate. But they left some beer.'

He twisted the tops off the bottles. 'Where's Connor?' His voice was soft, kind, unthreatening. He pushed one of the bottles into my hand.

I put it on the coffee table.

'I forgot,' said Travis with a smirk. 'You don't drink. Perhaps you should start. You look like you need to relax.'

'What do you want?'

'To talk.' He took a long swig from his bottle. 'Where's Connor?'

'I don't know,' I said. 'We had an argument last night. He's not speaking to me.'

'What did you argue about?'

'I broke his telescope.'

Travis chortled. 'Nice. Pass me your phone.'

'I don't have my phone with me.'

'Stand up.'

'Why?'

'I'm going to pat you down and see whether you're telling the truth.'

I didn't want his hands anywhere near my body. I handed it over. Travis spent a couple of minutes looking at it and then dialled a number.

He passed it back to me. 'Tell him to meet you here.'

I hung up. 'No.'

I felt something hard hit the edge of my jaw with enough force to knock me sideways on the couch. A searing pain began to radiate along my face.

'I need to talk to Connor,' he said.

I sat up. My jaw ached and my mouth was dry. 'Why? He doesn't know anything.'

'I'll be the judge of that.' He stormed out of the room.

I held my jaw. There was no blood and I could move my mouth, but the pain was intense.

'I'm sorry I hit you,' he said, coming back into the room. He placed a small wet hand towel against my jaw. He smelt like sweat and cigarettes, and the sour smell of beer lingered on his breath. 'I don't make a habit of hitting girls, but you were not being very cooperative.'

I took the towel from him and held it to the side of my face. He stared at me. For a few seconds I stared back. I'd never really looked at him before. He was Miranda's smart-ass boyfriend. Not really worthy of my attention. Now I really saw him. His upper body was broad; his blue T-shirt tight against his body showing the outline of large biceps and pectorals. This was not the physique of a chef. He obviously worked out or did some sort of physical activity. He could overpower me with one arm.

A sneer made its way up one side of Travis's face. 'Like what you see?'

I felt the old flush start on my chest. 'I don't know what you're talking about.'

'You were checking me out.'

'No, I wasn't.'

'Ryan's only been gone a few hours and already you're looking for fresh meat. Nice dress, by the way.'

I looked up and caught his leer. Self-consciously I pulled at the hem of my dress trying to make it longer. This was not the Travis I thought I knew. This was an entirely different person.

'Pass me your phone,' he said. 'We're going to do this again. And this time you're going to tell Connor to haul ass over here.'

He dialled Connor's number and passed me the phone.

'What do you want?' asked Connor.

The phone was on speaker.

'I need to see you.'

'I don't want to see you.'

'Tell him it's important,' Travis whispered in my ear.

'Please, Connor,' I said. 'It's important.'

'I have plans with Megan. I'll call you in a few days.'

Travis shook his head.

'I really need to see you today. Please, Connor. You're my best friend. I wouldn't ask if it wasn't important.'

Connor sighed down the phone. 'We're going to see a movie in a bit. It doesn't finish till ten.'

Travis whispered in my ear again. 'Tell him to take a taxi and you'll pay the driver.'

'Take a taxi,' I said. 'Meet me at Ryan's farmhouse half-way down Trenoweth Lane. I'll pay for the taxi.'

'What's going on, Eden?'

'Just come here later, OK?'

I hung up.

'Good girl,' said Travis. He checked his watch. 'We have a couple of hours to kill. I'm hungry. Are you hungry?'

'No. And Miranda is going to wonder where I am.'

'Let's sort that out first then, shall we?'

He opened his own phone and dialled a number.

'Hey, baby,' he said. 'I'm still working. I probably won't get to see you until tomorrow.'

He was silent while Miranda said something on the other end of the line. For a second I considered shouting for help, but the pain in my jaw reminded me what could happen if I tried something on. I'd have to come up with a different strategy.

'I just saw Eden. She's going to the movies with Connor and some other friends.'

I stared at him. He winked at me.

'She asked me to let you know she'll be home late. I'll see you tomorrow, baby. Love you.' He pressed a button to end the call.

'How could you pretend to like Miranda? How could you pretend to be our friend?'

Travis shrugged. 'I arrived nine months before Ryan and the others. Nine months of just waiting around. That's a long time to do nothing. I needed a friend.'

'Did you choose Miranda because she was my aunt?'

'Yes. She was my second choice. I briefly considered Connor's mother, but she wasn't my type.'

'You're horrible. How can you do that to someone?'

'You're just a kid,' he said. 'You still believe in true love. One day you'll realise that we're all just looking for someone to keep us warm at night. But let's talk about food. I'm starving. The only place that's willing to deliver to this godforsaken hellhole is Perran Pizza. Ben was thoughtful enough to leave their menu by the phone. Choose something.'

The pizza arrived at eight o'clock. Travis went to the door to pay for the food. Connor would be here in two hours. Maybe the two of us would have a chance against Travis, but I doubted that.

I called him while Travis paid for the pizza.

'What now?' he said.

'Forget what I said earlier,' I said.

'Fine. You're acting really weird.'

'I know. I'm sorry. Just don't come to the farmhouse, OK?'

'Fine. I'll call you in a few days.'

I hung up and slipped my phone back in my pocket, out of sight.

Travis carried two boxes of pizza into the living room.

'Cheese for you and meat feast for me,' he said, placing both boxes on the coffee table.

'I'll go and get us plates,' I said.

He didn't try to stop me. I went into the kitchen and took two plates from the cupboard. Then I quickly looked through the cupboards and drawers for something I could use as a weapon. There was nothing. No bread knives or meat knives. Just ordinary knives and forks. I was about to settle for a fork when I noticed a corkscrew with a sharp end. It might do a good job on a cork, but I wasn't sure it could harm a strong man. It was all I had to work with so I put it in my pocket next to my keys.

Back in the living room, I handed one of the plates to Travis.

'I'm going to get another beer,' he said. 'Sure I can't tempt you?'

I shook my head. He returned with two more bottles. He'd already drunk the bottle from earlier as well as the bottle he'd brought for me. If he drank these, that would be four. Maybe he would drink too much and pass out. I looked at him again. He was big. Lots of muscle. The bigger you were, the more alcohol you could tolerate without becoming drunk. It would take a lot for Travis to pass out. But perhaps if he drank enough, he would get sloppy. And then I could stab him with the corkscrew. Would it do enough damage if I could? Maybe if I went for a soft place like the inside of his nose or his eye it would hurt him enough for me to make a run for it. What if he overpowered me and stabbed me instead?

257

'You're checking me out again,' he said with a grin. 'We have a couple of hours to kill. I wouldn't say no if you're interested.'

I ignored him. But his comment made something clear to me: if he was going to hurt me – or kill me – he wasn't planning to do it until Connor was here. He must need me to lure Connor to the farmhouse. But Connor wasn't coming. What would he do when he realised I'd called Connor back and told him not to come?

I picked at my pizza. Usually I love it, but there was no way I could swallow more than a few bits of stringy cheese.

Travis finished his pizza and lit a cigarette.

'Smoke?' he asked, offering the pack to me.

I shook my head.

'You're so uptight with your good-girl routine. But it's starting to unravel, isn't it? Getting drunk in the park, lying to Miranda, checking out older men.'

I picked my drink up off the floor and sniffed it. Perhaps if I played along, pretended to loosen up, I would be able to get him drunk and escape. I sipped at the liquid and swallowed. It tasted sour and I pulled a face.

'You don't like beer?' he asked.

'No. I prefer water.'

He took another drag on his cigarette and exhaled in my direction. 'You're no fun.'

But he fetched me a glass of water.

'Let's talk,' he said, pushing the glass into my hand. He sat on the couch, close, so that our knees were nearly touching.

'About what?'

'First of all, when are you planning to attack me with the corkscrew? We can get that over with now if you like. I can put my hands in the air and let you try and stab me with it.'

I blushed. 'I don't know what you're talking about.'

Travis laughed. 'Go ahead. Stab me.'

'I'm not going to stab you.'

'In that case would you mind giving me the corkscrew?'

I pulled the corkscrew out of my hoodie. Travis removed his jacket. 'Come on then,' he said, winking at me. 'I think I can handle a corkscrew.'

I put the corkscrew on the table and sat back down on the couch.

'Like I said before, you're no fun.'

He sat back on the sofa next to me. I could smell his deodorant or soap, the faintest hint of sweat.

'What are you going to do to me, Travis?'

He put his hand on my bare knee and squeezed it in a gesture that he must have meant to be reassuring. I tensed. 'I'm just going to talk to you, OK? I need to know how much Orion told you. And then we're going to figure out how to keep the future safe. Does that sound OK to you?'

I nodded.

He stood up. 'Right, I'm going to take a leak. And then we'll talk. Don't try anything stupid. I know you think you're a good runner, but you can't outrun a car. And there's nothing to be afraid of. All we're going to do is talk.'

He strode out of the room and I heard him thumping

heavily up the stairs. A bolt of adrenalin surged through me. I clutched the car keys in my pocket and calculated the time it would take me to reach the front door. Perhaps ten seconds. To get to the car? Another ten. To fire up the ignition and drive away? Another ten. Thirty seconds.

This was my chance. He was upstairs. He could probably zip his fly and run down the stairs in ten seconds, but he would only do that if he knew I was trying to escape. And he didn't know about the car. I tiptoed into the hall and quietly opened the front door.

I bolted. I pressed the unlock mechanism on the car as I ran. The lights of the car flashed like an erratic heartbeat and I heard the locks unclick.

'Eden! Wait!'

I pulled open the driver's side door and threw myself inside, banging the door shut behind me. I pressed down on the central locking just as Travis reached the door of the car. He pulled at the door handle.

'There's no need for this!' he yelled. 'You're overreacting. Open the door!'

Trembling, I pushed the key into the ignition. Travis banged so hard on the window that I was afraid it would shatter. The engine shuddered to life. Clutch. First gear. Gas. Release brake and clutch. I slowly released the clutch and the car crept along the gravel driveway.

Travis walked alongside the car, continuing to bang on the window.

'You can't drive. This is ridiculous. Stop the car! I won't hurt you. We need to discuss how to deal with this.'

I dipped the clutch and moved into second. Travis began running. Once I reached the lane I could shift into a higher gear and there was no way he could outrun me.

My instinct was to go home to Miranda. Lock the doors and tell her everything. She had always kept me safe. She would know what to do. But what if she wasn't home? What if she'd given Travis a key? And if I told her everything, she would just become part of the 'mess' Travis wanted to clean up.

At the top of the lane, I stopped. Miranda's car was in the driveway. Decision time. I checked my rear-view mirror. A black car with tinted windows was approaching at speed. I put the car in gear. And stalled. Travis approached from behind. He had slowed down, but not enough to stop. I was thrown forward with a jerk as he rammed into the rear bumper.

Shaking, I turned the key in the ignition again, and the engine roared to life. A red light flashed on the dashboard but I didn't know what it was. I ignored it and pulled on to the coastal road. He followed. I had no idea where I was going or what I would do. The coast road led to Perran and stopped. There was nowhere else to go in this direction. My only option would be to stop in Perran or turn around and head back out of town on the bypass. There wasn't even a police station in Perran.

I checked my mirror. He was matching my speed, not attempting to ram me again. He must have realised I had nowhere to go.

It began to rain. Great sheets of water fell from the sky

and my windscreen was awash. Frantically, I pushed buttons and hit the sticks either side of the steering wheel. My indicators came on. Then my headlights. I kept the headlights on. It hadn't occurred to me that I needed my lights. Finally, I found the wipers.

As I shifted down and took the corner above Lucky Cove, the car shuddered. We were passing Perran golf course now. Rain glistened on the road. My wipers raced frantically from side to side. The engine roared, and then shuddered again. I was losing power. I shifted down to first gear and the engine screamed. And then stopped.

I turned the ignition, but it sputtered and refused to come to life. The red light on the dashboard was still flashing. Taking a closer look at it, I realised it was the low-fuel light. I was out of petrol.

Checking my mirror, I could see Travis undoing his seat belt. He would be on me in seconds.

I unclicked my seat belt, flung open the car door and hurled myself across the road towards the golf course. Without looking back to see if he was behind me, I launched myself over the low fence. He couldn't follow me over the golf course in his car.

'Eden!'

I could tell from his voice that he was close. I was not a sprinter; I was an endurance runner. If he was faster than me, I was done for. I pushed myself harder, not saving any of my energy for the long haul. My chest ached and the rain slashed my skin.

'Eden!'

He sounded a little further away. Resisting the temptation to turn around and check his position, I pushed myself on. The rain was in my eyes and the footpath above the cliff top had turned to mud. One slip and I would either be over the edge or flat on my face.

If I could just get to Perran, if I was among people, he wouldn't be able to hurt me. I could see the streetlights bright in front of me. It was nine o'clock in the evening and raining, but it was June. In June there were always tourists. Even in the rain, there had to be tourists. But what if there weren't any? Then what? I would go to Connor's.

I passed the end of the golf course and the path narrowed. I was running alongside fields of potatoes. I couldn't hear Travis so I risked a glance backwards. He was a couple of hundred metres behind me, running slowly and panting. Too many cigarettes.

I had found my rhythm and if I had been in my running shoes, I could have kept this up for miles. But I was wearing sandals that were soaked and muddy. I could feel my feet slipping inside them with every stride. I wouldn't be able to keep this up for long.

Travis was probably three minutes behind me. The field petered out and I was on the seafront road. The street was deserted. Where were all the tourists? I blinked hard to squeeze the rainwater out of my eyes and aimed for Connor's house at the other end of the seafront road.

I slammed into his door and pounded on it.

'Connor!' I shouted.

I banged my fists against the door.

'Connor! Open up!'

Nothing.

I looked behind me. Travis was halfway along the sea-front road. He would be on me in a minute.

'Open up!' I screamed. God, he must still be at the cinema. He couldn't help me.

I looked back again. Travis was close. Desperate, I turned towards the beach. It was deserted; the boats bobbed and dipped on the high water, their masts clanging together eerily. In seconds I would be out of options. I got myself ready to run again.

Tears joined the rain in my eyes. I ran. I ran back down to the seafront road, which was towards Travis. We passed within a couple of metres of each other before I hit the sand and headed towards the harbour wall. The sea was high and I had one chance. One slender thread of hope. That I could jump off the harbour wall and avoid the deadly rocks. That Travis would follow me in without knowing where to jump.

The wall was slick with rain. I paused to kick off my sandals and took a quick look over my shoulder. Travis was about ten seconds behind me. He was walking. As if he knew I had nowhere to go.

I reached the end of the harbour wall and looked down. When the sea was flat calm, you could just about make out where the rocks were under the water. But now, with the sea sucking and surging below, I couldn't tell with any certainty where they were.

'Eden! Don't jump!' Travis yelled. 'No one's going to hurt you!'

He was only a metre away from me. I looked down at the sea again, trying desperately to find that safe place between the two groups of rocks. I felt his hand grab for my hood and then I hurled myself towards the place where I had seen my friends jump so many times before.

The cold water opened up to swallow me. I sank deep, down beneath the seething surface. My eyelids closed and then reopened. A pearly brightness high above me suggested twilight. I kicked hard and aimed upwards. By the time I broke the surface, my lungs were exploding with pain. I gasped.

I squinted up to the top of the wall. Travis was there, watching. I swam towards the opposite headland, the way I had seen my friends do countless times before. Glancing back, I saw Travis shrug off his jacket. Someone else was approaching him. I swam hard. I'd never been a strong swimmer. I'd always been terrified of deep water, intimidated by large waves.

There was a deep splash behind me. Travis presumably. I didn't waste time looking behind me; I swam harder.

'Eden,' I heard Travis yell hoarsely.

My arms ached as I parted the water, my mind focused on one thing: reaching the opposite headland. Waves lifted me up and threw me down. I tried not to panic.

I felt a hand on my shoulder. It touched, barely, and slid off. I swallowed a scream and a mouthful of water. When I caught my breath again, Travis was swimming alongside me, a bloody gash to the side of his head. His eyes were wild with panic. He reached out to grab me. One of his hands grasped my shoulder and pushed. My head sank beneath the surface. I struggled, but he had a tight grip on my hoodie. I hit upwards towards his face but the water stopped me from getting any power behind my punch. I tried to swim away. His hand held tight to my hoodie. Bubbles escaped from my mouth and drifted upwards. Above me, red radiated around his head like a bleeding poppy. I panicked and dug my fingernails into Travis's hand. He gripped my shoulder tighter. My chest was tight with pain. I needed oxygen. My legs began to kick randomly as I used my arms to push for the surface. Travis continued to push me down.

I closed my eyes. My lungs were empty. I felt a heavy movement in the water nearby, but couldn't register what or where. Saltwater was in my nose and mouth. In my ears. I thought of Ryan. I pictured the sticky pink of blood above me. I saw a blue planet spiralling away from me.

This was the end. I knew it. I had been under too long. The light was too far away. But Connor was safe. The future was safe. The planet would continue to thrive. Ryan. His face swam into my mind. I wanted it to be the last thing I thought about, but a jumble of images floated through my consciousness: my mother's windblown red hair; the photograph of Connor on the last day of school, a seagull gliding through the air.

And then I felt pain on my arm. A dragging. Brightness in my eyes and cool salty air. Still in darkness, I sensed cold water in my hair. My lungs aching. A tugging that hurt the socket where my arm met my shoulder. And then darkness.

I don't know how long the darkness lasted for.

The next thing I was aware of was a sharp pain between my shoulder blades and then saltwater again, warmer now, leaving my mouth instead of entering it. My lungs burned. I tried to breathe but couldn't. A sharp strike to the back was followed by more water. My eyes were streaming, my nose bled saltwater and I couldn't breathe in because water was still coming out.

I heard voices in the distance, was vaguely aware of people around me. And then I was lifted on to something soft and carried away and I drifted out of consciousness.

CHAPTER 17

I awoke to a room washed with fluorescent lights and the voice of a bright, chirpy nurse checking my chart at the foot of the bed. I turned my head to the side and saw Ryan sitting in the chair beside me. His forehead was creased with concern, but his rich brown eyes were filled with light and warmth and the corners of his mouth were turned up in a crooked little smile. I wanted to reach out and touch him, but he was too far away.

'Oh good, you're awake,' the nurse said brightly. 'I'll be back in a moment to take your blood pressure.'

If this was a dream, I had survived. Unless this was heaven. I didn't even believe in heaven. But if it existed, Ryan would be there. I smiled to myself. Heaven or a dream. I didn't care. I just wanted it to last as long as possible, so I could enjoy gazing into his perfect face.

'Good morning, Sleeping Beauty,' said Ryan.

'Am I dreaming or am I in heaven?' I asked.

He raised one eyebrow.

'I don't care which it is so long as you're there.'

He gently brushed my hair back from my eyes. 'You're not dreaming. And you're not in heaven.'

'Am I hallucinating? Did they give me morphine?'

He smiled. 'No. I'm really here.'

'You can't be. You left.'

'I came back.'

I blinked. He was still there. I touched his hand. It was warm. It felt real.

'What do you remember?' he asked, running his thumb across the back of my hand.

'Everything. Up until Travis pushed me under the water.' An image of blood, pink and foamy, fanning out around his head, filled my mind. 'Where's Travis?' I asked.

'Travis is dead,' he told me.

'In the water?'

Ryan nodded. 'He was concussed and then he drowned.'

I shook my head. 'That's awful.'

'No,' Ryan's voice was hoarse. 'It's the best thing. He would have killed you, Eden. He's dead and you're safe.'

He leant over and kissed me gently on the mouth. Right on cue, the chirpy nurse came back to check my blood pressure. Ryan stood up to give her space.

'Too much excitement will raise your blood pressure,' she said, winking at me.

'Can I go home?' I asked.

'The doctor will be doing her rounds soon,' the nurse said, smiling at me. 'If everything is OK, you should be free to go right after breakfast.'

I still had so many questions. How could Ryan be here? Who saved me? Where was Travis's body?

'It's a little high,' the nurse said, taking my reading. She glanced at Ryan. 'But nothing to worry about. Breakfast will be here in just a few minutes.'

'Is Miranda OK?' I asked once the nurse had left the room again.

'As well as can be expected.' He took my hand again.

'Does she know anything?'

Ryan shook his head. 'She thinks that Travis was walking along the harbour wall, trying to take a photo of his restaurant. You were there too, helping him. Travis slipped and fell in and then you jumped in to try to rescue him, but he had hit his head on the rocks. Then I jumped in and managed to save you, but it was too late for Travis.'

'And how come you were there?'

'I told Miranda that we changed our minds and decided not to go back to America.'

'But really, how come you were there? How can you be here?'

'I came back for you.'

Breakfast arrived, putting an end to our conversation. Then the doctor. And finally Miranda.

She looked tired and drawn. Her hair was pulled back in a ponytail and she wore no make-up.

'Thank God you're OK,' she said. 'Let's get you home.'

'Ryan,' I said.

'Get some rest, OK?' he said.

'I don't want any rest. I want to be with you.'

'Eden,' said Miranda wearily. 'Travis is dead and I have to try to contact his relatives. I don't know where to start. I need you.'

I looked at Ryan. I'd said goodbye for ever. I couldn't do it again.

'I'm not going anywhere,' he whispered in my ear. 'Ever. Help Miranda. And come and see me tomorrow.'

'You promise you won't leave?'

He nodded. 'I promise.'

CHAPTER 18

He was stripped to the waist, wearing nothing but a faded pair of blue jeans and a few splashes of white paint. Long ribbons of pink wallpaper were strewn all over the floor around him and one of the walls was painted white.

'I didn't think I'd see you until tomorrow,' he said when he saw me standing in the doorway of the living room.

'I couldn't wait that long.'

'You should have called!'

'Am I interrupting something?'

He shrugged. 'I would have cleaned up, rather than have you see me looking like this.'

I ran my eyes over his body. 'You look fine.'

He raised an eyebrow. 'I'm going to have a quick shower.'

'Why are you doing this anyway?'

'If I'm going to be living here long-term, the wallpaper has to go.'

I almost allowed myself a glimmer of hope. 'Define "long-term".'

'The foreseeable future.' He grinned at me. 'Make yourself comfortable. I won't be long.'

* * *

Five minutes later he was back downstairs in a clean white T-shirt and fresh jeans, his hair wet.

He just looked at me. 'You're here,' he whispered.

I rolled my eyes. 'My being here is not extraordinary. It's you being here that requires an explanation. You left for the future. No going back. Goodbye for ever. And then you show up in the nick of time to save the day. You've got some explaining to do.'

Ryan peered through the window. 'It's a beautiful evening.'

'Ryan. I don't want a weather forecast. I want an explanation.'

'And you're going to get one. But we don't have much time. Come on.'

He took me by the hand and led me into the kitchen which was beginning to look lived in again. A small stack of dirty dishes was piled up next to the sink and a half-eaten loaf of bread stood on a wooden chopping-board. Ryan opened the fridge which was jam-packed full of food. He crouched in front of it, moving things to one side until he found what he was looking for. A bottle of champagne.

'I thought you didn't drink?' I said, when he placed two champagne flutes on the table next to the bottle of champagne.

'I never said that.'

'But I never saw you drink. I saw you accept bottles of beer occasionally. But you never took a single sip.'

'I was working then. You don't drink on the job. Not when the existence of the planet is at stake.'

'So does this mean you're not working any more?'

'I am definitely not working.'

I narrowed my eyes at him. 'You're not back here to fulfil another mission?'

He grinned. 'I have a mission. But it has absolutely nothing to do with work.'

He carried the bottle of champagne in one hand and picked up a large punnet of strawberries.

'Can you carry these?' he asked, passing me the two champagne flutes.

Although the sun had set an hour earlier, a deep red stained the western sky, like spilled red wine.

'I replanted our tree and the time capsule,' he said, as we walked across the lawn. 'It was the tree that tipped me off something was wrong.'

'How so?'

'We planted the tree because you said it would last a hundred years. When I went to the house, there was no tree. I realised it could have died or been chopped down, but it set off alarm bells when there was no sign of it ever having been there. Then I dug for our time capsule. It wasn't there. So I looked you up, the way I said I would.'

'And?'

He reached for my hand. We walked down the gravel driveway to the lane.

'You weren't in any of the census returns. There was no marriage certificate. No children. It was as if you had disappeared from the Earth without a trace. Which is exactly what a cleaner would do. Eliminate you. Kill you and destroy the evidence.'

'Are you trying to tell me that Travis killed me?'

'Yes.'

'He killed me.' I whispered the words.

Ryan squeezed my hand. 'In the first timeline. But not in this one. He's dead.' We had reached the lane.

'Where are we going?'

'Down to the cove.'

'Why? There's no one at the farmhouse but me and you. No adults. No Cassie. No one to interrupt us.'

'There's no rush. We have all the time in the world.' He smiled. 'Indulge me.'

I shrugged. 'So how did you find out that it was Travis?'

'I went through my father's files. We changed the future, but my father still runs Westland Travel, the only four-dimensional travel company on Earth. As one of the senior members of the Guardians of Time, he still has access to confidential files on all time missions. I accessed the files on my mission and saw his name. Travis returned to 2122 forty-eight hours after I did. His mission report said that clean-up was straightforward. One female to eliminate. It had to be you. I checked the newspapers from that time and you were reported missing.'

God. I was supposed to be dead.

'How did you get back here? You said that time travel was difficult. That almost no missions ever get approved. That fuel's hard to come by and that travelling back to a time where you've been is dangerous.'

We'd reached the cove. The tide was high and the water flat and still. There was no suggestion of the storm from the night before other than the seaweed strewn along the high-water mark. I followed Ryan across the pebbles to the rock I'd once seen him sitting on while he sketched picture after picture of me.

'I stole a ship. The one we used to get here the first time. It was supposed to be scrapped because it had sustained some damage during our portal home. I tinkered with it a bit. I got hold of some fuel.' A shadow crossed his face. 'But it took months to get my hands on it. They don't just leave these things lying around.'

'But you were only gone for a day.'

'One day in your timeline. Nine months in mine.'

'You were gone for nine months?'

He nodded. 'I knew I had to get back here, but I knew there was no way an official mission would be sanctioned. My dad – the board – would have considered one life an acceptable price for the future of the planet. But it wouldn't have been fair. You're the one who saved the planet.' He smiled at me. 'You're the one who made a fool of herself ensuring that Connor didn't get to look through a telescope.'

'Thanks for reminding me.'

We sat on the rock, side by side. 'So I came back. To change history one last time.'

I frowned. In the last ten minutes Ryan had told me that he would be living in the farmhouse for the foreseeable future and that we didn't have much time. Much as I didn't want to know when he was leaving, the not knowing was worse. 'When will you return to your time?'

He shrugged. 'I won't. I couldn't even if I wanted to. There was only enough fuel for a one-way trip.'

I let that sink in for a moment. He was here for ever. 'You've given up so much for me. Your destiny. The life you're supposed to live in the time you're supposed to live.'

'Eden, I haven't given up anything. My destiny might have been in the twenty-second century, but my heart was back here with you. Do you remember you once asked me if I believed in Fate?'

I nodded. 'You said to ask you in a hundred years' time.'

'Well, I've seen a hundred years later and I know the answer to that question. I don't believe in Fate. I believe that we make our own destiny. And my destiny is with you.'

As we sat on the beach, the sky charred and blackened as the world turned away from the sun, towards the feeble light of distant stars.

'These Guardians of Time. Won't they be able to tell that you're here?' I asked, gripping his arm. 'You said before that they looked for energy signatures.'

'Yes. But I portalled in yesterday. Just one day after we originally portalled out. With a bit of luck the energy signatures will be muddled and they won't be able to tell.'

'And what about Travis?'

'His funeral will be in the newspaper. They'll see that he died on the job. His wife will get his death benefits.'

'He was married?'

'Apparently.'

'What if they do come for you, Ryan?'

'I'll cross that bridge when I come to it. But I'm not planning on getting caught.'

'But . . .'

Ryan put a finger on my lips. 'No more worrying about what might happen. I'm here to stay. And you're alive. I'd say we have quite a bit to celebrate.'

He pushed the champagne cork out of the bottle with a pop. I held the two glasses while Ryan let the champagne spill into them. I wondered if I would like champagne, if it would taste the way I'd imagined. Above us a million stars turned on like possibilities.

'You once told me that your perfect date would be spent drinking cold champagne and eating warm strawberries while watching the sun set over the ocean.'

I felt my heart surge.

'With someone I love,' I said.

He looked me in the eye. 'I'm making assumptions here – I guess I'm hoping that you feel the same way about me as I do about you.'

'You don't really need to ask me that, do you?'

He smiled shyly. 'I've made quite a leap of faith.'

I clinked my glass against his. 'Here's to making our own destiny. And watching the sun set over the sea with someone you love.'

And then he kissed me and time stood still.

About the Author

Helen Douglas was born and raised in a small beach town in Cornwall. After leaving home to go to university, she lived in London, California, New Jersey and New York. She is now back in Cornwall, where she combines writing books with teaching secondary school English. A keen star-gazer, one of her first memories is of getting up in the middle of the night to sneak outside and watch the Perseid meteor shower with a friend. It was a telescope that she received as a birthday gift that helped inspire *After Eden*. She is currently writing the sequel, to be published by Bloomsbury in 2014.

Don't miss

CHASING STARS

The breathtaking sequel to AFTER EDEN

'This is my niece, Eden,' Miranda told the woman. 'Eden, this is Lauren.' She paused and then added, 'Travis's sister.' For a moment, I was confused. Travis, obviously, didn't have a sister in 2012, because he was from the future. He was a cleaner sent back to 'clean up' anything the time agents left behind. Which meant that anyone who knew anything about Travis was either an impostor or from the future too . . .

Coming in Summer 2014